The distance between fiction and memoir is
measured in self-delusions.

COWARD

Jarred McGinnis was chosen by Kei Miller, on behalf of the National Centre for Writing and British Council, as one of the UK's ten best emerging writers. His debut novel *The Coward* was selected for BBC 2's *Between the Covers*, BBC Radio 2's Book Club and longlisted for the Barbellion Prize. He is the co-founder of The Special Relationship, which was chosen for the British Council's International Literature Showcase. His short fiction has been commissioned for BBC Radio 4 and appeared in literary journals in the UK, Canada, USA and Ireland. He is an Associate Writer for Spread the Word, a fellow of the London Library's Emerging Writer Programme and a Writer-in-Residence for First Story. He also has a PhD in Artificial Intelligence, but mostly he inspires the able-bodied by using public transport and taking his daughters to the playground.

@JarredMcGinnis | jarredmcginnis.com

'Efficient, bracing and bleakly comic' *New Statesman*

'Jarred McGinnis finds truth and humour in the brutal honesty that makes for a compelling read' Mark Strong

'Brutal, tender, moving and funny. Life as a novel' C.D. Rose

THE
COWARD

Jarred McGinnis

CANONGATE

This paperback edition published in Great Britain in 2022
by Canongate Books

First published in Great Britain in 2021 by Canongate Books Ltd,
14 High Street, Edinburgh EH1 1TE

canongate.co.uk

1

British Library Cataloguing-in-Publication Data
A catalogue record for this book is available on
request from the British Library

ISBN 978 1 83885 154 5

Typeset in Bembo 11.5/14.75 pt by Palimpsest Book Production Ltd,
Falkirk, Stirlingshire

Printed and bound in Great Britain by Clays Ltd, Elcograf S.p.A.

For S_

1

When I woke up in the hospital, they told me my girlfriend had been killed. She wasn't my girlfriend, but I didn't correct them.

The first weeks were a confusion of morphine and fluorescent strip lighting. A scrubs-clad stranger told me I wouldn't walk again. She said something about a wheelchair and I said I preferred crutches, still not understanding.

Each morning arrived too early and too loudly, delivered by the clatter of the curtain being pulled back: nurses gossiping, machines beeping, patients calling out, mop-bucket wheels squeaking, relatives arguing, doctors talking, toilets flushing, my own voice in my head counting over and over the stupidities that got me here. I resented being pulled from vivid dreams where I walked, wasn't in constant pain and hadn't met Melissa that night. Steeped in painkillers, muscle relaxants, anticoagulants and anti-spasmodics, my brain turned dreams into staged re-enactments of my life. I took every chance and every pill to see what vignette of my past that sleep would play for me. These dreams were more real than the washed-out moments awake in a hospital. The characters' wigs were askew and the cast not quite right for the parts, but I was the director. When the dialogue turned against me or the narrative galloped away, I stopped the action, repositioned the players and began again from the top of the page. I edited dialogue so I said what I should have said. I cut whole scenes from my life. I was redrafting the story, because I didn't like the ending.

My neighbour was a good ol' boy who broke his neck on a fishing, mostly drinking, trip. His fishing buddies, his family and girlfriend visited every day, and every day I opened my eyes to his nightstand full of greeting cards. Every day: a card with a cartoon dog surrounded by smiling sunflowers; another card with a smiling sun; another sun; one with flowers – all cheerily commanding 'Get well soon'. Fuck you, dog. Fuck you, flowers. Fuck you, sun.

For the first months, I had to be put into a back brace before being sent downstairs for physical therapy. The orderly adjusted my legs one by one. My damaged nerves reported an ambiguous pull at my hips, but when he touched my feet it felt like they were dipped in scalding water. My feet would turn bright red from the gentlest of touches. The doctors and physical therapists assured me this was normal.

At the centre of the physiotherapy room, a set of three steps stood like an altar. An elderly man, lopsided from a stroke, with a driftwood gnarl of a left arm, struggled to lift his leg onto the first step while three therapists hovered around him murmuring encouragements. Half a dozen wheelchair-bound patients – old young fat thin white brown black – worked away at weight machines or hand cycles. A line of grotesques and the pitiable. And I was one of them, gooble gobble gooble gobble.

The therapist poked me with a pin. She marked on an outline drawing of a sexless body in my medical folder where insensate flesh began. She stretched my legs and explained which muscles she, not me any more, was working. She encouraged me as if she was toilet training a puppy. Good job. That's it. Hurray for you.

Hurray for me. Hurray for this cockless creature measured by whether I'm avoiding pressure sores, constipation or foot drop. When our sessions finished, she pushed me over to the weight machines and warned me not to overdo it while still wearing the brace. I waited for the therapist to leave, then asked a patient's mom to push me outside where the orderlies smoked.

I fist-bumped with Ricky. His green scrubs were tight against the thickness of his arms and legs. He looked like a thug, but I had seen that barrel of belly, Marines flat-top, cauliflower ears, cradle in those arms an old lady, tiny and ashen in her thin hospital gown. He had gently lifted her from wheelchair to bed. Brushing back the loose wisps of grey and in answer to her repeated thank yous, he had wished her good night.

'You ain't doing PT?' Ricky said and handed me a cigarette. I nodded my thanks.

'Why're you all trying to shove a basketball in my lap? I didn't give a crap about sports when I was over six foot. I'm sure as hell not interested now that I'm four foot gimpy. God clearly wants me sitting on my ass doing nothing. Who am I to argue?'

'Who's talking about basketball?' Ricky took a long drag, watching me. He blew the smoke over his shoulder. 'Your tris and delts are your legs now.' He straightened an arm and pointed at the flexed muscles with two fingers, his cigarette between them. 'You can't be expecting other people's mommas to push you around.'

'Duly noted,' I said.

'Shit,' Ricky said. 'Where your people at?'

'I got no people.'

He sucked his teeth. 'You got people.'

I looked away and took a long drag. After our smoke, Ricky brought me back to my bed. He positioned the chair and locked its brakes.

'A lot of guys try to pretend this ain't happening. They ignore everybody's good advice, but the quicker you get your head right the quicker you can get back to normal.' There was that word again. You can't tell an able-bodied person that being a cripple isn't momentous. It's impossible to accept. At the time, I didn't. All your understanding of living assumes two working legs. Newly disabled, you can't know that with time and practice you won't need to think about how to manoeuvre a wheelchair off kerbs or pull yourself over a step. You adapt and move through the world differently but as easily. Depending on who you are, the disabled are a memento mori, the good deed for the day or a vessel into which you pour pity or curiosity. The last thing you want to hear is that it's no big deal.

I struggled to keep my balance as Ricky lifted my legs onto the bed.

'All this . . .' He waved his hand around the hospital room and pointed at the wheelchair. 'You think this is the end of the world? It ain't. You ain't even that bad off, but you don't want to hear that.'

'No, I do not.'

'Light off or on?'

'Off.'

I was awoken by a woman from the finance office. She shoved my shoulder roughly and repeated my name. She wore a fleece jacket covered in cartoon pugs playing sports and yet, with an inch extra of working spinal cord, she was better than me in every way.

'Are those pugs playing soccer?' I asked.

'My husband bought it for Christmas.' She held the lapel out and looked down, smiling.

'Are you guys still together?'

'Yes,' she answered, her forehead wrinkling.

'Amazing,' I said.

'Sir, sorry to wake you. But we need to arrange your discharge.'

I sat up sharply, ignoring the slashes of pain. 'I can't,' I blurted.

'The doctors are very pleased with your progress. The brace can come off.' She smiled. She handed me a letter from the surgeon. Her polite grin disappeared as she watched my hand shake. I couldn't focus on the words.

'They said six months. I've been here three. What happened to six months?' I asked.

'With your insurance situation—'

'I have nowhere to go,' I pleaded.

'You were aware this was a possibility. We've discussed this.'

'Is this because of the hot dog thing?'

She shook her head.

'I was trying to cheer the old lady up. The nurse was being a jerk. It was funny.'

Her lips tightened. She looked to the ceiling and sighed.

'Is it because the guy across the hall gave me his meds?'

'No.'

'I'll take PT more seriously.'

She set her folder on the bed rail. She looked tired. 'This isn't a disciplinary action. We have a limited number of beds available.'

Her weariness sapped the fight from me.

'What do I need to do?'

She opened the folder of papers to be signed. I followed her finger to the dotted lines and the check boxes.

'Is there someone you would like us to call?'

'No. I'll do it. Can you see if the nurse will bring me some pain pills?'

Without the back brace, I could get myself in and out of the wheelchair, but the months of being in bed, the Dilaudid and cigarette breaks when I should have been doing physical therapy made the distance to the payphone across from the nurses' station a chore. After ten years, I still knew his number by heart. On any day for the past ten years I could have dialled the number and he would pick up on the third ring and say . . .

'Hello. Jack here.' The wall around the phone radiated rays of squiggled phone numbers. What did the person who had to dial 'Ackroyd 781-2307' say when Ackroyd picked up? How did Ackroyd respond? No good news could come from this phone.

'Hello?' the voice in the receiver repeated.

'Hello,' I managed to say without my voice breaking.

The phone went silent until Jack said, 'Okay,' unsurprised, as if he knew he would get this phone call one day. 'What's happened? What do you need?'

'Are you around tomorrow morning? I need you to pick me up.' I choked up from hearing my father's voice after so many years. Me calling from this hospital phone, from this wheelchair, became a weight pulling me towards my bed ready to let pain pills whisper me back to my stage-managed dreams.

'Okay. What's the address? Wait, let me get a pen. Okay.'

I breathed deep and rubbed at my eyes. I read him the hospital's address from a piece of paper taped to the face of the phone. In tiny squared letters someone had written 'fuck this'.

'Are you okay?'

I picked at the address and peeled away a thin strip of tape. I wrote Jack's name and number on the wall. I don't know why.

'I was in a car accident.'

'How serious?'

'I'm okay,' I said, fighting to keep any emotion out of my voice.

'Can you tell me what happened?'

Ricky was coming down the hallway. I turned away and put my head against the wall. I didn't want him to see me crying.

'You still there?'

'Yeah, I'm here. Is it possible to stay with you for a week or two while I recover?'

'Okay. We'll get you home. You need me to bring you anything?'

I tried to say no, but when I opened my mouth I sobbed. I cried with gratitude, but a good chunk of self-pity was in there too. I mourned my life, as messed up as it was, because it was over. I wanted to tell Jack I was afraid, but I couldn't. I wasn't ready to admit ten years of failure were my fault. Being a cripple in a hospital amongst all the other damaged can be endured. Out in the world, you must process what it means to be a fuck-up and now a fuck-up permanently confined to a wheelchair.

'It's a few hours' drive from the house, but I'll be there first thing in the morning,' Jack said.

'I'll be here. I'm not going anywhere.'

'Okay,' he said.

2

In the dream I couldn't direct or rescript, paramedics stood over me. The buildings and people in waterproof coveralls were washed in the alternating red and amber of an idling fire truck. There was no pain, yet. There was confusion. There was fear. There was my heart trying to escape my chest. But no pain, and that scared me too. I was going to die. I knew that. I wanted to ask if I was dying, but I didn't know the words. More people nearby. People speaking to the driver. People speaking to Melissa. Melissa, was she okay? Ask if Melissa is okay. Every thin thought fell apart before I made sense of it. A voice to my left. I looked. A middle-aged woman. Her helmet, so yellow it glowed, loomed closer until I saw only her sun-hardened face. The deep crow's feet at her eyes made her look kind and gentle. I thought maybe it was going to be okay.

It was not going to be okay.

'Can you hear me? What's your name?' Behind her safety glasses, her black eyes shone in the glare of the headlights. 'Can you tell me your name?'

'Jarred.'

'Hello, Jerry. Can you tell me if you're allergic to any medication?'

'No.'

'No, you can't tell me? No, you're not allergic?'

'No, not allergic.'

'Jerry, I'm going to put this tube between your ribs to inflate your lung. Your ribs are broken. It's going to hurt. Ready? One . . . two . . . three.'

Pain arrived as promised. A fiery Fourth of July bloom of hurt burst from my side. It vibrated down my ribs, spreading along my spine, shoulders, arms, neck, skull. My teeth loosened in their sockets. It awoke all the other agonies. A jolt of electric pain shot from the break in my arm and churned my stomach. I didn't want to be sick. I was going to be sick. I needed to tell them I was going to be sick. The kind-eyed woman set my arm in a splint and I heard the terrible yelp of a dog being punished. It was me who had made that noise. Scared, I was very scared. Golden sparks swam and fizzled in my vision and each time she adjusted the tube between my broken ribs the pain rippled new and fresh. This couldn't possibly go on. This couldn't get worse. I was wrong. Every root and branch of nerve hummed hate and each shallow sip of air that burned my throat reassured me that what had happened was not a dream. My body shook.

'I'm cold,' I said through chattering teeth.

'We're going to take care of you,' she said.

In the darkness my body drifted up. The sounds of that night faded and there was a steady beeping of an unseen machine. I felt the flicker of tv light behind my closed eyelids. I opened them and I was in my hospital bed. The sheets were damp with sweat. The redneck roommate snored away on the other side of the curtain, dreaming of beer and bass. The harsh light from under the door kept the room in a yellow gloam. I had to reassure myself that

9

I was awake and this was not the dream. But I still felt pain.

My head was being compressed. At each throb, pain jabbed my eyes. Nausea churned my stomach and I fumbled for the bedpan. My heart tapped out a triple beat before stumbling back to its steady rhythm. I mashed the nurse call button. My unfeeling, unmoving legs were being twisted. I was lying on my back, but my legs were pinned up behind me, curling like a withering plant. My left leg twisted away from my body. The bundled straw of my muscles snapped one by one under the torture. I tried to climb the bed to escape the attack. I mashed and mashed the call button. I could hear the bell ringing at their desk down the hall. My howls resonated in my skull and drowned out the snores of my unperturbed roommate. I yelled a little louder, partly for the relief, partly to hurry the nurse and partly to wake the redneck up. A nurse arrived and casually walked to my bed. I felt an urgency that this suffering should be shared.

'My legs! What's happening to my legs? They're breaking. They're breaking!'

She pulled the sheets away. She touched my legs, still irritatingly calm, while I struggled in bed pulling at the skin of my stomach. She felt my head. How could she be calm right now? How could my roommate be sleeping?

'Do you feel like you have a hangover? Nauseous?'

'Yes,' I said, teeth clenched.

'You need to sit up.' She pressed the button on the bed. Another nurse came in and took my blood pressure. 'Have you peed?'

'My fucking legs. They're twisted. Straighten my legs, straighten my legs!'

'They are straight. It's neurological pain, probably dysreflexia. I'll go see if you can have some meds.'

'I can have meds,' I screamed, as the unseen hands twisted my legs into another impossible direction. Paraplegia isn't just the golden ticket to great parking and people's condescension. It comes with surprises like autonomic dysreflexia and phantom pain. Though it was the phantom pain that was torturing me, I found out later that it was the dysreflexia that could kill me.

She came back with two yellow pills. I gripped the rails so tight that my fingers hurt and tried to pull the rail from the bed. I wanted something besides me to be broken. I wanted the nurses to be as scared too. I wanted my roommate to be awake and witnessing. The pain in my head started to fade, but my legs were still being twisted off.

'The pills aren't working.'

'They will. They will.'

'No! They won't.'

The two nurses looked at each other, looked at me, wordlessly conferring. I wanted to shout, 'Why are you so calm? Look at my legs!' A nurse left and came back filling a syringe. She gave me the shot and calm and peace and a floating goodness spread through my rebelling body. My legs drifted back to their normal position and I felt warm and exhausted and happy to be going to sleep and, as I drifted off, I heard my roommate's thick Texan drawl say, 'Welcome to the shitshow, partner.'

Later that night, the crack of light under the door flared into full sun then quickly died back to its strip of harsh glow. The curtain around my bed squeaked open, closed and a woman giggled.

'Hey, babes,' the woman said. By the outline of shadow, I knew her hand was on the bed. Maybe on my legs. Touching me. Even though you are paralysed, you still sense the presence of your legs. They are there and you vaguely know their positions, but the details are scrubbed. She touched my foot, maybe, then I guessed she ran her hand up to my knee. She patted my knee, I think. Was she touching my thigh? I didn't speak or move. She drew closer, and I smelled the freshness of her soap and shampoo. I realised my mouth was hanging open. I swallowed.

'Wakey, wakey, eggs and bakey,' she whispered as she brought her face to mine. I opened my mouth to speak.

She said, 'Shit, wrong bed.' Her shadow disappeared. My neighbour's curtain squeaked. 'Hey, babes.'

The grumbling of my roommate waking up, a hushed conversation, their kisses, the hiss of two beers opening. I thought about her touching my leg, leaning in to give a kiss that wasn't mine. Longing filled me. Their bed creaked, creaked again, giggles, creak, creak. I didn't want to listen, but I did. The bed's motor whirred, too loudly, as I raised the top half. She moaned and I stopped. I felt embarrassed at my arousal and want. Quietly, carefully, I moved my legs over the side of the bed. I was afraid that the unseen hands would start their tortures again, but only a lingering ache in my legs and back remained. Those pills were doing their job, but my balance was off. The noises on the other side of the curtain became steady, gaining in urgency. I took my chance to leave them alone to enjoy this moment.

3

I watched in the rear-view mirror as Jack retrieved the wheelchair frame from the trunk, then the wheels, the arm rests. Fingers thick as tap roots manipulated the parts to click into place as if he knew by instinct how this all worked. The broad shoulders and thin frame made him look younger than his sixty-something years. I saw the face I remembered despite the wrinkles he had accumulated in a decade. Age suited him. His black hair was now mostly white but the thick eyebrows had kept their colour. He parted his hair on the right, the cowlick in the back still untamed. He should have been a fisherman somewhere Baltic and wind-swept and not the elderly widower living for decades in an unremarkable two-bedroom one-storey house in the Austin suburbs. At the hospital, he didn't ask any questions, just, 'You ready?' The car ride was silent.

Jack opened the passenger-side door.

Brick-coloured shingles capped the white rectangle of his house, which sat at the end of a short driveway marked by an aluminum mailbox. The carved number 99 on the wooden post smacked of Jack's handiwork.

'C'mon,' he said.

I managed a nod.

Jack pulled the wheelchair back a couple of feet.

'Jump for it. You can do it . . . no?' He shrugged off his ignored joke.

The pecan tree was still front and centre, but smaller and unremarkable. In my memories of childhood, it had been a behemoth of rough grey and red bark that dwarfed the house. Its wide canopy of leaves hung with the beards of catkins put the entire front yard into shade so that the grass grew only in patches. Beneath it, I saw an eight-year-old me cracking nuts between two chunks of cement. His fingers were stained black from the too-green husks. From the corner of my eye, a thirteen-year-old me sneaked out of a side window as a police car pulled into the driveway. By the front door painted butter yellow – I remembered it white – the shadow of a younger Jack held sixteen-year-old me by the throat. This house was haunted with memories.

A heaviness pinned me to the car seat. My body knew that if I went into that house there was no pretending. I was a twenty-six-year-old paraplegic with no money living back home with a man, my father, whom I hadn't spoken to or seen in ten years. It would be Jack's bad jokes, the accusing ghosts and the premature decline that awaited an invalid like me.

At the hospital, scattered amongst us newly damaged were the returning patients. Men, and they were always men, who had been in wheelchairs for a decade or more. They were back because of kidney stones or pressure ulcers or dysreflexia or thrombosis or embolisms or osteomyelitis or whatever. I had seen my future self in the beds on the ward. A fat, stubble-faced future with a sour sweat smell. A future that burped into the glow of his cell phone, dabbing at it with a crooked swollen finger.

Jack lifted my legs from the car. The laces of my red

Adidas had been removed to make it easier for me to get them on and off. When he set each foot down, the bump against the ground registered at my waist. It unnerved me.

'Hold onto my arm. Grab the oh-shit handle and lift yourself up.'

My arms trembled with the effort. I shook my head. The wishing you were dead comes at random moments like these. It's just a flash of pining for nothingness and it's gone before you can ransack the medicine cabinet for a bottle half-full enough. These moments fade eventually.

'All right. Let me help you.' He leaned in and lifted me out of the car without effort. He wore the same cologne as he had when I was a teenager. Once in the wheelchair, I concentrated on keeping my balance as I lifted my feet and placed them on the footplate.

'I'll get some wood tomorrow and build a ramp to make it easier for you to get in and out of the front door.'

Mom's rose bushes were no longer where I remembered them. After my mom died, the house always had a smell of emptiness, dust and paint. As Jack brought me into the living room, there was also an oily scent that I couldn't place until Jack cleared away his shoe-shine kit: a white gym sock stuffed with tins of shoe polish. A single sharp knock rattled the front door.

'You expecting company?' Jack asked.

I shook my head. He stepped outside and came back holding a pink training toilet. The three princesses in full evening gowns on its lid were weather-faded. Disneyesque shades doomed for eternity to watch toddlers foul before their royal visages.

'Amazon's really phoning it in these days,' Jack said.

'Why would someone throw that at your door?'

'Neighbourhood kids screwing around. There's a whole gang of them that live a few streets down. Jackasses. I'm going to put it out by the trash.'

'You're just rearming them.'

Jack went outside. The strangeness of my childhood home fought against its familiarity. I knew this place. I didn't know this place. I belonged. I didn't. I felt a seasick queasiness from the to and fro. Jack returned, talking before he was inside the house. 'When we were potty training you—'

'Does this happen a lot?'

'What?'

'Toilets thrown at your door.'

'No.' Jack chuckled as if I had asked a stupid question. To be fair, I had. 'Listen, when you were little, we had this training toilet that would play music when you used it. You just refused to be interested. We were at it for months. I was desperate to have one less butt to wipe. Then one day, your mom heard "London Bridge" playing and rushed in to see her clever boy using the bathroom all by his big boy self. What did she see instead? You pulling water out of the toilet bowl with a cup and pouring it out into your potty. Clapping your hands every time "London Bridge" fired up.'

'A kids' toilet thrown at your door is one weird omen,' I said, looking out the window to see if the children were going to return.

'You were always too clever for your own good. Never doing what you were supposed to and still getting rewarded.'

'I think the parable here is there is more than one way to make the music play,' I said.

'That even rhymes; get that on a sampler,' Jack said. 'What do you want to do now? You hungry? You want to watch some tv?'

'Just some sleep,' I said, suddenly exhausted by the effort of speaking.

'All right. I set you up in your old room.' He pushed the wheelchair into the bedroom, past the door with a hole more than a decade old – as if I needed to be reminded that memories here have consequences. Cardboard boxes sat in the corners. The only evidence of its once having been my childhood room was a painting that I'd done in high school art class. My mother as a young woman, in a western shirt, covering her face from the viewer with one hand.

Jack said, 'I'll leave you be. You need anything? Coffee? Juice? A kick in the ass?'

I managed to say, 'Some pain pills?'

'Yep. Be right back.' Jack returned with the medicine and a glass of water. 'Anything else?'

'No, thanks. Just a nap. The drive wore me out. I'm sore.'

Jack nodded his head toward the painting. 'Remember painting that? Do you still do any art?'

I didn't respond. Jack was trying to tell me that our past was okay. He was searching through the ashes to show me something that was intact, but I was too newly broken to recognise the chance to heal old wounds.

He looked around, uncomfortable with the silence. 'Okay. If you need that kick in the ass, I'm out here. Going to close the door now, okay?'

On the back of the door was a full-length mirror and in the mirror was a face, thin as a Christ, with dark circles under the eyes. Sadness washed over me like a chill. On the left arm, a ladder of suture marks climbed the slash of flesh where the bone had broken through. Straining to lean over, my balance unsure, I took off my shoes and socks. Taking off my underwear was a struggle. With the muscles

17

wasted away, the skin of my thighs draped loosely over cudgels of leg bone.

One morning in the hospital, a nurse had woken me to remove the staples the surgeons had used to hold my skin together. The nurse had to help me roll on to my side. One by one, I felt the pinch and bite as he tweezed the metal from my body. Once he was finished, he showed me the kidney-shaped bedpan and the anthill of metal 'M's within. As if he was a prideful hairdresser, he asked if I wanted to see my back. He handed me a mirror to see the centipede of sutured flesh that clung to my spine. Its skin-graft of a head rested on the crushed vertebrae above my hips where spinal tissue had become scar. He ran his gloved hand down its length, said oh shit, and I watched him pull a missed staple, my skin stretching as if it didn't want to let go of that last sliver of metal.

I shook away the memory until my temples throbbed. In my old room in my old mirror, the cripple from the hospital had followed me. His cheeks were red and blotchy from crying. He looked pathetic. I saw how other people saw him. I positioned the wheelchair beside the bed and pulled myself over. I had to lift my useless legs, one by one. The chill returned and crawled into my chest. I took a huge breath and pulled the blanket over my naked body. The red-eyed cripple in the door's mirror was there in his bed, blanket up to his neck, staring back. I squeezed my eyes shut, not ready to believe he was me, until the pills pushed me into dreams about Jack and Mom and me and the past.

4

It was Christmas Eve. I don't remember exactly how old I was. That year my big present was a Tonka truck, yellow and indestructible. How old is that, nine or ten? My mom was still with us, that I'm sure of.

To the left, the tv. To the right, the plastic Christmas tree with its star kissing the cheek of the ceiling. Between the two, a fireplace with logs more smouldering than blazing. Mom and Dad sat on the couch. She had her legs in his lap. He patted her ankle or rubbed her calf while tinselled tv shows happy-ended. Every lost dog found a home, every orphan her parents. And in our house, every glass stayed full. On return trips from the kitchen, Dad got a kiss and a refill.

At an early age, I recognised that the love affair between Mom and Dad was unique. They flirted like high school students. As Patrick, my older brother, was finishing high school, Mom and Dad had been settling back into their life built for two when I defeated whatever birth control they were using to shield themselves from another eighteen-year distraction from their love affair. They drank and they loved. I just happened to be there.

'I'm going to fix the fire,' Dad said.

He brought a gasoline can in from the garage.

His eyes shone and reflected the tree's strings of flashing colours. He sloshed the can toward the smoking logs. A fireball burst forth and Dad stumbled back. I froze with panic, watching the crickets of flames ride the splashes of gasoline. They settled on a present, almost igniting the Christmas tree, and half a dozen greedily gnawed on Mom's handmade rag rug. I jumped around stomping out their fiery bodies. Mom shouted and pointed at a blue cord of flame climbing the side of the gas can. Dad cussed loudly and ran from the room, trailing burning puddles. He threw the can into the bathtub, turned on the shower and slammed the glass door shut.

'Put the phone down. It'll go out,' he said to her.

Eventually it did. The glass door shattered from the heat and a wide ribbon of soot stained the wall. The shower water didn't disturb the gasoline fire, of course, and the next day they laughed about Dad's mistake.

'And that, my boy, is how not to make a fire,' he said as the rainbow puddles burned in the bathtub.

They resumed their positions on the couch. Dad sent me to peek at the bathtub and give status reports as the remaining fuel burned away. Mom mourned her murdered rag rug, inspecting the holes with her toes, but neither she nor Jack removed it.

In the morning I saw that the rug was gone. Instead, the wheelchair cut twin wakes through a light blue carpet that I hadn't noticed yesterday. The house was silent. After months of hospital clatter, the stillness was unnerving. My tinnitus filled the void, and I forced a cough to give myself a break from the incessant ringing. Jack had already shifted the furniture to accommodate the width of the wheelchair. The coffee table was gone from the living room and stored in the garage, which because of one small step I couldn't explore.

The chair's front wheel nicked the doorframe of Jack's room. I rubbed at the gouge of yellow wood. It takes time for your sense of self to encompass the extra width. *The* wheels, *the* chair become *my* wheels and *my* chair. Well-intentioned people who push you up hills without asking first can't understand the invasion of personal space. Eventually, you gain a cat-whiskered awareness of the spaces you and the chair can fit between without breaking your stride. But that will take time, pinched thumbs and bashed doorways. In every room of Jack's house, the walls will tell this story in hieroglyphs of scratched paint and tyre marks.

Jack's bed was made hospital-corner crisp. Faded cherries on a field of white covered the bedspread. Mom must have bought this and somehow he had made it last. I smiled at the thought of always-thrifty Jack making the bed each morning with his cherry-covered sheets and following washing care instructions meticulously. In the bathroom was his worn-out toothbrush, toothpaste, two soap slivers mashed into one and a small bottle of white spirits, the liquid a cloudy white at the bottom.

After Mom died, how many mornings had Jack stood there, brushing his teeth while her toothbrush sat in the holder unused? How many toothbrushes had he worn out before he threw hers out too? There was no makeup, no hairbrush or dress on the back of the door to have its wrinkles steamed by a hot shower. The closet too was empty of her. I imagined the gaps between Jack's sparse wardrobe packed with Mom's clothes: the colourful silhouettes of dresses wrapped in drycleaner's plastic, her nurse's whites and rarely worn musky wool coats. What I thought was a women's shoebox was filled with paperwork and receipts.

Did Jack ever find someone else? Maybe he remarried and that other woman threw out Mom's clothes or, worse, wore them? Maybe the cherry-covered sheets weren't Mom's? I couldn't decide if I felt sad or angry or nothing. I wondered if the pistol was still stuffed in the back of the closet, wrapped in its oily cloth. I didn't have any concrete plan for it – it didn't work anyway – but it was hard to stay away from black thoughts.

'Good morning, Ironsides. You want to get out of my room and mind your own business?' Jack said, standing at the door. I rolled back to shut the closet but my chair bumped against the bed. I had to manoeuvre a three-point turn before I managed it. I didn't dare make eye contact with Jack for fear of seeing the pity I felt for myself.

'What are you looking for?' Jack asked.

'Nothing.' The closet door closed harder than I meant it to. Jack stepped aside to let me past, but he followed me into the living room.

'Okay then, sourpuss, how about you go investigate the mystery of the full mailbox? And stay out of my room.' Jack pointed toward the front door. 'I'll put the coffee on. What do you want for breakfast? What do you like these days?'

'I can't.' My world stank of can't and I resented Jack for seeing that. Now, recalling this memory, all I see is an old man as overwhelmed as I was.

'Right. Never mind. You do the coffee. I'll get the mail.'

Jack had to help me with coffee too. The coffee and filters were stored in the upper cabinets above the coffee maker. I filled the urn but from the wheelchair I wasn't tall enough to pour the water into the reservoir. I sat nearby, useless, as he brewed the pot, then followed him to the kitchen table.

'Patrick said he might come visit once things quiet down at his work,' Jack said.

'Oh good,' I said. Jack ignored my sarcasm.

'After breakfast, I'll go to the hardware store and get the wood for the ramp. I was also thinking I might switch out the hinges on the bathroom door so you can do your business in peace. I'll make it so the door swings out rather than in. What do you think about that? If any of the doors are too narrow, you tell me. We can widen them. If it's on a loadbearing wall it'll be a bigger job but Patrick knows people. How wide is your chair? Twenty-five, maybe twenty-six inches, that's my guess. The wheels look like they slant a bit. Do they do that for stability? Let me get my measuring tape.' Jack stood. His chair legs squealed across the terrazzo floor like bad brakes.

'Stop with all the handyman shit!'

Jack looked as if he had been slapped.

'I know you got some grand plan for a father–son reunion, but you can shove it up your ass. You had your chance, you fucked it up. The past's the past. My getting hit by a car isn't your ticket to family therapy time. Melissa is dead because of me!'

He stepped back, his palms facing me. 'You need to calm down. That's not what I was trying to do. Who is Melissa?'

'Can you please, just please, leave me alone? Don't pull your holy AA bullshit on me. Don't tell me Patrick's okay once you get to know him. Don't say anything about the fucked-up childhood you gave me.'

Jack opened his mouth to say something, but I cut him off.

'And don't you dare mention Mom.'

He turned and left. The back door slammed. I knew I

had gone too far but I didn't care. The adrenaline felt better than the constant lurking fear and sadness.

From the kitchen window, I saw him standing motionless in his greenhouse. At the time, I felt it a triumph but now the memory comes with regret and embarrassment. I was twenty-six and yet still acting like a teenager. I found the large bottle of Vicodin perched at the top of the fridge. The only parting gift from the hospital that I needed. They could shove their blue egg-crate padding, their plastic urinal and their pamphlets covering the range of bodily functions from bowel programmes to disabled sexuality. I didn't want any of it. I grabbed a long wooden spoon. I knocked the bottle into my lap. I popped the lid. I poured the pills out. A palmful of teeth.

Late that night, Jack came into my room but I feigned sleep. He replaced the open pill bottle on my bedside table with an orchid, a blossom with small red-lipped petals surrounded by five large white ones. He went to the top drawer of the desk and removed a small sandalwood box. The stashed pills clattered back into the bottle. The lid snapped closed. Of course, he remembered my old hiding spots.

5

Jerry, I'm going to put this tube between your ribs to inflate your lung. Your ribs are broken. It's going to hurt. Ready? One . . . two . . . three.

———◆———

The pain threw me awake and back into Jack's house and the present. I peeled away the sheets, sticky with sweat. I sat up, drank water and threw my legs over the bed to go to the bathroom. All the things the nurses told me to do. The nightmare's panic ebbed and my breathing slowed to normal. Running my hand over the scar on my side where the paramedic stuck the tube, the skin thin and soft, as if by pressing hard enough I could push my fingers through.

For years it hits you anew that you must do it all over again. All the inconveniences and outrages are waiting for you. You'll figure out strategies and tactics to simplify the simple things. Like getting dressed in the morning. You'll set out your clothes for the next day on your nightstand so that you don't have to get up to get the clothes, only to lie back down to put them on. I hadn't figured out that trick yet.

Jack knocked on my bedroom door and opened it.

Following his eyes, I became aware of the stacks of coffee mugs and bowls with their thickened glue of milk and cereal. My few items of clothes were thrown everywhere. The sheets were balled into a pillow at the foot of the bed. I needed a shower.

He surveyed the room's windows, which I had blacked out with the legal letters, hospital bills and collection notices that gathered on the kitchen counter every morning. 'Well, this isn't creepy at all,' Jack said. He picked up his Garden Gripper that I had borrowed. The rubber-tipped claw obediently opened and closed as he gave the trigger a couple of squeezes. 'Yes, perfectly normal behaviour.'

In those first weeks back at Jack's house, I was too haunted by the guilt of Melissa's death to mourn the loss of my legs. I had deserved the punishment received. My depression was the relieved sleep of the condemned. Paraplegia gave me an out too. The hospital left me with enough prescription refills to make sure I never had to try and fail again. My problems would no longer be my fault. It was the wheelchair. The loss. The losses, plural. They were to blame, not me. Jack must have seen that transformation beginning. It had happened to him when Mom died. I see now that Jack's annoying, insistent nudging was to make sure I didn't lose what he had lost.

'You haven't been outside in a while. Let's go for a walk.' Jack said.

Above the midweek stillness that the suburbs do so well, a patchy grey sky dared the sun to burn it away. The interstate was a soft hiss in the distance. We walked in the street, hanging close to the rain gutter, skirting around the slanting concrete at the storm drains. The streets were wide enough for two lanes of traffic in each direction. Mostly, they were empty. The occasional car that crawled by moved far onto the other side as if the elderly man and wheelchair boy might throw themselves at their windscreen. Jack waved to everyone who passed. It felt good to be outside after so long in the hospital. My head swivelled back and forth to catalogue how the neighbourhood had changed/stayed the same. Each corner was marked with a cross of bright green street signs. Bold white letters announced roads with names of the native fauna this suburb replaced: Water Oak Lane, Red Cedar Road, Bald Cypress Street.

'Why aren't there sidewalks? Did there used to be?' I asked.

Jack rubbed at his temple as if he had a headache. 'God, no. When they built the neighbourhood, it was to show off. Look at us. We can all afford cars. Now stuck-up yuppies have moved in and they think only communists take walks.' Jack stopped in front of a small brick house trimmed in hibiscus bushes. A ten-foot inflatable Easter bunny stood smiling near the front door. In one air-filled hand was a paintbrush and in the other was an Easter egg. 'That's one for the nightmares,' he said. 'This is not how I thought I'd be spending my sixty-ninth birthday.'

'Happy birthday,' I said, pushing forward.

'I guess a present is a long shot,' he said. Before I could quip back, he continued, 'If you don't want to tell me what's happened for the last ten years or how you came to show up on my doorstep in a wheelchair, fine. I'll pretend I don't want to know.' He looked up and down the road and rubbed at his temple again. I turned away from his gaze. 'You don't want to be friends.' He grimaced. 'Fine. That's understandable. We're roommates and that's it until you are strong enough to be on your own again. We'll bullshit about football and the weather. After that, you go back to your life and I go back to mine.' He said all this in that rye-bread rumble of his until the sound of a leaf blower roared nearby. The man in the safety glasses and vest nodded to us. After we passed a few more houses, I held the wheel rims, vainly willing myself to keep going.

'How am I going to do anything? I'm exhausted just by going—' Behind us came a yelp of brakes and the crunch of a tail-light. A black Mercedes had backed out of a driveway and had hit a car parked in the street. A businesswoman in a pencil skirt and heels got out to stare at the damage. I bent over, my chin to my knees, with my hands covering my head. I heard the screech of the car the night Melissa died. I felt the impact. The noise. The screams. The panic and pain.

'Jesus!' Jack said.

'She's dead. I hate this. I hate it. I'm going to be sick,' I said, and retched.

Jack, fear in his eyes, got behind me and pushed us home. We moved quickly. I couldn't stop sobbing.

'The lady was fine. She just bumper-bumped a parked car. Jarred, talk to me. You're gone for ten years. You come home like this. I don't know what to do.' Jack struggled with each short sentence, trying to catch his breath.

I rushed to my room with Jack close behind.

I turned on him. 'Here's the deal. I can't walk. Melissa is dead. Jack, that's my fault. She was doing fine until I came around. I did it. Her husband has got his lawyers after me. The driver is changing his story. God knows what happens if the cops charge me. A cripple in jail. Can you imagine? The hospital bills are all on me.'

'We'll figure it out. But you got to talk to me. Who's this Melissa?'

'No!' I shoved the door closed.

6

Boxes laced with cobwebs and the earthy whiff of attic had appeared in my room while I slept. Neither of us acknowledged this gesture or the continued weeks of me sleeping all day. I struggled to shift the box. Without muscles in your legs, your back and stomach must do the work. Your centre of balance is thrown off for months until the new muscles are strong enough to take up the slack. The box was heavy with old sketchpads, neatly packed by Jack, that I had filled when I was fifteen. On an empty page, I sketched the orchid that Jack had left on my nightstand. My pencil tried to mimic the curves of the petals, but it had been a long time since I had drawn. For the shading, I dipped my forefinger in the remains of a coffee and dabbed at the paper.

Jack was in the living room, leaning back in his recliner with the leg rest popped out. I formulated the question in my head. A simple sentence: 'Jack, what's up with the flower in my room?' But, no. I wasted so many chances to talk to Jack.

His hands in his lap held a pamphlet, 'Spinal Cord Injury: Guide to Functional Recovery'. His eyes were closed. I moved closer to Jack and picked at the cracked leather armrest with clouds of stuffing bursting out. I remembered when I had stood over him as he slept in this chair in this house with a brick in my hand and my arms trembling with hate. As I watched him sleep now, it was sadness I felt: thick, cloying and constant.

The coffee table, nicked and gouged, was the same one from my childhood. The couch, the tv, the same. So much of the house hadn't changed. Like Jack, it had only aged.

'Jesus!' Jack started. 'What the hell are you doing creeping up on me?' He slid the pamphlet in his back pocket.

'This house hasn't changed in years.'

'Because it didn't need to.' His eyes closed again.

'Don't you ever get bored of looking at the same four walls?'

'What kind of moron pays attention to walls?' he said, his eyes still closed.

I wheeled over to the few hung photos and drew smiley faces in the dust on the people in the pictures: Jack and Mom on their wedding day, my older brother graduating from high school, my older brother graduating from college, a picture of me on one knee in a Little League uniform but no picture of all four of us together. That would have been an impossibility.

'It's boring around here.'

'Only stupid people—' Eyes still closed.

'Get bored,' I finished his sentence.

'All right.' His eyes popped open. His hand dropped to the recliner's lever and the footrest folded back in with a sproing and a clunk. 'Since I'm not getting my nap, you're going for a walk with me.'

'I can't.'

'C'mon. You've been hiding out in your room too long. Sleeping all the time is not good for you. You should be cutting down on the goofy pills and starting to build up your strength.'

'My back hurts.'

'I'm awake. You got no one to blame but yourself.' Jack said. 'We'll aim for the donut shop and make it as far as we can.'

Two streets down from our house, Jack hesitated.

'Too late. Brace yourself. She must have been waiting behind her curtains for us.'

'What?' I said.

'It's the neighbourhood busybody. She thinks that goddamn dog is the messiah.'

Coming down her driveway was an old woman with a blue-rinse puff of perm perched upon a bag of leathered skin. A small yellow dog looked at us with disappointment from the cradle of her arms.

'Hello, Jack. Is this your son?' she asked in her smoker's grumble.

'This is my youngest, Jarred.'

'Jarred, would you like to meet Lulu?' The dog was in my lap before I could respond.

'Lulu is a cocker spaniel mix and a certified therapy dog.'

The dog stared gormlessly between the woman and me.

'Lulu is the world's bestest, most devoted therapy dog,' she said to the dog.

Its stillness, its warm weight was pleasant. Its black marble eyes shone. The dog gave a few timid licks to the air between us. Softening my look, I patted it on the head. The golden fur was soft. The tail picked up speed, swishing across my jeans.

'Hello, Lulu,' I said.

Lulu's owner beamed at Jack, who looked down the road.

'Lulu, you're a little fur baby. Aren't you?' I said. Jack furrowed his brow, confused. I petted the dog. The tail was a lie-detector needle going nuts.

'Lulu, should we show the nice lady where the bad man touched us? Yes, I think we should.' I lifted the animal. He covered my face in doggy kisses. I cradled him in my arm, his belly up. The dog licked my neck. 'Let's see. First he took me out for ice cream and then he took me to his naked puzzle basement.' I scratched and rubbed the dog's belly.

'He told me to take my shirt off, and he touched me here and here.' I pointed to the dog's nipples. 'I don't remember there being so many. It was definitely these two,' I continued. 'Then the bad man touched me here.' I twanged the carrot-top tuft of hair on the dog's penis. Lulu's tail and tongue were full tilt. The owner squealed in horror and rushed forward. Jack stifled a laugh. The owner and I tussled for the animal, who was loving the attention.

'Wait! Wait! That's not everywhere,' I shouted as the lady retreated back up her driveway. 'Lulu! Lulu, call me!'

'Can't wait to see her community newsletter item about that one,' Jack said. We continued for a few more streets before the pain became too much and Jack pushed me. When we got home, I don't remember if we bullshitted about football and the weather. I hope we did.

7

When I was ten, my mom had an aneurysm and it was my fault. I was sitting in the nurse's office staring at the jar of goat eyes on her desk.

Earlier in the week, the nurse had brought the jar to our fifth-grade class to explain the anatomy of eyes. She talked about the function of each part and handed dissections to my classmates. The lens peeled off like a sticker. The clear jelly disc sat in my palm and enraptured me. At the end of class, she held out a plastic bedpan for us to deposit the remains. I hesitated, not quite finished with this small wonder, and all that day I had sniffed at the sour chemical smell on my hand.

The nurse painted my scraped knees with iodine.

'No more fighting,' she said and sat at her desk to write her notes. A boy, pale and green, came in, holding his stomach. His cheeks puffed and the nurse rushed him to the adjoining bathroom. Violent splashes hit the toilet's water while the nurse encouraged him to get it all out. I unscrewed the jar's lid to fish out an eye.

The principal, Dr. King, rarely spoke. Someone said it was because of the Korean War. I didn't know exactly what that meant, but it felt like an explanation. He stood at the door and motioned for me to follow. I covered the wet spot on my shorts, but he had already noticed. He frowned and pointed at the pocket.

I dug the eye out and placed it in his palm. He furrowed his brow at the glistening white stone. He jerked his hand away and it plopped onto the ground. The corners of his moustache fell. His disgust moved from it to me. He pointed at the eye then pointed at the jar. I obeyed.

We walked through the school with his hand on my shoulder. I stepped carefully amongst the sidewalk cracks, pretending they bubbled and oozed fiery lava.

In his office, Dr. King opened a folder on his desk and dialled the phone. He handed me the receiver.

'Hello, Mom.'

'What have you done? I don't have time for this. Why can't you behave? Your dad is going to kill you.'

'I got into a fight.'

Dr. King raised his eyebrow. I covered the wet spot on my shorts.

'And, I stole an eyeball from the nurse, but I gave it back.'

'What do you mean an eyeball? A real eyeball?'

'A real eyeball.'

'I don't know what you're talking about. Jarred, I have such a headache right now. Let me talk to Dr. King.'

They spoke. He explained why there was a real eyeball in the nurse's office. Mom agreed that my punishment should be spending the rest of the week helping the janitor during recesses. He thanked her and hung up. I went back to my class. All the other kids watched me as I took my seat.

Near the end of the day, the PA speaker above the teacher's desk crackled awake and announced, 'Jarred McGinnis, please come to the principal's office.' I looked at my teacher nervously. She nodded and I retraced my steps through the empty halls toward Dr. King's office.

When I arrived, the secretary came from behind the desk and approached me. Her eyes went wet and she hugged me. I flinched against the fleshy press of her body. Her sweater was soaked with the smell of menthol cigarettes.

'There's been an accident with your mom. Your father called and will meet you at the hospital. It's last bell in a few minutes. Dr. King is going to drive you, okay? Do you want some water? Have a seat in the hall. Just a few more minutes and Dr. King will take you to your mom and dad, okay?'

I blankly did as I was told. As I sat in the hallway outside the principal's office, my thoughts circled. My mom was dead, because I had misbehaved. It was my fault. My mom was dead, because I had misbehaved. It was my fault. My dad and my brother would hate me.

The bell rang, ending the school day and setting off an explosion of noise. The children's laughter, yells and chatter built to a roar as they followed the hall past where I sat. Their staring shamed me. The need to cry churned inside me, but I fought it down. At the exit, a line of yellow buses greeted the students with the ignition of their fat diesel engines. When the last bus had pulled away, Dr. King came out of his office. He knelt in front of me and put his hand on my knee.

'It's not your fault. I'm sure she's okay.'

Startled by my thoughts being read, I began to cry.

'I'm going to take you to your dad,' he said.

Dad was sitting in the hallway of the hospital, just as I had been sitting outside the principal's office. Both places reserved for those to be punished.

'Mom?'

'No, she's not okay. Not at all.'

I bawled and bawled. My body convulsed, but he held me firm. He stared into my eyes, and his tears came silent and single file. That is still the only time I have seen him cry.

Everything in her hospital room was temporary. All the furniture had wheels: the bed, the chair for visitors to come and go and the machines leased to bear witness.

'She's in a coma,' Dad said. She looked happy under her cap of bandages, as if she was playing a trick on us, amused by our gullibility. He explained aneurysms to me while we watched her. They had put a clip in her head to stop the bleeding, and it was now a wait-and-see. She could die. She could stay like that; he pointed at her. Or, she could improve. Improve meant anything from permanent brain damage to same as before. Wait-and-see.

Our wait-and-see lasted a month. Each day after school, I took the bus that dropped me off near the hospital. The other kids acted as if I was a trespasser. I looked out of the window, counting the stops, and watched their stares and pointing in the reflection. While I waited for Dad to finish work, I climbed into her bed, bracing myself against the railing.

'Mom, I'm sorry,' I whispered. I followed the fine lines at the corners of her eyes and lips and thought they made her beautiful. She had a chocolate-chip freckle on her jaw.

'I haven't done anything bad this whole time.' I made deals with her and excuses for why I got into the fight. I offered impossible promises in exchange for her forgiveness. I listened to her breath for whispers, and every muscle twitch was a message to decode.

While we lay wrapped together in thin white sheets and

the smell of the baby shampoo the nurses used to wash her hair and between my deals and promises, I told her about the kids at school who bugged me, the teachers who were unfair and my current fixation, drawing comics. Wait-and-see was the first time that I didn't have to snatch her attention from Dad or the phone calls to my brother Patrick at college. Mostly I felt guilty and fearful but in that bed with us was the thought, carefully ignored, that I liked wait-and-see.

When the clock had sped toward Dad's arrival, I disappeared to look at the others who had been prescribed wait-and-see: newborn babies in clear plastic cribs (huge tubes and tiny bodies), old people in hospice rooms decorated like fancy hotels, the bandaged, the braced, the dying and the ones who would recover. I stole syringes and used them as squirt guns to terrorise my reflection in bathroom mirrors. In the tv room, I got giddy and ill from the cigarette haze.

The nurses and doctors suggested that we talk to her, but when Dad and I were there together, we couldn't. Instead, we held her hands. I mimicked Dad and brushed my thumb against the mother-soft flesh. Sometimes we sat for hours. Sometimes for five minutes. The time to leave was marked by Dad standing and saying, 'C'mon.' Before going home, we ate in the hospital cafeteria, which I liked. Every night I had my favourites: pizza, tater tots and chemical-green Jell-O.

The day Mom awoke I was telling her how I had a new voice in my head. I told her how at first I would hear the voice say 'stop', but I would already be doing something bad. Now the voice warned me beforehand, and it was working.

'Aren't you proud of me?' I touched the tip of her nose and felt the bounce of its cartilage. 'Since the voice has been helping me, I've only gone to time-out a few times.'

Her eyes fluttered. Her mouth opened and closed. She turned her head, and I watched comprehension cutting through the grogginess. Blinking out tears, she slurred, 'My baby, I'm so sorry.'

Her eyes rolled back. The exposed whites beneath the fluttering lids scared me, and I flung myself out of the bed.

I shook her, but I didn't like the way her head lolled. I ran to the nurses' station, yelling that she was awake. When they came to Mom's bedside, she was flailing her limbs as if acting out her dreams, and by the time Dad arrived, they had strapped her wrists to the bed, and she was back to her smirking stillness.

'Then what did she do?' he snapped.

'I went . . . I went and got the nurse.'

'Was she still awake when you left?'

I shook my head.

'You have to stay by her at all times. What did you say to her? It's up to us. Everything is for her now.' His voice was rising, angrier and angrier. 'Don't ever leave her side. Do you hear me?'

I stayed motionless, afraid to speak.

He swallowed his next sentence and left the room shaking his head.

It wasn't long before Mom woke again and stayed awake. The joke over, her coma grin gone. She slurred like a drunk. She couldn't walk. The shaved two-inch strip on the side of her head made her look stupid. She still slept a lot. She said everything was blurry and her head hurt.

★

Mom was finally meant to be coming home the next day. I found myself on the couch when a clatter in the kitchen woke me up.

Dad stood in his undershirt, which was dotted with ancient stains and new dribbles.

That was all he wore.

Framed by a fluorescent square of untanned flesh, his penis and balls hung from a dark clot of hair. He was taking a long drink from his favourite glass, a plastic tumbler with Mickey Mouse on the side. I watched as he emptied it and gave a satisfied 'ahhh'. In his other hand, he held the silverware drawer like a briefcase. Spoons, forks and knives pooled at his feet. He looked at me, frowned and kicked at the pile of silverware.

'What now?' he asked.

He pulled the junk drawer from its slot. Batteries, playing cards, pens and pencils spilled from it. He tossed the drawer over his shoulder, and it knocked down the pots and pans hanging on the wall. I fled and hid inside my bedroom closet. The fury of breaking glass, slamming doors and thumps against walls only stopped when he howled, a long and anguished 'what now?'

I fell asleep crumpled inside the closet. In the morning, the back door was open. Dad gone. Drops of blood marked the counter tops, the refrigerator, the broken plates and glasses. Every drawer had been pulled out and emptied. The cabinets hung wide-mouthed and cleared of their china teeth. Broken against the stove's backsplash, bags of flour and sugar spilled their contents and covered everything. I picked up a box of Cheerios that had been stepped on, ate a few handfuls, and left to catch the school bus.

When I got home, an ambulance was in the driveway. The kitchen was tidied, but hints remained. Drawers sat crooked in their place. A dusting of flour clung to the corners and here and there slivers of broken glass sparkled.

In my parents' bedroom, the EMTs talked to Mom like she was an idiot as they moved her to the bed. She didn't or couldn't acknowledge them. Dad stood in the corner nodding at their instructions. I stared at him with disgust. Like the kitchen, he had put himself in order. An Ace bandage bound his right hand and a dark seam of blood had seeped through.

'Go to your room,' he barked, noticing my gaze.

The EMTs left, saying good-bye to the senseless Mrs. McGinnis. There was a knock on my bedroom door, the creak of it opening and Dad calling my name. His voice haunted the house as he looked for me. He went outside. He came back in, calling for me with growing worry. My closet door slid open.

'What are you doing? Get out of there. We got some things to figure out.' He took me to their bedroom, which was usually off-limits. Mom lay sleeping in the centre of their bed. 'She's had a long day.'

I held her hand like when we were in the hospital.

'Your mom still isn't all the way better. There's a lot of helping out to do. That's our job now. She's always taken care of us. Now we're going to take care of her. Do you understand? Good.'

I stared into his eyes and tried not to cry.

The doorbell rang.

'That's probably the nurse,' he said.

The starched white uniform fought to put straight lines into the nurse's jumble of ellipses. Clipped to her right breast was a nametag, 'Daisy'. Her sunny hellos irked me. Her questions, read from a form that Dad had to sign, were delivered irritatingly singsong.

'We're ready to get started,' Daisy said. She put her clip-board away and, without asking if it was okay, walked into my parents' bathroom to wash her hands. She was near my mom's age and, even then, I wanted to know why Daisy wasn't the one with the aneurysm and my mom, who was also a nurse, wasn't at Daisy's house, asking questions about food allergies and washing her hands in Daisy's sink.

'Mrs. McGinnis. Mrs. McGinnis. We're going to give you a little stretch now. There we go. She's waking up. Hello, Sleepyhead. How are you feeling, Mrs. McGinnis?'

Mom nodded. She looked at Dad and smiled.

'Now, because your mom doesn't move around so much, you need to help her stretch her muscles. You want to help her, don't you?' Nurse Daisy said to me.

My hate complete, I looked at Dad to see if he felt the same, but I couldn't read his expression.

'Watch how I give your momma a good stretch.' The neon cords that hung from her glasses quivered as she manoeuvred to cradle Mom's calf in one hand and press Mom's foot against her bicep.

'Come around to the other side and put her foot in your arm like I'm doing. That's right. Like that. Hold it for the count of ten. Then relax and do it again.' Mom's feet were cold and clammy; touching them felt inappropriate, an intimacy we were forcing upon her. Dad nodded to reassure me. Mom remained impassive as Nurse Daisy and I stretched her motionless limbs.

One day I came home from school and Dad and Nurse Daisy were yelling at each other in the living room. Dad was calm, but his voice was raised. Nurse Daisy was flushed and, in her white uniform, she looked like a grub with CPR training.

'I'm not paying you to take care of Pat fucking Sajak,' Dad said.

'She was taking a nap.'

'That doesn't mean you get one too.'

'What would you like me to be doing?' she asked in a tone that illustrated one of the ways people can say 'go fuck yourself'.

Dad, preferring simple and direct, said, 'Go fuck yourself.'

'Sir, I don't have to stand here and—'

'No, you certainly don't. Jarred, get out of the way.'

'You will—'

'Lady, less talking and more leaving.'

She left.

He walked into their bedroom, and their laughter was interrupted by Mom coughing.

'Jarred, get your butt in here,' Dad called. 'The good news is Nurse Ratched isn't coming back. The bad news is that we got to take up the slack. I'm going to take some time off work and be the mom for a while.'

He patted her arm and smiled.

Even at ten years old I understood the look of worry she gave him.

Dad was the perfect nurse to Mom despite the Mickey Mouse tumbler following him as he did his chores. It sat in the garage as he separated the laundry. It sat near Mom's head as he cared for her.

We measured progress daily by a word pronounced that hadn't been yesterday, or by the extra minutes that she wasn't tired. The freezer was stuffed with my hospital favourites of pizza and tater tots. Most nights, Dad and I made Jell-O together. I stood on a chair to stir in the mix, pale gelatine dust turning vibrant as it poured into the water. Mom's steriliser with its cartoon rubber ducky trimming hissed beside us.

Now when I came home, I lay in their bed and Dad would be there already or come in shortly after with Mickey Mouse refilled and a watered-down whiskey for her.

'Do you want to see what I made?'

Mom nodded. Dad stopped reading the paper and looked over. He was wearing her apron decorated in shamrocks and hearts.

'It's a gun.'

My gun was a twelve-inch wooden ruler with a clothes pin glued to one end. I stretched the rubber band from the end of the ruler, but as soon as I clamped the rubber band, the clothes pin launched across the room in a sloppy arc.

'Glue won't hold, huh? C'mon,' Dad said.

The garage air was pleasant, cooler than outside with the sweetness of motor oil and sawdust. At Dad's workbench, tools hung on the wall, outlined like murder victims. In front of us, coffee cans of to-be sorted nuts, nails, screws and bolts sat.

'We need some epoxy. But, what you got here . . .' He held up my ruler. 'This here is bush league. Go get me a refill. My glass is on your mom's nightstand.'

When I returned, he took a drink and set it amongst its nest of ring stains. I sat beside Dad, snapping a rubber band against my cheek, increasing the tension each time. He jigsawed two scraps of lumber into the silhouettes of rifles. The scream of the saw drove excitement into my boy's heart. He helped me glue the clothes pins on with an epoxy syringe and spin the handle of the vice.

'While this sets, let's get some elephant-gun ammo and set up a target.' He looked under the workbench and dug around until he pulled out a bouquet of long red rubber bands. He drew a target on a piece of newspaper and taped it against the garage door.

'Hey,' he said. 'Want a sip?'

I considered the shining coal of his eyes.

'It's going to be okay now. Your mom's the strongest person I know. Ten times stronger than me. A hundred times stronger than anyone out there.'

Long seconds passed.

'Hey, look at me. You okay?'

Dad held me as I cried. He kissed my head and breathed promises into my hair. 'I promise you. I promise she's going to be better. It's up to us. I love you, son.'

'I love you.'

'Here, blow your nose on this,' he said and handed me an oil rag. 'Time to check our handiwork.'

We stretched rubber bands along the length of the wood and set them into the grip of the clothes pins. When we hit the target, the paper would snap and leave a rectangular hole. We'd cheer and reload.

'Does Mom want to have a turn?'

'Good question.'

We lay in bed with her and took turns shooting a stuffed dragon that used to be my favourite toy. When it was her turn to shoot, I held the gun while she unsteadily pinched the clothes pin to release the rubber band. Dad took a few turns too, but soon was answering the buzz of the washing machine, refreshing their glasses, or phoning the insurance company to argue about a bill.

For several weeks, we three floated on the raft of their bed past this hostile territory. Mom improved every day.

The tv was pulled into the bedroom and set up on their dresser. We ate our dinners from our laps watching game shows and sitcoms. We played board games spread across the sheets. Alone together and separated from the world, we were happy. Until finally our wait-and-see ended.

Mom died.

A second aneurysm while I was at school. A second wait outside the principal's office until he could drive me to the hospital, and the first time I ran away.

8

'Today's the day,' Jack announced as he helped me over the rain gutter. Our goal was still the donut shop at the edge of the neighbourhood. It had taken weeks but with every walk I had gone a little further.

Jack took a letter out of his back pocket, shoved it in the mailbox and raised the metal red flag. He tried to be quick, but I saw the letterhead of the hospital. He had been making the minimum payments to staunch the flow of creditors. I didn't have the courage to tell him to stop, and he wouldn't have listened.

Our walks were mostly silent, but occasionally Jack talked about his 'kids', the orchids.

'The thing to do is leave them alone the best you can. Other than that, it's about knowing where they come from. The one in your room comes from the Philippines.' His hand jabbed at a point on an imaginary map. Jack brightened. 'How much rainfall and how much light they're used to. Yours doesn't need much light and just keep its roots moist, not wet.'

I leaned forward for the last few pushes, my arms quivering and my legs crying wolf.

'How're you doing? Not too sore? Think you're going to make it?'

'I think so.'

We crossed the parking lot and passed the empty units with their glass fronts suggesting 'For Leasing Information Contact Ed'. The strip mall was a copy and paste of every other strip mall from every other town in every other state I'd been to: surrounded by a near-empty sea of parking spaces, a border of squared hedges at the edge of the road, a covered sidewalk in front of shops with their neutral-coloured paint jobs and each with a name written in backlit letters. 'Mr. Do-nut's' is after 'Goode's Chiropractic' and 'Tae Kwon Do Grandmaster D.D. Jones'. My muscles quaked, but it felt good. A few steps ahead, Jack was fighting the urge to look back and check on me.

I reached the shop and exhaled triumphantly. 'Made it.'

Jack opened the door. 'Not there yet. Donuts are inside.'

The small shop's glass counter stuffed with trays of donuts separated the few tables from the back of the shop, where Mr. Do-nut and an elderly Laotian woman stacked trays onto racks. A self-serve coffee urn sat beside the soda machine. Behind the counter there was a daily trivia question. The correct answer earned you a free donut. An asterisk was added in a different pen, 'No Using Inter-net'.

'Good morning, Jack. The usual?'

'Yep and whatever this young man would like,' Jack said.

'Is this your youngest? I haven't seen him in forever.' Mr. Do-nut flipped up the counter-top and stepped through to shake my hand. I waited for the 'What happened to you?', but it didn't come. Maybe Jack had already told him, maybe he knew enough to not ask, or it didn't matter. God bless the incurious.

I suspected they knew each other from AA. While he and Jack chatted, I went over to a table and pushed a chair out of the way. You don't need furniture when you bring your own.

Amongst the posters showing the team rosters of the local high school – the one that had kicked me out years ago – a clipping of the local newspaper, decades old, showed a young Mr. Do-nut holding his paper hat and grinning widely. Jack joined me with two coffees and a bag of donuts.

'A toast,' Jack said. We raised our donuts and tapped them together. 'Today donuts, tomorrow the world.' We sat and read the newspaper like a normal father and son.

Jack popped the last bite of a donut into his mouth with a satisfied hum. He wiped the sugar glaze from his fingers.

'How are you doing with your goofy pills?'

'I'm cutting down. One or two during the day. Two or three to sleep. My legs feel like they're on fire at night.'

'Just go easy on that stuff.'

'Your concern has been noted,' I said tersely and he knew when to stop pushing.

A greasy-haired blonde, pulling a small girl behind her, approached the counter. Ignoring Mr. Do-nut's greeting, she pointed at the display case and called out her order. When asked if that was all, she said a dozen donut holes as if that should have been obvious.

'I got a hot batch of plain coming in two seconds. Is that okay, ma'am?'

'Yeah, I guess,' she huffed. I felt her staring and was determined to cow her into politeness. Unfazed, disgust crept onto her face as she surveyed my legs and the wheelchair. Her bellybutton peered from under her tank top like a squint-eyed cyclops. She hiked up her sweatpants and blinded the monster. I hid behind Doonesbury and Garfield, angry at the shame that she should've been feeling instead of me.

She approached the table.

'What happened to you?' she asked.

''Nam, ma'am. Goddamn V.C. booby trap took my fuckin' legs!' I said.

The woman looked at me doubtfully and turned to Jack. 'Isn't he too young to have been in the Vietnam War?'

'Tell that to Nixon, lady. Now could you and your donuts fuck off and leave us alone?'

'Excuse me. Let's go, Laura. Some people don't have any manners.'

I laughed at her retreat. Jack smiled.

'That's right. Keep walking,' Jack called after her.

9

Jack was in his greenhouse by the time I woke up in the afternoon. Ten by thirty feet and shaped like an old-fashioned barn, its roof and walls were all glass. When I was a kid, his greenhouse was a small wooden structure with thick plastic sheets staple-gunned on. Then, he grew a few vegetables and flowers for Mom.

I craned my neck, lifting myself from the wheelchair, and watched him from the window. He was wearing a smock over a button-down shirt while he gardened. I was trying to remember if the Jack I knew as a child was as fastidious. Through the greenhouse panes I saw him with his head bent, a man in prayer, talking to his plants. Was he a lonely man or content or both? I had never gotten to know my father and that now seemed a mistake.

At two o'clock on the dot, every day, Jack hung his still perfectly clean smock on a peg near the door and came into the house calling me to take our daily walk to the donut shop.

I wheeled into the living room with my shoes in my lap.

'You need help?'

'No,' I said as I pulled my leg up and set it across my knee to wrestle a shoe on.

Jack said, 'Think of the money you're going to save on shoes alone.'

Our afternoon routine was interrupted by the arrival of a black Cadillac Escalade that dwarfed Jack's little Honda. My brother Patrick knocked then strode into the house just as I got my laces tied. He shook my hand as if I was a business client.

'Hey, Pops,' Patrick said.

'Where's the wife? My grandkids?'

'They're all at home. The twins have a cold but no biggie. I was just in town for a meeting. Thought I'd swing by to see how you and Jarred are getting on. You need anything?' he asked as he sat down on the couch.

Jack was in his usual chair. I was already sitting.

'How are you feeling, Pops? You okay? Did you make an appointment yet?'

Jack frowned and gave a quick shake of the head to Patrick. I pretended not to notice.

'I could get my guys over to take care of your lawn. They can do the tree trimming too.'

'I can do all that. I'll strap a lawnmower to this one and get him to do it.' Jack pointed at me.

Patrick turned his head. 'You're so brave. Our church has been praying for you. How are you?'

'Fine and dandy,' I mimicked his overly friendly tone. 'I don't know why I didn't break my spine sooner. How about you? How's Katie and the 1.8 kids?'

'Katie?'

'Your wife. She's got to be a Katie or a Deborah.'

'Karen.'

'I was close. How's Karen?'

'Fine.' Patrick turned to Jack. 'How's life with a roommate?'

'You can see for yourself. He's an asshole.'

'I noticed.'

'Brother, when I was in the hospital begging the nurses for enough morphine to knock me out, do you know what I found in the drawer next to my bed? A Bible. Do you know the story of Abraham?'

Patrick smiled and said of course. Jack gave me a look of caution.

'So, the Almighty tells this guy to drag his ass up a mountain saying he just had to have a sacrifice. And, oh yeah, he wants the sacrifice to be his kid. The same kid that poor Abe and his wife waited forever for.'

Patrick's smile turned stale, but he didn't stop me. We all knew how this played out, falling into decade-old roles. I was ashamed of myself but I couldn't stop either.

'Abe, the prick, does what he's told,' I continued.

Patrick opened his mouth to say something but didn't.

'Don't worry. He'll wear himself out soon,' Jack said.

'He straps the kid down, who is probably screaming his head off, wishing he grew up with those nice idol-worshipping neighbours next door and, just as Abe raises the knife, Isaac thinking "I'm fucked", God comes out, shit-eating grin, and says, "Just kidding."'

Patrick looked at Jack, who shrugged his shoulders and shook his head.

'Abe, stunned but thankful, drops the knife. Falls to his knees and is in the middle of thinking how to tell the Almighty where he can shove all this prophet business when the Lord, the sicko, winks and says, "But I am going to need a bit of his dick back. You know, for a covenant and stuff."'

Jack said, 'You feel better? How long have you been practising that one?'

'I'm sorry, Jarred. I was trying to be supportive.'

'Well, tell your church to pray harder; I'm still in this wheelchair. Jack, I'll be in my room.'

I came back out when the SUV pulled from the driveway. Jack, his feet up in his recliner, was reading one of his gardening magazines.

'That guy is a walking stereotype.' I pointed toward the window. 'All-American boy with his patriotic Republican beer belly.'

Jack put down his magazine and watched me.

'Does he just come over to brag about how rich he is? He was here for how long? Thirty minutes. He mentioned his SUVs, his Mustang for the weekends. His life is numbers: interest rates, price per square footage – you should have hit him up for some money.'

'What do you know?' Jack said sharply.

I paused, taken aback, and I realised that Jack had been borrowing money from Patrick, which must have been why he stopped over.

Jack sighed and put down the magazine again. 'What's it to you? He's happy.'

'His life was easy.'

Jack stood up. 'This isn't about Patrick. Stop being such a clever prick for five seconds and you'll figure that out.'

10

On the day of Mom's funeral, the house was full of family and co-workers. Patrick was there, not quite thirty, but looking very comfortable in a suit. He greeted every visitor. Each one was bearing sombre expressions and casserole dishes. To this day lasagne means death to me.

I had just escaped the clutches of an aunt who was battling to make one of Dad's ties fit me. Her last attempt, a knot the size of my fist, was good enough to satisfy her. I said thanks and fled. I found Dad in their – now his – bedroom. I sat beside him. We stared at the wall for answers.

'I'm not going to the funeral,' I announced.

'No? Why not?'

I shrugged, took Mom's pillow from the bed, and buried my head into it for the scent of her. We sat together and stared at the wall; still it gave nothing away.

'I'm definitely not going to the funeral.' I stood up and left.

In the kitchen, I took a sandwich from the pile and a can of Coke from the counter. A woman who I didn't know suggested there were cold ones in the fridge. I shook my head, put the edge of Mom's pillow in my teeth and went outside.

The neighbour across the street always left their garage door ajar to let their cats go in and out. I set my sandwich, Coke and pillow inside, then squeezed through. A narrow space meandered between the stacks of boxes and junk. The workbench was a pile of rusting tools and I compared it to Dad's orderly system of having a place outlined on the wall for every screwdriver and wrench. I thought someone should tell the neighbour about this system.

I moved between the stacks of boxes, opening them to examine the contents: photos and papers, canned food, newspaper-wrapped knick-knacks and ancient appliances. A marquee that advertised 'PIZZA' leaned against the back of a gun cabinet storing golf clubs, which created a space big enough for me to lie down. I moved boxes to seal one side, and I had my fortress. Shortly after, the calling of my name stopped, and the cars drove away.

I left her pillow in my fortress and shoved the empty can into a box of junk. Our house was left unlocked, but it was empty. The dining-room table was full of Tupperware and Pyrex domed with food. I pressed my finger into the Saran-wrapped broccoli cheese casserole and smushed a hole into it. I ate a cookie and smushed more holes. I ate some chips from a bowl and made more holes until the well-wisher's comfort food looked like a pegboard.

I went into Mom's closet, stumbling on the piled shoes, and was enveloped by her hanging clothes. The hangers clattered and her long dresses fell to the ground as I tripped and tangled myself into them.

In her bathroom, I uncapped and unscrewed and sniffed the menagerie of bottles and tubes that mothers need. I twisted the pink bullet of a lipstick up and down. I spread it on my lips and looked at myself in the mirror. I put two sharp streaks of war paint on my cheeks and one down the centre of my nose and forehead. I nibbled and chewed the waxy tip before returning it to its basket.

I crawled under her side of the bed, lying on my back, and imagined her sleeping above me. I was awoken by Dad pulling me out by the ankle. He wiped away the lipstick on my cheek and sniffed his fingers.

'Your brother is going to sleep in your room and drive back tomorrow. Okay? You can have the couch or sleep in here with me.'

'In here.'

'Hey, we gave Mom a fighting chance. You took good care of her. She's gone now, and we have to figure out how to deal with it, but she died knowing how much we loved her. That's more than a lot of people get.'

I nodded, but I didn't understand.

He continued, 'Think of all those extra days we had lying beside her, holding her hand. Remember? You should know just how special that is. Do you hear me? I mean it.'

He waited for me to respond.

'How about you go clean your face off? Unless you got a date or something.'

For a few months after the funeral, there was the flickering light of a dying bulb from Dad. It would fade until he was nothing more than a thin red filament when he and the Mickey Mouse glass disappeared into the garage to sort his coffee cans of junk. Sometimes he'd brighten, speak to me, be the adult, the parent, but each time his light returned, it was dimmer and dimmer. As far as I know, he never went back to work. Insurance money kept the electricity on and Mickey Mouse tanned whiskey brown.

I heard Mom's voice too often. I'd shake my head to get rid of the painful whispers and a few times I was sent to the school psychologist with teacher-scrawl notes of concern. We talked about stages of grief through picture books.

'Which stage do you think you are in?'

I gave the answers the little man with the gull's-egg head seemed to want and left as quickly as he would let me.

I heard her most often at home, singing, calling for Dad, who had more pet names than an ancient god. Sometimes it was the echo of her nurse's clogs on the floor.

Sadness ambushed me daily.

I was eating my after-school snack and watching a montage of the A-Team wielding their makeshift weapons driven on by their jaunty theme song. Bad guys flew in slow-motion non-lethal somersaults. I was crying so much my body shook. Dad picked me up like I was a baby. He looked confused and scared, not sure what to do with this strange child who was now his responsibility alone.

'Let's go see your mom.'

We left the house.

'We're going to walk it.'

I hesitated.

'I'm too tired to drive.' It was later that I figured out that tired meant drunk. 'C'mon, it's not that far. It'll be an adventure.'

The weather was warm and clear and the puffs of cotton-wood seed staggering on the wind made the world seem safe. We walked the sidewalks along the main road. We stopped for drinks at a gas station. Dad pulled a Coors off the six-pack like a ripe apple and emptied it in a gulp. I tried to match him, but the Coke's fizz burned my nose. A huge burp erupted.

'Say excuse me,' he said.

'Excuse me.'

He let out his own, loud and powerful, then he excused himself.

At the graveyard, the rows of headstones were lined up waiting for somebody, anybody. Mom's grave didn't have a stone yet. A red scab of clay amongst the grass and trees marked her death.

'I got another letter from school,' he said. 'You need to keep your head down and stay out of trouble.'

As if crawling into bed beside her, Dad lay on the ground. I sat, the rectangle of Mom's grave between us.

'Tell me something nice about your mom,' he said.

'She smelled nice.' I picked blades of grass then laid them in a row, 111111.

'Yep. She did. She had pretty eyes.'

'She had a chocolate chip right here. Her lucky freckle.'

'Her beauty spot. Do you think your mom was perfect?'

I thought about it. I nodded.

'I think so too. I've loved your mom all my life. I don't know how to be without her. She made me want to be a good man. I'm having a hard time believing why I should keep it up.'

I didn't know what he wanted me to say.

'You're growing up. Soon enough, you're going to start liking girls. You're going to love them and if you're lucky one'll love you back. You're going to be stupid. There's no avoiding it. A boy's hands are too callow for a thing as fine as a girl's heart. You're going to take for granted women who are too good for you in the first place. You aren't a man until you have enough regrets to shame you into it. Boys have no regrets.'

I wanted him to stop talking.

'I know this is all nonsense and I'm talking to myself here, but I hope you meet a girl as perfect as your mom.

I had so many, so many good years, more than any man is due.'

No, I wanted him to keep talking so I didn't cry.

'I'm glad she died first though. I think of her being left behind and feeling like this. I can't breathe sometimes, it hurts so much.'

I wanted to be here, but alone.

'I couldn't have done that to her. When she was real sick, before she woke up the first time, I should've loaded us all into a car and driven off a cliff. I hate myself for thinking like that.'

I wanted to run away. I wanted that, most of all.

Dad found me in a mausoleum arranging the niche vases so that all the flowers were on one side of the room.

'I don't know. What now? Donuts? Let's get some donuts. Mom would want us to be happy. Fat and happy.'

Still licking the sugar from my fingers, I had a kind of happiness. Back at the house, full of fried dough and remembrances of Mom, we were son and father. We were watching tv in the living room. Dad asked about school, but my lack of interest defeated him. I could see him straining to think of something to talk about. I didn't mean to discourage him, but I didn't know how else to respond.

During a commercial, Dad left and went into his bedroom. He came out wearing his old Navy uniform and boots. Bright flesh winked between the straining-buttons. He went into the garage wearing a motorcycle helmet the shape of a turtle shell. Curiosity stole my attention from the empty flickering of the tv and I went to find out what the tearing noises were.

Shredded cardboard boxes surrounded him.

'Come here. You need battle armour for Armageddon.'

He placed a sheet of cardboard with a hole in the centre so it fitted like a poncho. He tied it down with twine. He made me two tissue-box greaves for my shins and wrapped my forearms in the remains of a banana box. He nodded appreciatively at his work.

'Stay here.'

I fiddled with my armour, excited by whatever he had planned.

He returned with a plastic colander and sunglasses.

'Put these on, soldier.'

He dug out of his pocket Mom's lipstick and gave my cheeks two slashes of tutu-pink war paint.

'Go get your rubber-band guns.'

I did.

We loaded.

'Now we are ready to hunt the most dangerous game,' he said and walked back into the house.

'Armageddon!' he shouted. He jumped into the garage, gave another war cry of 'Armageddon!' and fired his gun. The rubber band snapped me in the shoulder.

'Oww,' I said, but it didn't really hurt.

'Ten . . . nine . . . eight . . . seven . . .' he counted while stretching another rubber band.

I shot at him as he bolted from the doorway.

We ran around the house, shouting 'Armageddon!' before each shot. We knocked over framed pictures, bumped into shelves. We hid behind furniture and ambushed each other.

When he put me to bed that night my cheeks were sore from smiling.

11

'You want a sandwich or something?' I asked as I wheeled past Jack sitting at the kitchen table, going over a store's receipt.

'A ham and mustard, please.'

'Thanks for going to the art shop for me. You want to see the watercolour I did?'

'There was a girl there with her ears stretched out like she was an Amazon tribesman. Why would you do that to your own head?' Jack opened the watercolour pad. 'This is good. How's your orchid doing? Do you remember the name?'

'Jack, the grumpy moth orchid,' I said, spreading the mustard.

'The real name.'

'Jack, the grumpy Phalaenopsis Aphrodite.'

He nodded, impressed. 'Bonus points for the species.'

He took a bite of his sandwich, hummed appreciatively as he chewed. I pulled the watercolour toward me. The green looked too washed out.

'Good news.' I pulled the denial letter from my sketch pad. 'According to Social Security, I'm not disabled.'

Jack said, 'You'll always be special to me.' He read the single sheet of paper and looked at its reverse side. 'That's it? They don't say why they think you aren't eligible any more. Jesus Christ. I thought you said that woman at the hospital had this all figured out.'

'I tried to call her and the social security office but couldn't get hold of anyone.'

Jack's voice rose. 'That's just great. Great.'

'Don't get pissed off at me. I can't get much more disabled.'

Jack looked from the paper to the corner of the room.

'It's fine. We'll figure it out.' He set it down. The back door slammed. I took the rest of his sandwich and threw it in the trash.

All our afternoon walks started with Jack helping me over the gutter. That tiny, shallow insignificance that toddlers and the elderly stepped over without a thought was impossible for me to manage alone. I had hitchhiked across the country back and forth a hundred times, jumping trains a hundred more times. One wheelchair later and I couldn't leave the driveway by myself.

I jerked the chair back and balanced on its large back wheels. It was a satisfying feeling as if my body was weightless, untethered from earth, floating inches above it. My arms held me and the chair at a point of equilibrium. I felt the glee of a toddler at his first steps. Inch by inch, I pushed the chair toward the gutter. A small acceleration as the back wheels went down the slope. At the vertex, I shifted my weight again and returned the front wheels to the ground. I smiled, genuinely pleased at my victory. Small wars deserve donuts.

'Where's your old man?' Mr. Do-nut asked.

'He's on his way,' I lied. 'Can you spot me a glazed until the old dude gets here?'

I ate my donut and thought of nothing. Children zipped past the window dressed in their Tae Kwon Do gis.

'Can you tell me when you wander off?' Jack said as he entered the shop. 'Don't worry about the bills. We'll figure something out. It's not your fault.'

'It is. It is absolutely my fault. You were fine until I came back. The last thing you said to me, the last time you saw me, you said that I'll always be a fuck-up. I never forgot that.'

Mr. Do-nut hailed Jack from behind the counter. 'The usual?'

Jack straightened up. His expression smoothed to a friendly smile. He called back, 'Thank you, sir. Coffee for this one too.'

After Mr. Do-nut delivered two plain glazed on a paper plate and two black coffees, Jack said, his voice low, his expression regretful. 'That was a long time ago.'

'No. You were right. Now look. You don't get more fucked up than this.' I slapped the wheelchair. 'Which is fine. I deserve it, but you shouldn't have to put up with it.'

'Good, bad, it isn't ever about *deserve*.'

'I know they have homes for people like me. I'll get my social security back. See if welfare will pay to put me in one of those.'

'If that's what you want, Jarred, that's what we'll do. But I'd rather have you home.'

We drank our coffees. The silent tv hung above us showing cable news. I picked apart my Styrofoam cup and created a mosaic on the table.

'When I was trying to sober up, I started growing orchids. At first, it was just about making the hours not drinking disappear. You remember Thomas? He was into orchids and got me started.'

'You don't believe that, do you?' I dropped my eyes back to tearing my cup.

'Believe what?' Jack finished the last of a donut and the remainder of his coffee.

I edged a Styrofoam piece into place with my finger. 'I don't remember it so neat and tidy. You used to hide out in your greenhouse to drink and get away from me.' I brushed the pieces into my hand then dropped them into the remainder of the cup. 'You grew orchids long before you got sober.'

'No.' Jack shook his head, but I could see memories were coming back.

'Once after you gave me a black eye, I blew up your greenhouse with a garbage bag filled with acetylene. The explosion blew out my eardrums and burned off my eyebrows. My ears still ring.'

'Maybe,' Jack said. 'The past is the story we tell ourselves to get through today.'

Mr. Do-nut was in the back moving trays to a cooling rack.

'Is that some AA fortune-cookie wisdom?' I went back to tearing at the cup.

Jack took a drink, but the cup was empty. He looked at the bottom and frowned. 'Maybe, but that doesn't make it wrong,' he said and went for a refill.

He returned, talking as he sat. 'When you were little . . . Really little. Maybe three. We were by the ocean, the three of us. Patrick must have been in college. I told you over and over again to stay away from the seawall. But you were a shithead, even back then. Still you went back to the edge, throwing stones or something.

'I yelled at you to stay away from the water. You looked at me. You said, "If I fall, will you save me?" I said, "We should be so lucky." You looked at me funny. I could see your little brain trying to work out my meaning. Then you tottered off to get more rocks and stand by the seawall and throw them in.'

'Did I fall in?'

'No, of course not. But I'm sorry I said that. I didn't mean it. When you're a parent sometimes you say shit you don't mean. Kids are exhausting, but I'm sorry.'

'Is that what you want to apologise for? Because I can think of other things.'

'I'm sure you can. Jarred, goddamn it,' he said without anger. 'Quit picking old fights. Right now, I need you to let me say what I need to say.'

I nodded then returned my attention to my cup. I felt his eyes on me, but I stayed focused on tearing up pieces of Styrofoam and putting them in the remains of the cup.

'I called the cops a few times. I filled out the missing juvenile forms. No one cares about some drunk and his delinquent son. They said there was nothing they could do until you broke the law.'

'They never waited long,' I said.

'But, to be honest, near the end, I let you run off. It wasn't like you were ruining your chances at a Harvard scholarship or anything. I let you run away, because I wanted you to run away. And you know why? Because another year in that house, holed up in my room, wondering what the crap you were going to do to spite me next, another day of that and I might have gone back to drinking. I wasn't strong enough to be a good father and a good husband. When you have kids, you'll understand better. Being a parent means always being wrong, no matter what you do. I was ready for it to be someone else's fault for a change.'

Mr. Do-nut was in the very back of the shop. He was

standing at an industrial sink and staring at the wall. His hands rested on the corners of the stainless-steel tub.

Jack followed my eyes.

'What's he doing?' I asked.

'Probably thinking the same thing we're all thinking.'

'What now?'

'What now, what now,' Jack said, 'C'mon. Men who stare at walls are best left alone. Let's take the long way home now that you're a world traveller.'

12

A magnet in the shape of a frog held a ten-dollar bill to the fridge. Some weeks instead of lunch money it was a case of Capri-Sun, variety packs of potato chips and Little Debbies with a note 'For the week. Make it last'. One week it was a hundred-dollar bill that got me an accusation of theft by the lunch lady and a confused phone call from a teacher where Dad's slurred shouts blasted from the receiver. On occasion Monday's lunch money for the week appeared Tuesday or Wednesday.

I took the money, packed my schoolbooks and waited for the bus. As we left our neighbourhood, I pretended that Mom was an acrobat running beside the bus. She did double, triple, quadruple somersaults over cars and buildings. Swinging on a lamppost, her white jumpsuit with its red stripe looked like a pinwheel. In her path, my father was shambling back from the 7-Eleven with a case of beer, already drinking one. She cleared the shameful figure with an effortless hop and cartwheeled through the intersection to keep up with the bus.

13

I dug around the junk drawer in the kitchen looking for something to write with. There was a box of matches, which I took, which made me think about cigarettes and having at twenty-six to ask my father if I could borrow money for smokes. That was too much reality for this early in the day. I found a metal pen with surprising heft. It was a freebie from Patrick's business. 'McGinnis Properties' written in a fancy John Hancock script. I wrote 'Jack. Going to take a walk. Jarred'. I thought about the sentence. Take a walk. What else do you write? I crumpled the paper and went to find Jack in his greenhouse.

'Jack, I'm going out for a bit.'

He said, 'It's almost two. If you wait until I clean up, I'll go with you.'

'I kind of want to be by myself.' There was worry on his face. He was trying to calculate the right thing to say. 'Calm your old balls,' I said. 'I'll be fine. I won't get far on foot.'

'Yeah, that's true,' he chuckled. 'You need some money?' Before I could answer, Jack fished out his wallet from his back pocket and handed me a soil-smudged twenty.

'Thanks.'

I crossed the gutter at the end of the driveway a little more easily this time. Left was how we went to Mr. Do-nut. I went right. There was a grocery store at the end of the neighbourhood, and I could get smokes. I pushed myself along the street. This was the first time since the accident that I had been alone. Before the accident, I preferred solitude. Now, with the chair, being alone scared me.

At the crosswalk the zipping traffic made me flinch. I hated myself for the cowardice as I waited for the light to change from DON'T WALK to WALK. My palms were sweaty. I looked left, right, left, right, scared that at any moment a car was going to slam into me. With every push across the intersection, panic fluttered in my chest. When I reached the other side, I had to wait for a few seconds for my hands to stop shaking enough so that I could continue pushing my wheels.

In the grocery store, I went up and down the aisles from produce to dairy with no real purpose. It had been so long since I had been shopping that it felt novel. A teenager in the store's uniform stopped stacking cans of tomato soup as I passed by.

'Hello, sir. Can I help you with anything today?'

'No, I'm fine.'

'Okay. Let me know if there's anything you can't reach,' he said as I continued down the aisle.

In the meat section, I manoeuvred to try to lift a ham into my lap. Before I could, another teenage employee, a girl this time, appeared, her ponytail swinging behind her.

'I can bring that up to the front for you, sir.' She reached to take the ham from me.

'I got it. Thanks.'

'You sure?'

'Yes, thank you,' I said.

'You sure, sir? Okay. Have a nice day,' she said and bounced away.

I was stopped once more before I decided to leave. At the service counter, I was carded for the cigarettes. I showed him my ID.

'Are you here by yourself?'

'Yes,' I said testily.

'Was it a car accident?'

'Really?'

We stared at each other.

'The ham too?' he said, pointing at my lap.

'No, this is my ham. There are many like it, but this one is mine.' I slapped the meat.

'Sorry, sir.' He took my money and gave me my change and the cigarettes. 'Have a nice day.'

'You too,' I said, moving away, the weight of the ham making it difficult.

I sat outside the grocery store and had a cigarette. Shoppers went in and out, and nicotine reverie tugged my thoughts along. I wasn't ready to go back to the house. Across the street from the grocery store, there was a 1950s gas station and garage that had been converted into a coffee shop called the Filling Station. Inside it had everything expected of a coffee shop: raw wood tables, exposed brick and a roasting 'philosophy' chalked on a large piece of slate. Above the tables, bromeliads hung instead of light bulbs at the end of electrical fixtures. Some had turned upwards to form red-leafed Js.

The barista was about my age. She was singing along to the music and wiping down the coffee machine. She was pale. She was red-haired. Her t-shirt read 'sexy senior citizen' in tiny letters. When she turned, I noticed that her belt had missed one of its loops in the back.

She greeted me with: 'Nice ham. What would you like?'

'Black coffee for me and Señor Jamon here will have a water.'

I picked a table with a view of the counter. I set my ham in the chair next to me and drank my coffee.

Jack came out of the garage when he heard the front door.

'Hey, how'd your first solo flight go?'

I held out the meat to Jack. 'It was pork and gimp day. Bring a cripple, get a ham. What luck, huh?'

He took it from me and put it in the fridge without comment. I lay on the couch. The locking of brakes, the positioning of the feet on the floor, the transfer over, the pulling the legs up one by one, had become automatic.

Jack came back with a letter in his hand and sat in his favourite chair. My stomach turned as I tried to guess what kind of letter.

'You promise not to freak out on me?'

'I don't know. Freaking out is my thing.' I tried to stay calm, shifting so that I was lying on my side and I could see him better. My knees clunked together and there was a flash of electric fire from my damaged nerves.

'You don't have to tell me,' Jack said.

'However, I did meet the love of my life today. So now is the time for bad news.'

'Oh yeah?' Jack nodded. 'That's good.'

'Very good. Fingers crossed she has a thing for men and aluminum. Hit me. What's in the letter?'

I stretched my arm out and Jack handed it to me.

'A gentleman by the name of Farooq Al-Thani, or more exactly Mr. Al-Thani's lawyer, writes to say that he is performing an asset search and is asking me for my home insurance policy details.'

I clenched my jaw so hard my teeth hurt. The letter mentioned Melissa's death, my responsibility and referred to civil case law as if quoting Bible verses.

'That car should have killed me too.'

'I got two things: doodley and squat. He can have them both. Listen to me, I'm not worried about it. I'm worried about you.'

'I think I'm done for the day. I'm going to bed.'

14

I went most often to the Filling Station coffee shop. At the time, I convinced myself it was because it had a wheel-chair-accessible toilet and was mostly empty save for the businesspeople popping out of their idling cars for to-go lattes. Of course, it was to be around the barista and the hope for our occasional customer–employee chitchat. It was also good to be away from the house and the muddle of Past Jack, Present Jack, and the confusion of whether I resented him, was angry with him or wanted to beg his forgiveness. I stayed away to give him a break from the black spot of me moving through his house, eating his food, leaving wheel marks on the floor and walls.

Shortly after I arrived, an old woman entered the coffee shop. She struggled with the weight of the door then shuf-fled to a table nearby. Her head was bowed by the weight of a red knit cap. The barista brought her a coffee and biscotti. The old woman cooed with excitement.

'On the house,' the barista said to the old woman and winked at me as she slalomed between the tables and back behind the counter.

I sketched the old woman on a napkin. Her magnified blue eyes swam behind thick lenses as she leaned forward to blow on her coffee. Her whole being was focused on her tremoring hands and not spilling. Tipping the cup to her lips, her eyes widened in pleasured surprise at each sip. A bolt of eyebrow and a gleeful rubbing of the hands followed each bite of biscotti.

'That's amazing,' a voice said from behind, surprising me. The barista was pointing at my sketch.

'She's adorable,' I said as an explanation.

'Can I show her?'

I shrugged. 'She can have it if she wants it.'

'Trudy,' she called.

The old woman pulled the picture to her nose. 'Very nice,' she said, and returned to her coffee.

'It's you!'

'Oh my!' she said.

'That young man drew it. He says you can have it,' the barista said slowly and clearly.

'Oh, thank you,' the old woman said toward my general area.

'You're welcome,' I said and earned another wink from the barista.

Besides the coffee shop, I went to the graveyard where Mom was buried.

Her grave was beautiful and it was Jack who had cared for it. Alternating grey and red stones, the size of fists, half buried, marked the perimeter. Within the stone border, a thick blanket of chamomile, studded with plush yellow buttons and white petals, scented the air with bubblegum. Beside the plain headstone, two white-blossomed and red-lipped orchids stood guard in their pots. A freshly cut spike of tiny yellow orchids rested below the carved dates marking the limit of my mother's life. I was part of it for a small fraction. The blooms, intricate as watch gears, were still full of life. Jack probably went daily. I didn't know. We never talked about it. Even as the remnants of our family fell apart after her death, this place was hallowed ground. Here we paused the terror, sadness and confusion and thought about her. She, beatified and canonised, was no longer able to fail us. Only death perfects us that way. When I picture Mom, even now, she is crowned in bandages with the coma-sleep grin as we lie together in her hospital bed.

I wanted to lie beside the grave, but I didn't know how to get down out of the chair, even less how I would have gotten back up. Thinking about the dead weight of my legs overwhelmed me with hopelessness.

The pot-bellied, baseball-capped elderly caretaker made his way along one of the rows of gravestones in a golf cart. He paused at a grave, leaned cautiously, one hand anchored on the steering wheel, and plucked the small American flag marking the grave of a veteran. He put it into the back of the cart, which jolted forward and onto the next grave. He passed me with a nod, and I pushed myself back to the house.

There was Jack now and Jack from when I was a child. Nothing in between. It wasn't dissimilar to how I became disabled. One day I walked and the next I couldn't. In one way, it was better than if I had had a degenerative disease with function slowly leaching away. Having constantly to readjust to a slightly worse status quo, over and over, accumulating resentment every step down. Running away gave me, gave Jack, ten years of scar tissue. It was damaged but functional flesh. The body as a whole could be saved if we left the past to pulse beneath old wounds.

I entered the greenhouse by popping my wheels over the small lip at the entrance. It was getting easier to manoeuvre around the everyday obstacles like sidewalk cracks, a small step here or there, and grass or dirt.

A jasmine sweetness peeked out from under the smell of damp earth. Potted plants packed the table. Digital-faced devices measuring temperature and humidity hung along the wall. Wood chips and soil covered the squares of concrete that made the floor. Plants with their sparse white beards of roots hung from the beams of the ceiling. Zigzag branches strung with prehistoric blooms blasted from waxy green leaves. The flowerpots, wire pot-hangers, bags of soil, a box of woodchips and a rusty fold-up chair were tucked away – everything fitting perfectly – below the growing tables. I understood how Jack found solace here.

Jack's head and shoulder pinched a cordless phone to his ear.

'I'm fine. I'm not paying some doctor for the privilege of him telling me what I already know. I wouldn't have said anything . . . No, it's not that. I'm paying you back . . . I don't care. That's how it works . . . Patrick, give me a break here.'

'Jack.' I knocked on the doorframe to announce myself.

'I'm going to put bells on that machine of yours,' Jack said, turning to look at me. 'Patrick, Jarred is in here sneaking up on me. I'll talk to you later. Give my love to the babies.'

'Everything okay?' I asked.

'Yeah, yeah. Patrick just being mother.'

I thought of Mom's grave and the care he had shown it. Silences between us made Jack anxious and he was always eager to fill them with an innocuous quip. It used to agitate me but I appreciated his constant steering me toward neutral ground. I didn't have the strength then. I don't know how he did.

'How was today's wander?' he asked.

'Good, thanks. You want to get Mr. Do-nut after you finish in here?'

He smiled. 'Sounds good. Come here. Help me pollinate this Monk.'

I pulled up to the table. Jack showed me a square of paper. A dozen yellow grains of pollen rested along the crease down the centre. Jack handed me a jeweller's headband, a chunky pair of metal glasses. He placed an orchid on the table and, through the headband's magnifying lenses, I marvelled at the mottled green of the leaves that looked more leather than plant.

'Handsome devil, huh? Monk orchids are tough as nails. He started in Africa, made his way up South America, the Caribbean and now he's invading Florida. Florida is perfect for orchids. I would have moved there, but there's one problem.'

'What's that?' I raised the magnifying glass of the headband, thinking he was serious.

'Floridians. They're a cross between New Yorkers and rednecks. Arrogant and backward. No thanks. Take the tweezers.'

I rolled my eyes and snapped my head to make the lens fall back in place.

'You need to find the hole for the pollen. Have a poke around. It's called the "stigma". It'll be shiny. It should be underneath this bit.' Jack's huge gloved finger entered the fish-eyed magnified view. 'That's it. See? Now take a grain from the paper and poke it in. It should stick immediately but you might have to give it a nudge or two to make sure it doesn't fall out. Good.'

Jack put the flower on a nearby counter, explaining how with luck it would make a seedpod with a new cross species of orchid.

'Thanks for helping. My eyes are starting to crap out and my hands aren't as steady. My advice is don't get old. It's a pain in the ass.'

15

I remember it happened on a Saturday or Sunday. Above our house a thunderstorm abused the sky. I had wrung dry every distraction. In my bedroom, an eleven-year-old me lay on my back firing my rubber-band rifle at the scratch-and-sniff lemon stickers on my ceiling.

Now we are ready to hunt the most dangerous game, I thought. I took off my black t-shirt and fashioned it into a ninja's cowl. With the sleeves tied behind my head, my eyes peering from the neck hole, I put on black socks – now ninja shoes – and carefully, slowly, inch by inch, opened my bedroom door. Dad's lower half was visible, lying on the couch. I crept closer. His bare feet hung over the edge above me, one crossed over the other. I sneaked up beside him and placed the other rifle across his chest. He was a soldier dreaming of parade.

I stood up and faced my quarry, steading my aim, right between the eyes, his sleeping eyes.

'Armageddon!' I fired.

Dad shot to his feet, roaring.

He lunged. I turned. He stood to chase me but tripped on his rifle. The crash of his body rattled the house. I hid in the closet. He punched my bedroom door, leaving the rectangular hole in the flimsy wood. The house shook with the slamming of the front door, but I stayed in the closet that night.

16

'Hello, Jarred McGinnis?' a moustached man said.

'Is that Patrick?' Jack shouted from inside the house.

'No!' I shouted back. Bills had become collection notices, which had become phone calls to Jack pretending to be old friends of mine, which became visits from moustached men with golf shirts and khaki pants that screamed off-duty cop.

'He's dead. He blew his brains out yesterday.' I mime the back of my skull exploding. 'Word to the wise. When cleaning the gore of a beloved family member, you need the good stuff. None of the "ecofriendly" nonsense.'

He looked over my shoulder toward Jack's voice. He dropped a large brown envelope in my lap. 'Can you—'

I frisbeed it over his shoulder and slammed the door.

'What was all that about?' Jack asked.

'Jehovahs.'

'Bastards. Come out to the greenhouse. I want to show you something.'

I followed him across the yard.

He talked to me over his shoulder. 'When Patrick comes by this week, can you be civil?'

Inside the greenhouse, it was warm and humid and

comfortable. The sun shone through the glass roof. Jack pulled his smock off the peg and put it on.

'I tiered the table on this side so you can work in here too,' he said. One table was empty, lower than the others. Its wood, yellow and bright, was missing the soil-and-water-stain patina of the others. The shelves below it had been removed to accommodate my wheelchair.

'You built this? Took you long enough.'

'What you mean?'

'How long have I been in this house? And you're just building this now.'

Jack sputtered. 'Well, if you didn't spend all your time eating goofy pills, sleeping all day or having hissy fits any time someone tries to help you . . .' He stopped when he saw that I was smiling. 'You ass.'

'It's a nice thing to do. I appreciate it.'

'It's not too late to put it back and cut a moat. Now pay attention.'

He picked up a slipper orchid. Underneath its thick, waxed leaves, he examined the overgrowing roots. He explained what he was doing and why. Jack washed the lingering bits of woodchip and dirt from the roots, dunking it in a bucket of rainwater. He repotted the flowerless plant and set it in a shady part of the greenhouse.

'Do I have to wear the little outfit?' I touched the apron of his smock.

'It's a tradition,' he reminded me. 'I need you to help out around here. I'm going to work.'

'What do you mean? *Work* work?'

He nodded.

'You didn't tell me you got a job. Where you working?'

'I'm a security guard at a warehouse for dog food. Or something. A job is a job. I know that look.' My face must have done something to betray what I was thinking, because Jack said, 'Don't get heavy on me. It would be a big help if you can keep an eye on the kids for me.' He waved his hands over the orchid tables.

17

The school secretary presented me with a handful of potato chips on a paper towel holding their greasy shadows. I had resolved not to eat her pity gift, but as I waited for Dr. King to call me into his office, they found their way into my mouth. As soon as I was done she stood, her desk chair creaking, walked over, knelt to my eye level, and asked softly if I wanted more.

'No, thank you.'

She took my balled-up paper towel. Dr. King led two chastened third-graders out of his office, then motioned for me as the secretary handed him my file.

We sat across from each other. The front of his desk had shoe scuffs from the parade of fidgety children that his days were made of. My file was opened and turned to the latest report from the teacher. The ends of his moustache nodded as he read.

'You okay?' he asked.

I had been hearing that question a lot. At that age, what was okay? I was too young to understand that parents don't necessarily suffer horrible illnesses. I hated that Mom was dead, but I didn't have the additional injury of knowing the injustice of it. That it wasn't okay. That it didn't have to happen this way and that millions of people including the wicked and the undeserving never needed to mourn their mothers while their fathers drank themselves to death.

'He was a bully,' I said.

'Was he bullying you?'

I shrugged. 'Are you going to paddle me?'.

'Would it get you to stop fighting?'

Another shrug.

'Do you know your dad's work number?'

'He doesn't work.'

The way he was looking at me was worse than any corporal punishment. I toed the front of his desk to see if my shoes would also leave a scuff mark, wishing he would hurry up, paddle me and send me back to class.

'Is there someone else I can call?'

I started to cry.

He flipped through my file. 'What about your brother? Do you know his number? What's his name?'

'Patrick.'

'We'll look him up in the telephone book.'

Patrick arrived at the school office. Mom's dark-eyed dark-haired beauty was there in a tailored suit and tie. A handsome man full of command and confidence. An alien being to my world.

As we got into his car, he explained, 'Pops isn't feeling good. Do you want to have dinner with us? You can meet your new niece.' He was still married to his first wife and their first child had been born a few months earlier.

I don't remember the make of the car. A sports car, but to me it was a spaceship. Patrick quickly but gently admonished me for touching the row of buttons on the stereo's equaliser.

'Jarred, when was the last time you took a bath? You're

smelling pretty beefy, kid. While we're cooking dinner, how about you take a shower?'

'No!'

Patrick was taken back. 'The principal said that you got into a fight because the other kids called you stinky. How about this? Would you like to use our pool? You swim and Fran will make us some fried chicken and mashed potatoes.'

I swam in their pool. I looked at their baby, unsure what they expected me to say. It was small and bewildered. I said hello to it. I ate their dinner, which was good. I kept my eyes down, hoping his wife would stop talking to me with her eyebrows fixed with worry. I watched tv and ignored them talking under their breath about Dad and me.

'He's home now. Or, finally sober enough to answer the phone.' Patrick said to his wife, hanging up the phone. 'Not sure if I should take Jarred back there. What do you think?'

'You need to talk to your father. He's got a problem. He can't be doing this to your brother.'

Patrick noticed that I was listening. 'You ready to go home? Should we stop and get some groceries for the house?'

At the grocery store, I stood on the cart while Patrick pushed. He asked what I thought the house was out of from that aisle. He let me choose, but coaxed me toward sensible things: toilet paper, fruit and veg and frozen dinners. Patrick pushed the cart down the aisles, making tyre-squealing and engine-revving noises. We rushed around with Patrick calling out a food – Ritz crackers! – and as we zipped past, I would snatch the item from the shelf and throw it in the cart.

He was worried about how we would get into the house if Dad wasn't there. I told him the house was never locked.

'You need to make sure the house is locked. It's safer that way. Do you have your own key?'

I shook my head.

We put away the groceries. The last item to go into the fridge was the prize, a bottle of antifreeze-green Mountain Dew.

'Shall we do the dishes?'

'Okay.'

Patrick washed. I dried. Jack came into the kitchen and watched.

'Jarred, can you go to your room, please?' Patrick asked.

I hesitated.

Jack snapped out of his bleary-eyed reverie. 'Go!' He kicked me in the butt with the side of his foot. I buckled, banged my knees on the cabinet. I ran to my room and listened to them argue from my closet.

18

Around the age of twelve, he stopped being Dad, was demoted to Jack. I called him Jack because it irritated and wounded him. A single-syllable jab I knew he could still feel.

I was looking for detergent for the washing machine. I had a sliver of hand soap to throw in with my clothes if I couldn't find any, but I wasn't sure if that would work. It didn't.

On my tiptoes, I tugged at a canvas bag to see if there was any detergent on the top shelf. A full beer can rolled out of its case and with depth-charge precision hit me in the forehead with a humourless thunk. Tears burst from me. I picked up the can, dented from when it hit the ground, and ran for my father's comfort.

I found him in the hallway with the smell of burning coming from the kitchen. His chin shone with grease. Listening to my blubbering explanation, he took the beer and opened it, spraying the suds into my eyes, on the walls and himself. He wiped his bare chest, sucked a finger and drained the can.

'Man up, you got mopping.' He handed me the empty and moved unsteadily down the hall.

'Fuck you, Jack,' burst from me. I was shaking with fear at the huge silhouette of my father. He seemed to be fixed to the spot. His back was still turned. The hot welt above my eye from where the can hit throbbed. I was already crying for what would happen next.

He turned.

I stepped back.

He slapped me hard and left me alone with my heart bouncing against my ribs.

19

Jack knocked as he entered my room. He was wearing a plain blue tie. I was sitting in my wheelchair and sketching. He picked up an empty beer bottle, read the label and set it back on the nightstand.

'I'm heading to work in a couple of hours. You need anything?'

I continued sketching.

'Jarred, am I going to have to worry about you while I'm working? You were doing better. You were getting out and now you clam up in here again.'

'Do you want to see something magic?' I feigned brightness and excitement, wanting to avoid hearing said out loud what I was thinking.

Jack didn't answer. He wasn't in the mood to play along.

I transferred over to the bed, pulling my legs onto the mattress. I took off my sock while singing the 20th Century Fox theme. 'Are you ready?'

Jack stared.

'I said, are you ready?' I asked.

'Jarred, I'm not playing around. This isn't healthy—'

'Behold and wonder, mankind,' I said loudly.

After a moment of silence, both of us staring at my foot, my second toe wiggled.

Jack's face lit up. 'When did you figure out you could do that?'

'This morning.'

'Wow! Good stuff. Do it again.'

I concentrated. The toe took another bow. We watched the motionless digit for a moment before I said, 'Pretty useless muscle though.'

'We should probably keep making payments on the wheelchair.'

'That'd be best,' I agreed.

Jack sat on the bed and he put my feet into his lap. We watched the toe. He wiggled it. I forced it to make another almost imperceptible nod.

'Your feet feel cold. You cold?' he asked. Jack got a look on his face and it made me afraid.

I asked, 'Are you okay?'

'Where have you been for the last ten years?' Jack asked softly.

'Not here,' I said.

'I had no idea you were so close.'

'Only for the past year or so until . . .' It was absurd that I couldn't say 'the accident', but I didn't. I wasn't ready to admit what happened had happened. It took a long time to untangle the shame I felt about the night of the accident with the shame I felt about being disabled. 'I've been all over. San Fran. Chicago. Toronto. Down in Chiapas for a winter when I was eighteen. Patrick was always closer. How often did he visit?'

'You could've visited once. Or gone and seen Patrick. It would have been nice to know you were okay.'

'I wasn't.'

Jack took a deep breath. 'Even if you were still angry with me. The first time I hear from you is from a hospital. You still haven't told me what happened. The only things I know come from some rich guy's lawyer and police reports. Who was Melissa? Were you fooling around with this guy's wife? Is that why he's trying to pin this on you?'

'Show's over.' I pulled my legs out of his lap. My feet howled with false pain as I put on my socks.

'Shoes?' I snapped.

Jack leaned over with a groan.

He had to help me put on my shoes. My attempt to storm out and end the conversation became that much more ridiculous, which made me angrier.

'My chair.'

Jack moved the wheelchair closer.

As I left the room, I fingered the fist-sized hole in my bedroom door. 'Are you going to fix me? Ten years and you couldn't fix the door you broke.'

I wandered off and headed toward the convenience store. I didn't even try to be subtle. I had figured out that a wheelchair makes you invisible. People walk into you, talk about you as if you weren't there. I put the six-pack of Corona in my lap, pushed past the cashier and out the door.

I went and sat in Jack's greenhouse. The door opened and closed behind me.

'Ice cold, refreshing cerveza.' I took a long drink then went back to dividing up an overgrown Cattleya like he had shown me. 'Remember the good ol' days after Mom died? Good times. You want one?'

'Thanks.'

I handed him a beer, pretending to examine the rootstalks.

'You got an opener?' he asked.

I moved the bottle opener to the edge of the table.

The beer hissed. Jack snapped his fingers and the cap skittered and bounced around the greenhouse. Old nerves from long ago awoke and sensed danger. I looked to see if he would take a drink.

He poured his beer into a compost barrel and returned the bottle to the case, which he grabbed from the table and threw over the fence outside.

Pausing at the greenhouse door, he said, 'I left the hole there as a reminder to never let myself get like that again. You think you're the only one with shame and guilt? How long you going to pretend you don't need help, huh? Face it, you're in a wheelchair.' Jack held his fists at his sides. The tendons in his forearms were tight as guy ropes. His face was red. Most of the time our lives go wrong slowly, small incidents and decisions with enough space between to get used to a world a little less right. There are exceptions. A moment, a clear landmark, where you can look back and say there, that is when it went all wrong. This was one of those moments.

'Jack,' I pleaded.

'How about not being such a selfish prick? Huh? How about asking me how I fared the last ten years? What did I do? Where did I go? I'll tell you. I didn't go far in case the phone rang and you needed me. Ask me how long was it before I learned to stop worrying about you? How many years before I figured out every phone call wasn't going to be the cops or the hospital to tell me you were dead.'

Tears streaming down my face, I asked, 'Jack, did you ever find someone else?'

'No,' he shouted. 'Too little, too late. I'm done parenting for the day. You stay in here and I get the house and the

AC for a change. When I leave for work, you can come back in. I'll unlock the back door before I go. Until then, you're locked out – and don't make a mess in my greenhouse!'

20

I came home from middle school. Jack wasn't there. I did homework. I made dinner. I went to my room. I didn't give his absence much thought.

It must have been late and, if my family life was more sitcom-ready, I would have long ago been tucked into bed, kissed by both parents, and wished 'sweet dreams' by my tough-love older brother in a telling affectionate moment right before the commercial break. Instead, I was playing with Lego and the empty case from a twenty-four of Michelob.

The crash came from the living room. My heart bounced hard against my lungs with the smash-smash of window followed by the crunch of someone climbing through. I listened for Jack to confront the intruder, to keep us safe, but there was silence.

The medicine cabinet in the bathroom opened. Its contents clattered into the sink. I waited for each noise to be followed by the boom of Jack's voice commanding 'stop'. The intruder moved around the kitchen then into the living room. Yet, I heard no fearful explanation or pleading not to call the police. Light switches flipped on and off. My door handle didn't turn slowly, dramatically, like it did in the movies, but Jack was not going to save us. The house settled back into silence. Other than the blood noisily pumping in my ears, nothing stirred.

There was nothing in my room that could serve as a weapon. Maybe the thief was in the garage, rifling through Jack's tools. I made the plan to sneak to the door and lock him in there, phone the police and save the day myself. Inching toward the living room, my eyes adjusted and the dark house made itself known.

Jack was passed out in his chair.

The brick he had used to break the window sat on the couch like a house cat. Both of his fists were wrapped in toilet paper. His knuckles were marked by circles of drying blood. One eye was swollen, and the dash of a cut marked his bottom lip.

I had nothing but hate for him. He was a loser, a coward. I picked up the brick and stood before him. The need to hurt him vibrated through my body and hummed through my fingers.

I imagined what would happen if I hit him. The blood, the broken teeth. I lifted the brick over his head and let my grip loosen a little, willing gravity to do the damage. Jack's mouth opened. A thin white line of his bottom teeth peered just above the swelling of his bloodied lip. A low steady snore grumbled and ground from him. My arm fell and I stormed out of the house, making sure the front door slammed.

I went across the street to sleep in my fortress. I don't think the neighbours ever found out that I had set up camp behind their PIZZA marquee. My fortress was stocked with blankets, books, a flashlight and food sometimes pilfered by mice.

The garage was shut. I tried the side door, the glass sliding door in the back and the windows. All of them were locked. Back at the front door, I knocked and my heart raced, imagining the neighbour opening the door in his pyjamas. Something in me wanted conflict, an uncomfortable exchange. I had no idea what I was going to say. I knocked again with more force.

No answer.

I kicked the door. I continued to kick and the anger ebbed out of me with each thump. I didn't realise that I was still carrying the brick and, before I knew what I had done, it had gone through the window. I froze, wide-eyed at the damage. Then I was calm. I reached in through the hole and unlocked the deadbolt.

I stepped through the house. The floor plan was the same as ours. It felt like this could be my house. It should be my house. A house without a dead mother or a useless drunk for a father. I marvelled at how they had placed a chair in one corner where our house had a bookshelf. Their tv was bigger than ours. A hutch was full of china with a collection of porcelain hippos and elephants amongst the plates.

Where my breakfast cereal should be there were bottles of liquor. I opened one and wrinkled my nose at its astringent smell. As soon as it touched my tongue, I spat in the sink. I poured out the rest of the bottle, watching the clear liquid disappear down the drain. Once it was empty, I screwed the lid back on. I poured out all their booze and returned the bottles to the pantry. I went to the garage and flipped on the light switch.

I climbed into my fortress between the gun cabinet and the PIZZA marquee sign and fell asleep with my head on Mom's pillow, which no longer smelled of her but of dust.

21

The air collapsed behind Jack. The sour smell of the beer he'd poured onto the compost filled the greenhouse. I sat, rubbing my thumb across the wrinkled and waxy flesh of the orchid's bulb, and stared at the neighbour's house. From my position I could see a middle-aged woman with a thick braid of brown hair draped over her shoulder. She was on a couch, motionless, entranced by the tv. The spell was broken when her husband arrived with the stacked paper containers of Chinese takeout. Her face broke into a huge grin as he showed her the contents, spooning the glistening food onto plates. When he sat down beside her, she put her head against his shoulder, then kissed his chin. They both smiled, occasionally laughed, as they watched tv and ate, plates held in their hands. They were nondescript the way people from tooth-paste commercials are nondescript. Smiling easily, not attractive but not unattractive.

The woman stood and took his plate. She was heavily pregnant. Her jeans were pushed low to accommodate the perfect roundness of her belly. He kissed the bump and put his head against it. They talked for a while in that position, she standing with the two empty plates in each hand and he with his arms around her and his ear pressed to her belly.

Mom's death didn't have to be the milestone or the moment it all went wrong. It could have been worse; I could have witnessed two drunks inevitably destroying that unique love that sustained and enabled them. I rehearsed in my head what I should say to Jack as I replanted the bulbs. I pushed toward the house, feeling good.

The back door was locked. He had locked me out. He'd said he would and he did. I had forgotten Jack was not a man of empty threats.

Before the accident, I was skinny, but pushing myself around for those months had broadened my shoulders and filled out my chest. My arms thickened. Calluses hardened my hands. Proof that I could endure.

I had expanded my range beyond the nearby grocery store, Mr. Do-nut, the coffee shop with the redheaded barista and the cemetery. Inevitably, I ended up at the mall because there was nowhere else. I spent my time reading in the book stores, people-watching in the food courts and wandering until the pain in my back became too much. I learned to use the escalator by holding onto the rails and letting it pull me and the chair up. It made people nervous, which was why I did it.

In the food court, a woman greeted me with, 'I almost ended up like you.' I responded with 'What? Handsome?' and left to go to the art-supply store.

I was shoving a sketchpad up my shirt when I spotted a man at the end of the aisle. His thin body sat unevenly as he wrestled to push his wheelchair made mostly of duct tape and scratches. His legs were curled and withered. Two dirty grey socks insulted his feet.

'Hello,' the man slurred. He twitched. He bared his teeth

as rebellious nerves and muscles fought his will. His black hair, threaded with grey, needed a cut and a wash. 'Good . . . day.'

While the man battled his own body, I tried to fill the awkward gaps between his words with small talk. He read my discomfort and it aggravated the tremors. The clawed hammer of a hand shot up and hit him in the face. His surprise at the self-inflicted attack made me laugh. He finally mastered his eyebrows to direct a clear and unambiguous anger. He pushed himself backwards, unable to turn his back on me. Pushing by fits and starts, his furious expression remained fixed. Though we shoved ourselves around the world in the same way and dealt with the same stares and comments, he'd mistaken me for someone who understood. He couldn't have known that accepting his vulnerability would have meant accepting my own.

With an hour or so before Jack left for work and hopefully unlocked the house, I retreated to the coffee shop. I sat and thought about the man in the art-supply store. About the damage Jack and I had inflicted on each other. With my tinnitus singing, I thought about the damage I had caused to myself.

'You okay?' the redheaded barista said.

'Huh?' I said.

'You look glum, chum.' She set down a black coffee then sat at my table. 'On the house. Who are you?'

'Jarred.'

'I'm Sarah. Jarred, nice to meet you. You okay?'

'Not great, to be honest.'

'I don't know if this will help you in your situation, but sometimes when I'm sad I like to think about those bro guys who have the really big arms' – she flexed her biceps and continued – 'and the really big chest muscles but still have teeny tiny skinny legs. That makes me giggle and then I feel a little better about my life.'

I laughed and Sarah smiled. I felt an eagerness to keep her there and talking to me as if I was normal.

'My dad. He's too old to be doing shift work, but we need money because I had to move in with him after my car accident.' She looked at my wheelchair as I tapped its armrests as an explanation. It felt good to unravel the knot of me into words.

'Most of the time we avoid each other, because we're always getting into arguments. Although we used to fight a lot more when I was a teenager.' I took a sip of the coffee. 'Sorry, that was a lot to throw at you. I'm sure you have your own stuff.' I felt foolish for laying out all my problems to a woman I barely knew and more foolish for blurting, 'Thank you for the coffee.'

'Don't feel bad. We all have baggage. I don't know if you want or need advice. What I got was things with your dad aren't good, but they are better than they were. "Better than before" is something to hold on to. It sounds like you're worried about your dad and your dad is worried about you. That means you guys care about each other. That's a whole lot of something to hold on to.'

I nodded as she spoke. She was right. It was a relief to hear it spoken, allowing me to admit that I cared about Jack.

'Thanks,' I said. 'I mean it. I needed to hear that.'

'All part of our customer care pledge,' she said, smiling. She stood up and hugged me. She said softly into my ear, 'Hang in there, kiddo.' I froze, unsure how to react. No one had held me since the accident. I felt the weight of her shoulder, her hand, the outline of each finger. Her perfume smelled of sugar and coconut. She drew up straight and I felt the loss.

'You okay?' she asked again.

My eyes reddened, I said, 'Yes, thank you.' She went back to work. After I finished the coffee, I waved goodbye. She waved back from behind the hissing coffee machine.

In the driveway, Jack's car was replaced by an old Toyota Camry with a mismatched front wheel. The moustached collection agent got out and the solace I had gathered talking to Sarah was lost. He handed me a subpoena. I frisbeed it into the yard and went inside the now-unlocked house.

I was making a snack in the kitchen when I heard the front door. It was Patrick, carrying groceries and the subpoena. We greeted each other.

'This was on your doorstep,' he said as he followed me into the kitchen.

I took the thick envelope and threw it away.

Patrick said, 'Throwing it away doesn't change anything.'

I nodded.

He shrugged and I helped him put away the groceries. 'If Dad asks, tell him you bought them.'

'He'll think I stole them. He won't ask,' I said.

Patrick hesitated. 'I'm sorry I wasn't there when you needed me.' He handed me a box of oatmeal.

'Nobody was there. The accident was all my fault.'

As he was struggling with his next words, I realised he was talking about after our mom died and Jack fell apart. He grabbed an armful of canned vegetables. He spoke to the cabinets above the countertop as he set the cans inside. 'I was trying to get my company started and working a full-time job, eighty hours a week, week after week. I didn't have the bandwidth and I convinced myself that it wasn't as bad as it was.' He paused.

I picked up a plate from the sink, pretending to worry a chunk of stuck-on crud. I couldn't escape without an awkward manoeuvring of groceries, cabinet doors and this stranger called my brother.

'Mom and Dad were always drunks, right? That was nothing new,' he said.

I didn't dare look up or answer. A light-headed feeling rushed over me.

'Fran, I mean, there were lots of reasons we got divorced but, god bless her, she was the one who suggested you come live with us. That's with McKenzie just being born. That was the plan, but you know what Jack is like, was like. I don't know how many times he threw me out of the house, telling me to mind my own, excuse my French, goddamn business. Sorries are a dime a dozen but I needed to apologise. I'm sorry.'

I didn't say anything. He didn't say anything. The faucet ran. I scrubbed dishes. He put away the frozen burritos.

'Do you remember when Mom came home from the hospital and we all—'

A memory of all four of us on their bed watching cartoons and eating tv dinners flashed into my head.

'Stop. Stop. Stop. Motherfucking stop right fucking now. Stop,' I said.

He stopped. He folded the brown paper bags and tucked them behind the garbage like Jack does, like I do, like Mom did. If ever a paper bag was needed for whatever reason, there were always five or six neatly folded between the wall and the garbage. For ten years, I did the same thing, in

103

whatever shithole I lived. I did it here automatically when I moved back home.

The front door closed. I heard Patrick's SUV working through its gears as he drove off.

22

I was thirteen, and the year or so of hating him had diminished Dad, but I had grown. I was already as tall as him, if still a lanky uncoordinated copy. The dusting of a moustache was shaved by techniques gleaned from commercials. With the new strength in my limbs and the invincibility of youth I tested him. I picked fights daily, silently glaring, clicking a pen, or drumming on the table after he begged me to be silent. We'd trade punches, me always getting the worst of it.

'I'm staying at a friend's house. Is that okay with you, Jack?' I stepped close to his chair and knocked his Mickey Mouse glass over with my toe as I spoke. He didn't notice.

'Casanova was an asshole,' he said, talking to the tv. 'Any guy with money and bullshit can seduce a thousand girls. I seduced one woman, the same woman every night, a thousand times. That's what makes a great lover.'

'That's poetry, Jack. Pour yourself another.'

'Now, she's dead. Fucking stolen.'

'Now, she's dead.' I was determined not to be like him, even in grief. 'She's better off that way.' I said it to insult him, not her.

The alcohol burned from his eyes, now clear and hateful.

He sprang up and slapped me. The stinging outline of his hand marked my cheek. He parried or ignored my pathetic windmill of punches. He pinned me against the wall. His forearm pressed against my neck. The thud had knocked the breath out of me and a few family photos from the wall. Anger steamed from him. My shirt slowly tore from his grip. He slapped me on the other cheek and put a finger in my face.

'Even here, even in this house, there is a line you don't cross.' He dropped me. He went to pick up his glass, saw that it was knocked over and kicked it. The hard plastic clattered and bounced undamaged. He disappeared behind the slamming of his bedroom door.

Near the house, a rusty railroad cut north–south through a pine forest. I followed the grey spine of ballast. Each outing I travelled farther, scratching my initials into the trees. The 'friend's house' I told Dad that I was staying at was a campsite in my forest. At night, I made a fire, breathed the incense of smoke and earth until I felt a rare calm. I stared into the Milky Way and fought the terror of all those other planets, all those other worlds. I imagined myself being pulled up and away, spun from earth, to drift through the emptiness toward the spray of lights.

It wasn't long before I knew my way through that pine forest. A wilderness hemmed by suburbs, big enough to hold a few deer for rednecks to poach from truck cabs, but small enough for me to know that getting lost was for a day at most. Getting lost became the point.

On the opposite side of the forest was a neighbourhood of fat white houses packed tight as teeth. I was following the fence and looking for an opened window or some other way to climb into one.

Instead I found a doe-limbed girl. She had wild lying eyes and short black hair.

The first time I saw Melissa she was with the first girl I would ever kiss. They were playing under a tree thick with pink flowers, a scene irresistible to my fourteen-year-old self. I was already falling in love daily with other girls with short black hair and thick eyeliner, girls with skater shorts and Band-Aid knees and girls who happened to be smiling when I caught their eye.

Melissa had the other girl on her shoulders. Her bare feet curled into the small of Melissa's back as she stretched to shake the flowers from the branches of the tree.

They spotted me and stared.

'Hey, boy, what are you looking at?'

'You lost?' her friend said.

'Come here. What are you doing over there?'

'You live out there? You homeless or something?'

'Yeah,' I lied, wanting to be obliging as much as I wanted to be intriguing. The attention of girls like them powered boys like me for months.

'Stay there.' They walked to the middle of the yard, whispering unnecessarily, watching me all the time.

'Do you want us to feed you or something?'

I climbed the tree and dropped into their yard. We introduced ourselves.

'You don't smell like you're homeless,' Melissa said as we walked into her house.

They made me a sandwich, gave me Cheetos on a paper plate and asked me questions. 'Where do you shower?'

I sipped at their soda and made up answers. 'Truck stops.'

'Have you ever kissed a black girl?' Melissa asked and pointed at her friend.

My ears were hot coals. Luckily, her friend was more embarrassed.

'She's never kissed a white boy. She wants to know what it's like.'

'I didn't say that.' Her friend slapped at Melissa's shoulder and averted her eyes.

Melissa positioned us like department-store mannequins. I didn't dare move or speak, afraid that what was happening would end. She put her hands on our heads, playfully pushing us together. The girls' closeness and the anticipation awoke every cell in the most ancient part of my boy's brain.

I kissed her, and in the closed-eye seconds I had no doubts, worries or guilt. I suddenly understood what I previously had felt as a vague pull of gravity. As soon as it was over, I wanted more and knew I would always want more.

I looked at the girl. A wrap of cloth held her hair back and gave her a halo of curls. Her eyes flitted across my face.

She whispered a shy, 'Nice'. They giggled at me.

Melissa, still close to us, interrogated our expressions. She was satisfied by what she found, or more likely by what she had orchestrated.

'I think you like kissing black girls. A lot.'

Her friend stayed embarrassed and pretended to watch tv while Melissa sat beside me and continued asking questions. After a while, her friend said they had to talk.

Melissa looked annoyed as she followed her into the bedroom. When Melissa returned alone, she told me that I had to leave before her dad got home. I would find out later that there was no dad coming home.

'Let me get your number,' I said, my need greater than my insecurity.

Melissa wrote it down and tore out the page. I wrote down mine.

'What's this?' she asked.

'Oh yeah. I'm not there any more. It's a place I used to crash.' I went to scratch out the number, but she took the notebook away, smiling.

'Call me, yeah? We'll hang out,' Melissa said as we walked across her backyard.

I hopped the fence and hiked back, not thinking about Dad at home and his sloppy pronouncements on love but wondering if it was possible for other people to tell that I was no longer a kissing virgin. I concentrated on the memory of the girl and Melissa watching us and wondered how long I should wait before I called the number.

23

The morning after the incident with the Coronas and Jack locking me out of the house, I was eating breakfast when I heard his bedroom door open and close.

'You want some eggs and bacon?' I shouted.

The front door opened.

'Morning, Jack,' I called.

The front door shut.

'Well, fuck you too,' I said to the empty house.

I let Jack's change jar decide what I did that day. By the grace of some quarters buried below layers of pennies, I went to the Filling Station for a coffee.

'What's in the box?' I asked. Sarah was drawing on a cardboard box on the counter between us.

'Some guy left it here literally five seconds ago. Said God wanted me to have it.' She rotated the box. She had drawn a cartoon strongman complete with leopard unitard, thick belt around his waist and a dumbbell, its bars bending under the weight. Instead of a strongman head with twirled moustache and shaved head, his neck ended in a hole. In fat block letters, it read INCREDIBLE MISTER SHAKEY. I looked at her, trying to understand. She nodded toward the box. I pulled closer to look inside and a cat's head squeezed from the hole. The Incredible Mister Shakey had the body of a strong man and the head of a grey cat.

'The guy stood at the entrance and said, my dad was Santa and I am the Easter Bunny. He walked up to the counter, said God sent this, no need to sign for it. Before I could even respond, he went, Coffee Girl meet Mister Shakey, Mister Shakey, Coffee Girl, and he was gone. Now I own a cat named Mister Shakey apparently.'

'The Easter Bunny didn't get me anything.'

'I don't know what I'm going to do. My brother is super allergic. There's no way I can bring him home.'

'I'll take him,' I said.

'Really?' she said. 'That would be amazing. I didn't want to take him to a shelter. I just can't bring him home. I'll give you a ride. We can stop by a pet store. I'll buy the cat food and litter and all that stuff.'

I almost said yes. But I saw what would happen. We would go to the car. Sarah would stand behind me while I positioned these useless legs and gracelessly moved this body across from the chair to the car. The excruciating procedure repeated at the pet store and at the house. Every moment with nothing to talk about except the cat and the inevitable 'What happened to you?'. The next day she would gossip with her co-workers about taking the wheelchair guy out to buy litter for the cat she pawned off on him.

'That's okay. I'm not far from here,' I said. She asked if I was sure and I was sure.

I struggled through the neighbourhood. With every push, the box threatened to tip from my lap. The cat peeked from its hole after a few rough jostles, but mostly it was still and silent.

Jack's car wasn't in the driveway. I struggled through the yard and into the greenhouse. I opened the box and petted the velvet grey fur, which elicited a few chirps, but the cat remained asleep. I stared into the neighbour's house. The couch where the pregnant wife and husband ate takeout and watched tv was empty. The curtains of the bedroom were pulled shut.

A lifetime of bad decisions, like sneaking into houses, is a hard habit to kick. When I was a teenager, a psychologist told me that my breaking and entering was me looking for a perfect home, because of my own less-than-perfect one. The truth is I'm just nosy.

I set the Incredible Mister Shakey down, still asleep in his box, and wheeled to the neighbour's front door. Predictably, the key was under the mat.

The house had too much furniture, seemingly untouched, like a show house. The art was all the same, plain black framed watercolours of famous landmarks: Mount Rushmore, the New York City skyline, the Golden Gate Bridge, the Space Needle in Seattle. They looked like they came free with the furniture set. The dining room had place settings for six, complete with blue ceramic napkin holders. I went to the glass sliding door in the living room and looked out at Jack's greenhouse just as the grey cat skulked around the corner and out of sight. The tv took up most of one wall. I thought about how he had held her round belly while she looked down at him. Two baby monitor receivers faced each other on the coffee table. I clicked one on and listened to the static. I didn't know how to make things right with Jack. He was going to throw me out and I wouldn't have blamed him. I should apologise to Patrick but I knew I wouldn't. I wanted Sarah to hug me again and tell me 'hang in there'. I wanted her to call me 'kiddo'. I liked that. The static was soothing.

I thought about how Melissa and I first met. She was

my first love, my first heartbreak. She could have stayed that, but I had to ruin it. In the hospital, I had rolled around with the injustice that my accident and her death had happened when I was on the verge of making a change finally, no more fuck-ups, no more hurting people, no more running away. That was a lie and Melissa was dead because of that lie.

I looked around the house and imagined the couple bringing home their baby boy. Both exhausted but strengthened by the hope for the bundle in their arms. Who knows, maybe this kid was as doomed as I was. Maybe dead moms and drunk dads don't matter as much as we think. What was I doing in their house? I wasn't on the verge of changing anything, that night with Melissa or now. The truth of that was a sucker-punch and one that I deserved.

A car pulled into the driveway. I turned off the baby monitor and put it in my pocket without thinking. The glass sliding door out to the back patio had two steps. An impossibility. The car's engine turned off.

I pulled the sliding glass closed behind me. Two steps between me and an escape. Car doors slammed. Panic lit through me.

I imagined my two legs working beneath me. Left foot effortlessly dropping to the first step. Right foot, second step. Done. Step by step leaving the neighbour's yard and yet another mess I had made. Part of me thought it could be done. All I had to do was will it. I looked at my knees, expecting them to twitch to life. The locks turned. The front door opened. Voices heard.

I considered getting out of the chair, scooting down the steps on my butt then pulling the chair after me. No, it would take too long. I balanced on my back wheels with the idea of hopping down.

Two people, a man and a woman, were talking to each other, moving through the house. A jangle of car keys clattered into the bowl on the kitchen counter. Cooing sweet words from the woman.

I gripped my wheels and prepared to ease myself down backward. As soon as my weight was over the first step, gravity won. My back and shoulders slammed against the cement. My head hit with a thud. More stunned than hurt, my knees pointed to the sky above. I rolled out and my legs clunked to the ground. I mewed ohs and owws.

The woman passed the glass door holding a swaddle of blanket. She slid it open.

'Hello. Do you need some help?' she asked, then called behind her, 'Honey, there's a person, a wheelchair person, in our backyard. He's hurt himself, I think.'

The man came up behind her. The woman bounced and patted the newborn at her shoulder. She looked worried, eager to protect her child, as if my stupidity was contagious.

'He's from the house next door. Jack's son,' the man said.

'Can we help you?' she asked as if I was hard of hearing. 'Should we call the hospital?'

I shook my head.

'What do we do?' She conferred with her husband.

'Put him back in his chair, I guess.' The man righted my wheelchair then stood over me, trying to decide the etiquette for lifting paraplegics to whom you haven't been formally introduced. He put his hands under my armpits. We embraced as he struggled to put me back into my wheelchair. The man smelled nice. I couldn't bear looking at either him or his wife with their baby. Back in the chair, I adjusted my legs. My ears were hot and flushed with embarrassment. Slicks of sweat slid from my armpits down my sides. The man pushed me through the grass back to my front door.

'Are you sure you are going to be okay?'

'Yes, thank you. Sorry to trouble you,' I said as I hurriedly pushed myself inside and shut the front door.

Jack came home late that night. I was lying on the couch, pretending to read a book. Instead, I was thinking about Melissa and the night she died. The streetlights had cut hard shadows from the parked cars and buildings. Melissa's motionless body lay in the road. Below her arm, another shadow or blood, I couldn't tell. I tried to focus on when I had first met her. I saw her, young again, and her friend, the first girl I kissed, playing in her backyard. I wanted to replace the night she died with the thousand other nights we were together being stupid kids doing stupid kid stuff.

'How was work?' I asked.

'It was good. Had a nice chat with the neighbour next door.'

Oh shit. I still had the baby monitor in my pocket.

'They got back from the hospital today. Their little girl was born a couple of days ago. Eight pounds. Margaret. Always liked that name.'

'You want something to eat?' I asked.

'No, I'm tired. You get up to anything today?'

I thought about derailing the conversation by telling him about my new pet happily stalking squirrels in the backyard. I could also mention that I used the last pennies in his coin jar to buy cat food after the incident with the neighbours. I decided that would only compound the problem.

'Not much.'

'That's a shame. It was a nice day to flop about on the

neighbour's patio, scare the hell out of the new parents next door. They had a lot of questions that I couldn't answer. Do you want to explain yourself?'

'Not especially.'

'Fair enough, because I don't want to hear it. Stop with the stupid shit.'

'Stupid shit stopped.' I looked away, fearing he might change his mind and insist on answers.

'Good. Night night.'

'Night night,' I said. I wish I had said more to convince him that I did want to change. Jack's advice from a long time ago flitted into my head: 'Once is a mistake, twice is a decision.'

24

I climbed the tree and knocked on the back door of Melissa's house. She opened it and hugged me as if we had known each other for years. We went to her room. Dolls and toys still clung to the corners pushed out by teenage concerns like clothes and posters of listless men in black.

'I don't want you as a boyfriend.'

'I don't want a girlfriend,' I lied.

'Fine. Let's go see a movie.'

I bought a ticket, went to the fire exit, and let her in. We hopped between films. We ate from boxes of popcorn left on seats. We explored the storage spaces behind 'Employees Only' doors. I thought about us making out while watching her face in flickering colours of the movie. She caught me staring, called me 'freak', and pushed my chin toward the screen. We left after the last show at midnight. We slept in her bed.

She slept.

I lay next to her and faced the ceiling. My attention burned upon the feel of her knee pressed against me.

For months, we hung out every day. I never saw the girl I had kissed again. We stretched our legs in the petty crime teenagers call rebellion. We created missions like stealing houseplants from one neighbour's porch to put on the porch of another. At Christmas, the nativity scene of the nearby church was changed to a carnal orgy of shepherds, wise men, sheep and Mary, surrounding a lawn jockey statue in his manger. We shoplifted for sport more than gain: an enormous watermelon from a grocery store, a single ski pole from a sport store or anything that was as absurd as it was difficult. We sneaked into the pools of luxury hotels and swam in our underwear. Each night's adventure ended with a restless sleep beside her.

When we watched tv or a movie or just stared at the city lights from the top of a parking garage, she nibbled and sucked on the tips of her hair. While she slept, I once inched my face close to hers until I could feel her sleeping breath against my lips. I put that strand of hair in my mouth and sucked, but it didn't satisfy me either.

She told me her secrets. I told her my lies. Her dad was on to family number two and had no interest in Melissa. Her mom too had other things than parenting to think about. She never raised an eyebrow seeing me, this teenage boy, always in her kitchen eating. As I waited for Melissa to wake up, her mom would ask me to fix her a coffee and shuffle back into her room. Melissa complained about the way her mother wheedled money from her father and a parade of other men. Melissa was bored of her school. Bored of her friends. Of her easy comfort, of her prettiness, of her sidewalk-trimmed subdivision full of people she'd known since elementary school, of her emergency credit card used for shopping and her allowance, the fridge full of food, the closet full of clothes, the mall, the boys groping at her under the bleachers at football games, the after-school piano lessons and tutor two times a week. Bored of being bored.

To her I was a Ken doll that she could play grownups

with, trying to figure out the rules to this boy vs girl game. I was happy to be toyed with, but sometimes my unsatisfied lust became anger. Her refusal to acknowledge my need for her made everything she said irritating. I would snap at her and storm off to leave her alone for a few days until she called me crying, apologising for whatever she did to upset me. I'd say it was nothing, and we'd be back to planning our next adventure.

'Let's run away,' she said.

'Get your shit. Let's go.'

She hesitated before calling my bluff.

I led us to the train yard, a scratch of buildings at the end of a tangle of tracks among rusting heaps and diesel air.

'What do we do now?' she asked. She sounded fearful.

'Wait until one moves,' I said with weary knowing. One of my lies was that I hopped trains all the time.

That first time was exciting enough to sustain us through the shuffling hours. I told her train-hopping stories stolen from books and zines. When an engine lurched forward, we sprang from our hiding spot and flung ourselves into a boxcar's wide-open mouth.

It was years later that I learned that a three-hour wait was lucky. We had no idea of the danger we flirted with. Would my life have been different if Melissa or I had sprained an ankle jumping into the boxcar? If we had sat there all day, sitting on our haunches, socks bloated with rain, without a train moving out? If I had seen the future that is now my past, would that have been enough to keep me home? The time a tweaker attacked me with a rake handle while I was sleeping under an overpass. Or when two redneck cops with guns drawn, calling me faggot, stole my clothes and dropped me off in my underwear on the wrong side of town. If I had known I was going to watch a teenage boy fall out of a moving train and snap his spine miles away from any help, would that have been enough to save me and Melissa?

Instead, Melissa and I sang 'Movin' Right Along' and let our feet dangle out of the car. We chucked rocks at the blur of yellow and green landscape. We had jumped a shuttle between depots only half an hour apart. The train slowed to a stop and we jumped off. We ran through the yard as if chased, but only picked up a half-interested glance from the driver as he came down from the engine.

Our finish line to cross turned out to be a few streets of singlewide trailers surrounded by weathered picnic tables and trucks trimmed in rust and bumper stickers. At the edge was a convenience store called Big Bob's where we celebrated our adventure with Cokes and day-old donuts.

That night we lay in her bed together to giggle and recount our adventure. We planned other places to go and my knowledge of the tracks from my lonely hikes helped me falsify my image of veteran train-hopper.

We wrestled and horse-played. She held my wrists and used her body to pin my shoulders to the bed. She dug her chin into the nest of my shoulder.

She counted to two before I pushed her off and we struggled against each other. I slipped her grip. I jumped on top of her, held her wrists, looked into her eyes. One . . . two . . . three . . .

I still held her as I said, 'Hogan retains the championship.'

I became embarrassingly aware of my erection and that she too must have felt it pressing against her. Melissa's eyes darted across my face, and I ached for her to find what she was looking for.

We touched cautiously but grew bolder. We kissed hungrily, peeling clothes away. She took off her bra and panties, then pulled my underwear off. Those eyes of hers that always knew more than she said. Those eyes that dissected the stories I told to make myself someone else. Those eyes, they were uncertain and fearful. Her body was rigid and tense. She gripped my arm as I guided my penis into her.

This was her first time too.

I kissed her and whispered, 'It's okay.'

'Okay,' she agreed.

They weren't the most romantic words to say before we lost our virginity, but they weren't the worst. It was going to be okay and we needed that reassurance. We were children taking one of those irrevocable steps toward adulthood. A moment for both of us, never to be repeated or shared with any other person. Of course, I thought none of this as I pushed myself inside her. I moved softly and slowly and felt guilty when she winced.

It was over too quick but neither of us knew that yet. We lay embracing, surprised that it had happened.

'Excuse me,' she said and went to the bathroom. She returned and I drank in the vision of a nude girl, my first, climbing into bed with me. She curled into the nook of my shoulder, her body still heated, and ran her hand back and forth across my chest.

'I love you,' she said.

Melissa, the unattainable girl who had just taken my virginity, had said 'I love you' unprompted. How many times had I dared myself to say that sentence? Her 'I love you' burned so bright that she had to nudge me to make me realise that I left her in no man's land by not responding.

'I love you too.'

She smiled, nuzzled closer and sniffled. We fell asleep quickly.

Our time as girlfriend/boyfriend was brief. I hiked home in the mornings, every limb sore. My lips still feeling the kisses and the memory of her body like the ghosts of waves after a day in the ocean.

Dad had long ago been reduced to a spill, an unflushed toilet, the remains of a bottle, the tang of smoke from a pizza forgotten in the oven, a closed door, an inert body on the couch, a cut on my fat lip or bruise under my eye. The house itself began to disappear once I met Melissa.

25

In an attempt to avoid any more trouble with Jack or the new parents next door, I wheeled to the public library, took my spot at the rows of computers, and looked for a job. I had learned to go early to avoid the teenage boys taking up all the machines to play video games, but not so early as to have to sit next to the old man who watched online videos of women doing yoga while scratching at a patch of eczema on his neck.

The first email was from a book store. The subject line read 'I'm so sorry'. I deleted it without reading yet another email that blamed too-small employee bathrooms or a step at the entrance. They always felt terrible but not so terrible as to make their place more accessible. The second email was from a chain restaurant. They took a different approach and listed all the reasons that I was wrong to apply. There were three more emails to go through.

The middle-aged man seated across from me stared. I felt his eyes but it took a few beats for him to notice that I was staring back.

He gave a brief smile and dipped back to his screen.

'Were you wondering what happened to me?' I asked.

'Was it a car accident?'

'Gluten. One-way dinner roll ride to misery. Now it's a life of sitting in my own shit with nothing but people's pity and useless noodle legs,' I said.

He hid behind his screen again. I deleted the remaining emails.

'Motherfucker Betty Crocker,' I yelled and went home.

I sat at the kitchen table listening to the baby monitor, a small blue box with its one fat antenna-arm stretched to receive. It burbled electricity and static. Occasionally, a breathy coo, grunt or baby gurgle fired shooting-star quick from the speakers. I leaned in, waiting for those moments when the wife came in and spoke to her baby. I tried to recall my mom's voice. It felt like an insult that I couldn't. I didn't register Jack's key in the lock.

'What are you up to?' Jack feigned friendliness, but he looked tired. He eyed the bag of cat food on the table. He was looking his age. It was hard getting used to how suddenly Jack had become old. I had packed him and Mom away with everything else. Jack hadn't existed for me for a long time.

'Listening to the radio,' I said.

'Jarred, I'm going to get serious here. You need to pay attention: you and me both are too old for this shit. This is my house. You are welcome here, always have been. But it is my house, not yours. You need to quit horsing around the neighbour's house. You need to tell me why we seem to own a cat these days. And you need to stop treating me like a moron. You understand?'

I kept my eyes on my hands and the baby monitor. Jack leaned on the back of the chair across from me.

'I do.' I looked at him, hoping he'd see that I was sincere.

'I wish I believed you.'

My eyes fell back on the monitor.

'This stuff just happens,' I said.

'No, this stuff just happens because of you. Then everyone else has to deal with it. We're done with that. You're twenty-six. Aren't you tired of this? This is the same kind of nonsense that got that girl killed and you thrown into a wheelchair. How many more chances do you need? Get your shit in one sock, Jarred.'

I had nothing to say. Jack had said out loud what had been simmering inside me.

Jack calmed himself. 'What have you been doing for ten years?'

'Probably the same you have. Nothing.'

Jack tried again. He sat at the table. 'Do you remember when you gave your house keys to a runaway in Phoenix? The kid was maybe twenty-three, a guy named Eman.'

'No.'

'I do. Because he showed up at my door with a note in your handwriting: "Admit One. Signed El Presidente". You gave him your keys and said he could stay as long as he wanted.'

I chuckled nervously. 'What'd you do?'

He took the baby monitor from my hands and examined it. 'I let him stay. He was a mess. He had your room for about two years. I got him into the programme, my first sponsee. He met a French lady and moved to Canada. I still get letters from time to time calling me Dad. He's doing good.' He set the monitor back down.

'Maybe I should've come back from Arizona,' I said and turned the monitor on, but it received only static.

'Maybe.' He picked it up again and the monitor disappeared in the cradle of his rough hands.

'Truce?'

'Jarred, you're the only one fighting.'

I cleared the tears welling in my eyes. 'Let's take a walk. Get a coffee?'

'I don't know. I'm tired. Is anything even open now?'

'There's a place called the Filling Station across from the big grocery store.'

'Fine with me.' He stood and put his hand on my shoulder.

'One sec.' I wheeled into my room and returned. 'Check it out. Which one do you like better?' I held up a t-shirt with 'Not interested in Jesus or telling you why I am in a wheelchair' scrawled in Sharpie.

'Are those my goddamn undershirts?'

'Or this one.' I held up another shirt.

'Charming,' Jack said. 'The second one. It's punchier.'

'That's what I was thinking.' I exchanged my shirt for one that said, 'I am not your good deed for the day'.

At the Filling Station, Jack examined the art on the walls. He made his jokes about rabbit food and hippies as he looked at the vegetarian menu but marvelled at the bromeliads hanging from the fixtures like light bulbs. He stood on a chair to study how they were hung, talking about the species. He pronounced their Latin names like absolutions.

'I never knew this was here,' Jack said.

'Can't find new places if you don't get lost or new friends if you don't talk to strangers.'

'Where'd you pick up that little aphorism?'

'You, I think.'

'Well, it must be right then,' he said, still looking at the plants.

'How's Incredible Mister Shakey?' Sarah asked as she delivered our coffees to the table.

Jack raised his eyebrows.

'The squirrels are unimpressed but he's happy. This is my dad, Jack.'

'Is this coffee-flavoured coffee?' Jack said to Sarah.

'Hello, Jack. Drink your coffee and no sass,' she said, disarming him with a smile, and walked off.

'She's a keeper.' Jack took a sip. He put down his cup, clattering and spilling. He shook out his arm, his face worried.

'You okay?' I asked.

'Pins and needles.' He pumped his hand open and closed. 'It's fine. Too much coffee, not enough sleep.' He had been doing double shifts.

'Jack,' I said, concerned.

'If you're going to fuss, I'm sure as hell not going to tell you about the dizzy spells,' he joked.

'Not funny.'

'I'll cut down on the caffeine,' he said, took another sip of coffee, and winked.

'Or, I don't know, go to a doctor like a normal person,' I said. If Jack was talking about his problems, it was serious.

'Tell me about some of the places you've been. What was Arizona like? I always wanted to travel more. Your mom was agoraphobic, quite bad. She was scared of the world. I tried and tried.'

'Jack, you remember when you picked me up from the hospital?'

'Sure.'

'I almost ran off the night before.' He looked at me seriously. I continued: 'I was sad and scared. I was in a lot of pain. My roommate was with his girlfriend and I felt so alone.'

Jack gripped his coffee mug with both hands. He frowned and I thought he was angry. When he spoke, I understood.

'Well, I'm glad you didn't . . . didn't run off that night,' he said, his voice cracking.

'I wouldn't have gotten far on foot.' I forced a laugh to clear the sadness enveloping us. I wanted to tell him the truth about that night, about Melissa, everything, but I couldn't. I blurted, 'I have a job interview tomorrow.'

'Really? Are you up to it? Don't rush it if you aren't ready.'

'I'm ready.'

26

Melissa and I were walking past a shopping centre.

'Let's go bull-baiting for some hooch,' she said. 'I want to get drunk.'

'Pass.'

'You're going to be boring, aren't you? I bet you're cute when you're drunk. C'mon.' She put her arms around me.

'I don't drink.' Drinking for me was the broken man in our garage constantly following that Mickey Mouse glass and shaming Mom's memory.

'Boring.'

'So, I'm boring.'

She grabbed my hand and I let her drag me with her. 'We're doing this, McGinnis,' she said, looking over her shoulder.

'I thought we were going to break into the drug-dealer castle.'

'We'll do both. I am the woman. You have to obey me.' She switched tactics from commanding to cajoling. 'Please, please, please, with cherries on top. I'll show you my boobies.' She lifted her shirt to flash her bra.

'I'll steal but I'm not drinking.'

She kissed me. She set those eyes on me. 'You're going to drink with me.'

Unlocked and uninhabited, getting into the drug-dealer castle was easy. The neighbourhood gossip was that the house was unfinished because the drug-dealer owner had gone to prison. Knowing what the neighbourhood said about Jack and me, I had my doubts, but the amount of gold trim and pink marble made the rumours credible.

Already adept at the simple mechanisms by which boys operated, she got me to drink. Listening to a radio left by the construction workers, our legs tangled with each other, we sat in the master bedroom on the top floor and looked out onto my forest backlit by the glow of streetlights near the horizon. Between us was a bottle of orange soda spiked with shoplifted whiskey.

'You're a freak. Look how tiny your nipples are.' She pinched my nipple then pushed me away as I pretended to breastfeed her.

We sipped at the whiskey, enjoying our view and each other until a crash came from downstairs.

'Shh. Listen,' I said sharply.

'They're breaking a window,' she said.

'Quick, get dressed.' Wide-eyed, I watched the darkness beyond the bedroom doorway. There were more noises downstairs. Melissa held on to me.

'We'll go out through the garage,' I said. Another sound. A girl's laugh? We looked at each other and strained our ears. More laughter.

'It's kids,' Melissa said. We descended cautiously until we saw three guys and two girls stepping through the house.

'Hiya,' Melissa sang.

They jumped and turned. They fell over each other

laughing. Everyone spoke at once, Melissa explaining our fear, they explaining theirs. One of the girls told us that while the boys were breaking the window and crawling through, the girls went around and tried the door and found it open.

Melissa led us on a tour of the house, pretending it was ours. She talked about her days as a housewife, shoe-shopping, sleeping with her personal trainer, drinking banana-flavoured liquor with the housekeeper. Walking through the endless bedrooms, she made up children for us. I remember there was ten-year-old Roxy who still wet the bed and BananaHead, an unfortunate, misshapen first-born and the inevitable consequence of our being brother and sister.

As usual she awed me. She was fearless with these older teenagers who had achieved the giddy heights of being seniors and having drivers' licences. Everyone followed her, laughing hysterically, finishing our whiskey and starting on the beer they had brought. By the time we settled back to the master bedroom and the builders' radio, we were all drunk. I was envious of the ease with which Melissa won everyone's affection. Every time she got up to dance or leaned over to take a cigarette from one of the girls, the guys checked out her ass or looked down her shirt.

Those eyes of hers worked on everyone, girls included. It hurt most to understand that Melissa already knew this. I wasn't the only one she could make fall in love with her.

I put my arm around her, to claim her as mine, but she wriggled away. I tried to kiss her and she pecked my lips and turned her head. Her jokes became increasingly at my expense. Every retelling of how we first heard them down-stairs made me more cowardly. Still we drank, the seniors catching up with us.

She made a joke about my nipples. She teased me to show them.

I grumbled, but still wanted to be liked by the seniors.

She goaded. Everyone else joined in until I relented.

Melissa pinched my nipple and said, 'He's got baby nipples.' A joke shared between us was now a humiliation. I looked at the laughing faces.

'Look who's talking, Pirate's Treasure. They don't call you Mosquito Bites for nothing.'

The boys shouted 'damn' and 'snap'. She played it off, pushing forward her chest and frowning, but she ignored me after that. I grew sullen and quiet, drinking and watching Melissa being the centre of attention. The tall, handsome blond made a lame joke about my nipples.

'That's it. Let's fight. You're the tallest. Stand up.'

Everyone was laughing, because I was shadow-boxing and clowning in front of the guys.

'Me and my little nipples are going to fuck you up, Too-Tall.' I pulled my shirt over my head and thumped my chest. I slapped him hard; everyone froze. He was much bigger than me, but he was scared.

'What the fuck is your problem?' Melissa pushed me. I stumbled and fell. The senior girls were yelling too. The guys were telling me to chill the fuck out; the one I slapped stayed quiet.

'You need to leave,' Melissa said. 'You're being an asshole.'

'Fine. Fine.' I picked myself up sloppily. 'I'm sorry you got slapped and Melissa has little tits.'

I stumbled downstairs and into my forest where all the morning-after recriminations lined up beside the trees to greet me.

★

For days, I called her and left pathetic, wheedling messages. I waited across the street from her house trying to ambush her. I skipped class and took two city buses to wander the halls of her school with no idea how to find her.

I climbed the tree and dropped into her backyard. I knocked on the door. Nothing. I knocked harder. The curtain fluttered. She opened the door wide enough to let me see the guy I had slapped sitting on her couch, pretending to watch tv. Of course, it had to be him.

'What do you want?'

'I want to talk to you.'

'So?'

Her coldness stunned me.

'Are we done here? Go home.' I knew she had never believed my homeless story, but it was a lie that suited us both. 'I'm done babysitting you.'

'What did I do?'

She rolled her eyes and shut the door.

'Wait! I wrote you this.' I handed her a thick wad of folded loose-leaf paper.

She stepped outside, a small smile on her lips. My heart fluttered with hope.

'Can I borrow your lighter?' she asked.

She took the lighter and lit the square of paper. She watched me as I watched it. Once the flames caught, she dropped it and mashed it with the toe of her shoe. She threw the lighter over my shoulder. The door slammed.

I retreated to my side of the fence. I piled dry leaves around the trunk of the tree where I first saw Melissa and the girl I had kissed playing. My lighter's tiny flame was invisible in the sunlight, but its fire settled on the leaves and ate at the pile eagerly. It didn't take long before the tree was burning steadily. The flames climbed the branches and ignited the dead leaves that clung to them.

Melissa and her new boyfriend ran into the backyard. I gave her my brightest smile and a royal wave, enjoying their bewilderment. Melissa was screaming but I don't remember what. I pointed at the blond guy, did my best crazy stare then flipped him off and walked away.

By the time I had hiked home my heart was wretched. I sat in my room festering with ridiculous schemes to win Melissa back.

Dad and the Mickey Mouse tumbler were hiding in his room. I took his car keys and hurried back to Melissa's. Turning into her subdivision, I was stopped by a police officer who had blocked the road with his cruiser. Behind him was a fire truck parked in front of Melissa's house.

'How old are you?' he asked.

It was several hours before Jack picked me up at the police station. They made me sit at an officer's desk until he arrived. No formal charges were pressed. I got a standard-issue cop lecture before we left. We took a cab back home. I don't know if it was because they couldn't release the car or he was too drunk to drive. I didn't think about it then.

The entire journey I stared blankly out the window. I thought about Melissa, still contriving reconciliations. There was a part of me that wanted to tell Jack everything. Sitting next to him in the cab, I could have asked him what to do. He would have told me to forget about Melissa. He would have known that she was the kind of girl who would never love me back, not the way I needed. I tried to think of how to describe the hurt and need I felt for Melissa. I could ask about him and Mom. Maybe here, it could have been okay between us. Probably not, but it's hard not to think like that.

Instead, I didn't dare make eye contact, staying motionless as prey. When the taxi pulled into the driveway, I
prepared myself for the explosion that was my dad. He paid
the driver without his usual banter.

Would he swing at me first or start yelling and give me
some warning? I followed at a safe distance into the house.

He turned.

I stopped.

'Close the door.'

I closed the door.

I waited.

We stood there facing each other. I was cornered, but
he didn't move. I didn't dare. He was looking at me, but
past me. There was clarity in his eyes that unsettled me; I
expected the worst. I didn't know what he was going to
do.

I started to cry.

He went to his room.

I went to mine, not understanding what had happened.

27

The bus to my job interview passed Melissa's old neighbourhood while a small man with a thick Mexican accent critiqued the passengers – 'Fat, fat lady', 'Here comes smelly'. He had watched me from his seat behind the driver as I waited for the bus ramp to fold out. I positioned myself in the wheelchair space and locked my brakes with him watching. When we made eye contact, he nodded without comment and I took it as a benediction.

The address for the interview was a three-storey office building. I went to the room number on the contact sheet the agency had given me. Except for the room number, the door had no logo or sign to distinguish it from any other in the hallway. My lower back was already killing me, but I was determined to prove I could do this.

I sat in front of the office door debating whether to knock or just go in. The frosted glass revealed nothing.

I opened the door without knocking and was confronted by a lobby of sorts. Three chairs sat against one wall. Opposite, another door had 'ofice' written on it. Ceiling-high stacks of battered and water-damaged boxes crowded the rest of the room. Worn thin at both doors, the carpet's original colour, possibly cream or tan, had greyed to resemble the pelt of a disease-ridden wild creature. The air smelled of mildew and, confusingly, of dive-bar urinal cakes.

The room was too crowded for me to park myself without being in the way. I gave a quick smile to the man and woman already occupying the chairs and manoeuvred myself against one of the walls of boxes. A sedentary half-century on earth had left the woman a doughy androgyne. Her only distinguishing features were a wall eye and unwashed hair, calico from grocery-store hair dyes. Her bangs sloped to one side. I concluded she was the source of the urinal cake smell, maybe unfairly. The man beside her had the same figure, tits and all. He had wisely grown a goatee to mark out the chin that nature neglected. We three sat in silence. I gave up trying to avert my eyes and watched the man with disgusted fascination as he dug inside his nose as if polishing brass.

The interviewer opened the 'ofice' door and looked us over. I didn't blame him for the barely disguised disappointment. I was feeling despair for all of humanity at that moment.

The nose-picker stopped his labours when the interviewer called his name. Fifteen minutes later, the door opened again and the interviewer told him to wait in the lobby to sign some paperwork after he interviewed these other two. The interviewer flicked a pointed finger at me. I followed this captain of industry in the striped golf shirt and khaki shorts with his cell phone in a pouch attached to his belt. The 'ofice' was like the lobby. Stacks of battered boxes coughing up envelopes flanked the man and his desk.

The interviewer leaned on his desk and folded his arms. There was a dot-dot-dash of mustard stain down the front of his shirt. It was mesmerising. Arms still folded, he looked down at my application.

'Jarred McGinnis?'

'Yes, sir.'

'What happened to you?' he asked.

'The AIDS,' I said.

The interviewer's eyes widened. 'Are you going to walk again?'

'Not sure I want to. I get some pretty sweet parking spaces these days.' I did a fist pump. 'You know what I'm talking about.'

'Do you have any relevant job experience?'

'For stuffing envelopes?'

'Mmhmm.'

'Well, I don't have any industrial experience but I consider myself a talented amateur. I've been putting my own correspondence into envelopes for nearly twenty years. I'm talking about being involved in the complete process. Return address in the top left. Correct postage top right. Lick, stick and send. How much does this gig pay anyway?'

'The minimum allowed by law.' The interviewer chuckled.

I forced a laugh a little too long and a little too loud. 'Classic,' I said.

'Okay, thanks for your time.'

'Where do I pick up my cheque?'

'I think we have everybody we need.'

I went home and got undressed in my room. I fumbled my shoes and socks off. My feet were swollen and red, yet another boon from the gods of paraplegia. Without working leg muscles, blood and fluids pool into your feet. You can push your finger into the flesh as if it is risen dough. The divot lingers for a few seconds before filling in again. It's great entertainment for kids' parties.

Concentrating on the puffy red loaves, I curtsied my

second toe, my miraculous flinch. Maybe I could walk if I had to. With my arms I shoved my body up, thinking some secret need in my muscles would save me. Instead I awkwardly tumbled onto my bed and slid to the floor, pulling the sheets with me.

I thought about the night before Jack picked me up from the hospital. I had told Jack that I had planned to run away from the hospital. That wasn't true.

I had to leave my hospital room. I didn't want to hear the whispered coos and kisses as my roommate and his girlfriend lay together enjoying the warmth of each other. I was never going to feel intimacy again. The constantly hurting, useless body that the surgeons had left me with became over-whelming. They had saved my life but never considered whether it was worth saving. I pushed myself into the shining black lake of the parking lot. The air was rain fresh. A few cars and trucks lingered in their spaces but mostly the night was empty. A silent ambulance painted blue the archway of trees that lined the road. Should I have written a note? I thought, and rejected it as ridiculous. Would I be missed? Would I miss anything? One moment I would be here. Another, not. It felt clean and straightforward.

Under the streetlights, my shadow pulled and stretched across the width of the road. The outline of my head and shoulders were clear and recognisable. The lower half was a block of darkness. The wheels and spokes of the chair projected onto the asphalt as a pointless contraption of loops and crossbars.

It was hard to see through the tears, but headlights were turning onto the road. They got closer, dazzling me until a moment of stillness and clarity. The engine droned closer. The sticky sound of its tyres on the wet road neared. This was it. I was prepared. This make-do body was too painful. I squeezed my eyes shut as I pushed myself into the road.

Barely a squeak of brakes, then nothing but the idling engine and the shuffling of leaves in the canopy above us. The man in the car looked at me expressionlessly through his windshield. He was middle-aged with a neat blond quiff and black-framed glasses atop a stately nose. He got out and shut the door. He took a few steps before returning to his truck to turn on its hazard lights. He didn't say anything as he took hold of the handles on the wheelchair and pushed me back into the hospital. I was a stray shopping cart blown into his path by happenstance. In the empty lobby, he leaned over, locked my brakes, and left. With its hazard lights still blinking, the truck drove out of sight.

Back in my room, the redneck's girlfriend was gone or they were sleeping. In the silence and darkness, I pulled myself into bed and my breath became ragged and heaving. I felt the humiliation like a fever. I hated. I hated that driver. The useless failure of him. He hadn't kept the bargain we had made. The stupidity of my failed suicide overwhelmed me. I could have ended up not dead but just more hurt, more broken, a neck injury and unable to breathe without a machine. I wanted to rush through the world, find that driver and beg his forgiveness. Then, I remembered calling Jack. Oh god. Jack. He hadn't heard from me for ten years until that day. He would have shown up to find the wreckage of me. Did I really hate him so much to do that? I resolved to say sorry for being a terrible son and for torturing him. In the morning, when he arrived to pick me up, to save me once again, no questions asked, I broke that vow. I didn't say anything. No I'm sorry. No thank you.

★

Jack grabbed my ankle and yanked hard. 'Jarred!'

My head banged against the bottom of the bed. 'Ouch! Whoa, whoa! I heard you. One sec. I'm coming out.'

'What the hell are you doing under the bed?'

I pulled myself out. 'I don't know.'

'You don't know?' Jack yelled. 'I thought you might be dead. Took too many of your goofy pills.' His fear stung. I felt guilty but still I couldn't bring myself to talk to him.

'Bring it down a notch. I had another bad interview. I was feeling like shit. Felt like hiding. Calm down.'

'Crawling under the bed. What the hell is wrong with you?'

'Who doesn't like a little bedroom spelunking when they're depressed?'

'You idiot.'

'Take a walk?'

'Sure.'

I preferred the Filling Station to flirt with Sarah the barista, but Jack preferred Mr. Do-nut. He was buying so we went there. He ordered a decaf.

'Are you going to tell me what happened at the interview?'

'I'd rather not. Let's just say I wasn't mindless manual labour material.'

'You still waiting for a CEO position to open up?'

'For the right bonus package, I might consider it. Jack?'

'Yes.'

'See this?' I stretched my arms wide with fingers splayed.

'See what?'

'Imagine my arms are four times as long as this and my fingers are ten times as long. That's how big a fuck-up I am.'

'Jesus, Jarred. Lighten up.'

'I have some good news though.' I told him my good news. On the bus ride back from my disaster at the interview for the envelope-stuffing job, I had gotten a phone call from the detective investigating the accident.

'Does that mean the police aren't coming after you?' Jack asked.

'I think so. He said they weren't going to "pursue the case" any further. I got the feeling they never believed the driver's new version of the story.'

'That's good news then.'

'I guess. Doesn't help Melissa much.'

'No. It doesn't.'

'It doesn't stop her husband coming after you or me either.'

'Don't worry about that. I get the feeling he doesn't give a damn. He's rich and he can afford to make others miserable. He was hurt and angry and he sicced his lawyers on anything that moved. They'll get bored of trying to get blood from a stone. You okay?'

'Not sure how I feel about it. Relieved, but . . . I don't know.' Then I told him about Melissa. Not about what had happened the night she died, but how I met her when we were barely teenagers. I reminded him of the time I stole his car, and I told him that it was because she had broken up with me.

As we talked, I traced the cost of my return in the lines of his face. The bags under his eyes were half-moon shadows. His stubble was a day old, which was unusual for fastidious Jack.

'I remember that day in the police station as my first wake-up call. The cops looked at me like the piece-of-shit drunk I was. Sitting there, signing papers, getting lectured by those jokers, it made me realise how bad it had gotten.

That's when I stopped drinking and started to fix – try to fix – the mess our lives had become.'

Except he didn't stop drinking that day. I knew the real story of the night that he stopped drinking. Maybe he didn't remember telling me the story. Maybe he didn't remember the real story. Over the years the stories we tell ourselves change. They have to. Who wants to live as a foil or a minor character to their own life's story? We choose the scenes and chapters to tell a story where we are the hero. It's the only way to survive the gashes, nicks and scratches life carves out of us. And yet, here we are still with knife in hand.

We went home carrying to-go coffees. I held mine between my legs. I'd figured out how take a sip and put it back without having to stop. As we turned onto our street, I saw a car parked across from the house. The driver leaned against it with his arms folded and watched our progress. As we got closer, I recognised the cop moustache and comfort-fit khakis.

'It's that collection agent,' I said.

'Don't take it personally. He's just doing his job. I'll take his paperwork, thank him and we can all go on our way.'

As we approached, Moustache pointed at my coffee and said, 'No drinking and driving.' A splash of coffee brown painted his windshield and I hurried into the house, leaving Jack there alone.

28

A few weeks after I had set fire to the tree in Melissa's backyard and my arrest for driving without a licence, one day, just like that, Mickey Mouse's smiling face, unstained by whiskey, stared up from the trash. Jack's skin had turned sallow. There was more grey hair than I remembered and the stubble at his chin had skunk stripes. He was always on the verge of tears, which was the hardest comparison to the invincible father I remembered. It was the first time I thought of him as old.

'Jarred,' he said, 'I'm going to another meeting tonight. Can you be home?'

I stared at his bruised forehead. 'When are you going to win a fight for a change?'

He felt the tenderness on the bridge of his nose. 'Don't try to be smarter than you are. I asked you to be home tonight.'

'I'm spending the night at a friend's.'

I didn't ask what 'meetings' meant and now when I said 'friend', it no longer meant camping alone in the forest near our house. I had found other misfits my age and older roaming feral around our town. I had quickly become adept at finding girls just as ready as Melissa to exhaust themselves against my endless need. That night a friend and I were planning to steal a wheelbarrow full of flowers from the cemetery for the doorstep of a twenty-year-old I had made out with at a party.

'I'd like you to be home tonight.'

I didn't come home until after school the next day. A man was sitting in the living room with Jack. A pale creature birthed from a cubicle somewhere on the tenth floor of a tall glass building under strips of fluorescent lighting and textured ceiling tiles. He looked barely out of college. His wispy cowlick of sand-coloured hair twitched like antenna as he stood to offer his hand. The creature had a name.

'Hello. I'm Thomas.'

'I wanted you two to meet last night,' Dad said. 'I asked you to be home.'

'I told you I was spending the night at a friend's.'

'Next time I ask you to do something, I expect you to do it,' he said.

Thomas looked away, pushing up his glasses.

I held my response, unsure what this visitor meant. Was Thomas from school? Was he a social worker? A cop?

'I wanted you to meet Thomas.'

I turned to walk away.

'Sit down!' Jack yelled.

I sat.

Thomas pushed up his glasses.

'Stop being a shitty teenager and give people respect. You and I both know that things, that things . . . fell apart when your mom died. I know I hurt you in a lot of ways and I'm going to make amends. Thomas has been helping me to work the programme and not take another drink. I'm asking you for a favour. I need you two to get along. Okay?'

'Nice to meet you, Jarred. You should be proud of your dad. A lot of people never make it to day one, never mind week one.'

I stared at Thomas, eyes bugged. He looked to Jack and still I stared.

'Jesus Christ! Never mind,' Jack shouted. I felt betrayed that Jack invited Thomas to our house. I was used to being angry all the time, but with someone from the outside I had to feel shame. Of the two, anger was easier.

Months went by with Jack gone every night. Thomas picked him up and took him to AA meetings. I attacked and ambushed him with petty teenage defiance that had previously meant weathering a few slaps and kicks before he'd retreat to the garage or bedroom. Lately, it had been me retreating behind slammed doors unable to cope with this new calm, patient and sober Jack.

'Jarred, I would like you to be home after school tomorrow.'

'Are we getting a puppy?'

'Jarred, I'm serious.'

'Serious as piles?' We both knew I was going to defy him.

'Jarred.'

'How many times do I have to tell you to go fuck yourself, Jack?'

He smiled. I tensed. There was danger in that smile. He rubbed his chin then stretched, his balled fists spreading out. I flinched and took a step back. He frowned and turned, saying as he walked away, 'You're coming to a meeting with me tonight. It's important.'

'We'll see.'

'We will.'

After school, I was sitting on the kerb outside a 7-Eleven with my friends. Jack pulled up and stepped out of the car.

'Hello, son! Ready to go?'

I submitted meekly, cowed by embarrassment. We drove home, and Thomas was already there sitting in our living room. I hid out in my room, petulant and obnoxious, until there was a knock on the door and Jack saying, 'Ready to go?'

I followed the two men around a church – old and ignored, its stone shoulders rigid, trying so hard to impress. I felt sorry for it. We followed the sidewalk to a box of a building behind the church. As we approached, the lights from the windows halved in shadow the faces of the smokers gathered by its doors. They weren't all black or white, rich or poor, blue or white collar. One more of the Lord's little jokes: only in addiction is the brotherhood of mankind realised. Where else would Jack be hanging out with a guy like Thomas?

They shook hands and hugged their way through the group. Jack introduced me and their names flew past. The friendliness of these people was unrelenting. Puffy-faced and weary, they laughed and gossiped. Veterans of a war no longer celebrated.

Jack and Thomas went to sit in the front. I sat at the back near the exit. Every person who passed me made eye contact and smiled. I felt embarrassed for them.

At the front sat a well-dressed man flanked by two tatter-edged posters of AA's twelve steps and traditions. He sat up straight. His hands were folded with affected patience. On the table, a blue trilby was set to his left and a blue book to the right. When the crowd settled, he read from the book with a polished tone that made each slogan seem true and meaningful. Everyone except me knew how to respond to his prompts as he led the service or meeting or whatever they called it.

The well-dressed man invited people to share.

One by one, people stood and spoke. Every story scratched and scraped until I felt a rawness inside me. Each person standing to introduce themselves as an alcoholic was a family destroyed and a life broken. A goth-looking girl with a septum piercing said she was grateful to be an alcoholic. I didn't know what that meant, but I hated them all for the doomed hope their excuses bore. I absorbed the sadness of each speaker until my hands shook. Did their families agree to have their humiliations brought to this misery show-and-tell? Everyone talked about their selfishness when they were drinking, but none of them talked about the selfishness of recovery. Everyone in their lives had no choice but to support them. It was a room full of emotional extortionists.

I didn't dare look at Jack as he stood.

'My name is Jack and I am an alcoholic.'

Panic seized my guts when the room responded with 'Hello, Jack'. I wanted out of this room. What he was about to say would break something within me. I knew this.

'We never went to bars. My wife and I were quite happy to do our drinking at home. But we weren't alcoholics, no sir. Alcoholics didn't hold down jobs, pay their mortgage or raise two kids. My youngest is here tonight.'

I felt his glance, but I kept my eyes deep into the muddy pool at the bottom of my coffee mug.

'I don't mind telling you this scares the hell out of me. This is the second toughest thing I've ever had to do. The first was to stop drinking.'

The crowd made appreciative noises.

I hated them. I hated them. I hated them.

'I'm ninety days sober, and I'd like to tell you my story. I know now that my wife and I were drunks. Every day, we raced home from work to drink. We were high-school sweethearts and alcohol was always a part of our lives. We had a lot of great times together.

'She was an incredible woman. Even in the depths of our shared disease, she made sure everything was okay. She made dinner. Made sure our kids were doing their homework, had clean clothes, a kiss goodnight and all that stuff. She did all this for one simple reason: so she and I could get very, very drunk. The night wasn't over until we blacked out.

'We were going to drink ourselves to death. That was the unspoken plan. But she died, an aneurysm, and left me alone with a ten-year-old kid at home and a drinking problem. It is hard to describe the anger I felt at everybody and everything.'

Shut up. Shut up. Shut up.

'But I wasn't going to let a little thing like the death of my wife stop me from drinking. I took all that anger and pain to justify why I needed to drink more, forgetting about that little kid, my youngest, who needed his mom and, even more, needed his dad. Most of the last five years from the day I buried my wife to the moment, ninety days ago, when I stopped drinking are gone. Nothing but empty bottles and a list of wrongs. I hardly remember anything but pain and getting up shaking and sick and needing a drink.'

I sat on the edge of my seat. My legs coiled, ready to spring up and away.

'There's a lot of talk about a moment of clarity. I'm here to tell you about my moment of clarity. When I finally knew, I mean really knew, that I was sick and tired of being sick and tired.'

149

Someone clapped and said, 'Tell it.'

'I hadn't worked since my wife died. I didn't need much, just a house to hide in and a liquor store in walking distance. Now, I had been drinking all day, nothing new there, but that day I got it into my mind that I missed my wife so much that I was going to join her up in heaven. The kid, he'd be better off without me.'

I knew all the smiling smokers that we had met at the door were thinking of me with pity. If one of them turned around to look at me, I was determined to throw my coffee in their condoling face. They could shove their fucking donation box and every one of the twelve steps.

'I had an old pistol hidden away somewhere in our closet.'

My mind stopped ranting and tears betrayed me.

'I was digging around looking for the gun, holding on to the clothes rail to keep my balance. Snap! I crashed into the closet, banging my forehead on the wall and dumping all her clothes on top of me.'

I remembered seeing the bruised forehead and busted nose, and I had accused him of getting into another bar fight.

'I tore at her dresses, threw them around and kicked. Having a good old pity party. That was God having one more laugh at my expense. I was sure of that and, well, I found that gun, unwrapped it' – Jack mimed the action of holding the gun in one hand and pulling away the oilcloth with the other – 'and put it to my head without hesitation. I felt the resistance of the trigger. I felt it give way. I heard the snap and felt the click at my temple.

'But nothing happened. Nothing happened by the grace of God. I dropped the pistol, curled up into a ball and fell asleep. When I woke up, I dug through the Yellow Pages and found my first AA meeting.

'I realised a hard truth. My moment of clarity. I realised I hadn't mourned my wife. My disease was such that she meant less to me than drinking. I had been telling myself I drank because of what God did to me. He took my wife and left me alone. But my moment of clarity taught me otherwise. I was a selfish bastard. I wasn't drinking because of my wife or to spite God. I drank because I wanted to be drunk. It was all about me. When I realised that I cared more about drinking than being true to her and raising our boy right, I knew I had gone too far. I came to that first meeting shattered like most do, and as soon as I said it out loud, admitted that I was an alcoholic, I was revealed.'

Hearing my dad's voice break, I didn't dare look up.

'The dirty trick drinking plays on you is that it lets you feel the pain, but it doesn't let it settle into your system. The booze flushes out those feelings so you have to feel them again and again, which makes you want to drink more. So those first weeks, besides making sure that I didn't take a drink, I had to mourn that perfect woman until I cried blood. And the only reason I survived was by having a candy bar in one pocket and a list of meetings in the other. This is my ninetieth meeting in ninety days.'

The room clapped.

'Thank you. Thank you, all, and thank you, Thomas, my sponsor, for getting me this far.'

They were still clapping as I bumped into a fat man outside blowing his cigarette smoke at the moon. Wheeling around to scream fuck you at his stunned face, I ran into the night wiping away the tears and snot.

29

At a job interview to do filing and data entry for a machining company, the interviewer's high-pitched and nasal voice annoyed me. My back had been constant agony for weeks, and I no longer had the patience to pretend they might consider hiring me. In response to her question about 'employment gaps', I let out a long slow groan, my eyes rolling back, my mouth hanging open.

The interviewer pushed my wheelchair into the lobby as I disguised giggles as moans. She scuttled behind the door unlocked by the swipe of the ID card at her neck.

'The ambulance will be here shortly,' the security guard said.

I straightened up to make my getaway, the joke gone too far, but a sharp and genuine pain cut me in half.

By the time a tweedledee and dumb of paramedics pulled a gurney through the automatic doors, I was twisted into myself and holding my abdomen against white hot tentacles squeezing agony out of organs I didn't know the names of.

'I'm going to faint,' I said. The trip to the hospital and admission was a skipping stone, brief touches of consciousness before bouncing into blackness: the jerking bounce of being loaded into the back of the ambulance, siren ringing above while one of the tweedles filled in a form, the sliding force of a corner taken quickly, the blast of AC as we rushed through hospital corridors, a beautiful woman in a doctor's coat asking where it hurt, needles, a white one-eyed machine whirring above, stillness, quiet and then lots of black.

'Sir, can you get your pants off by yourself? We need to have a look at your pecker and the plumbing,' said an older man with a stethoscope and a thick Texan drawl.

'Doctor, I prefer Latin-based words when a stranger's looking at my genitals.'

'Suit yourself. Need help with your drawers?'

Jack entered my room with a nurse who was explaining, 'Your son had bladder stones and has been experiencing associated pain but he attributed it to his spinal-cord injury and stress. The surgery was simple and performed without complications.'

'Fancy meeting you here,' I said.

'Mr. McGinnis,' the nurse addressed me. 'You can leave as soon as you feel up to it. You'll be in a fair amount of pain. You can take two every four hours.' She shook a bottle of pills.

'Four every two hours, got it,' I said, and gave Jack a wink.

'No, two pills, four hours. No more than eight in a twenty-four-hour period. That's important. You should be drinking ten to fifteen eight-ounce glasses of water every day. Your urine will be pink. This is okay, but if it persists for more than three days you need to contact us. The phone number is on your discharge sheet. Do you have any questions?'

'Yes, ma'am. Will I . . . give it to me straight, will I ever walk again?'

'Um. Um. I think you know the answer to that.' The nurse fled.

I giggled.

'Feeling better, I see,' Jack said. 'Ready to go home? Let me find your wheelchair.'

I smoked while Jack pushed me.

'I tried to get a job. Do something right for a change. Let me do it,' I said as we came to the kerb, popping up my front wheels to edge myself off the sidewalk.

A woman walking past said, 'You need to be careful.'

Jack said, 'If he had any sense, do you think he'd be in that wheelchair?'

'I was just saying,' the woman retorted.

'Now you have,' Jack said and the woman gave us both a dirty look as she left.

'I can defend myself,' I said.

'That had nothing to do with you. That was all about her. I need my fun too. Anyway, I was about to say you got a phone call today. Sounds like you have a job.'

When we got home, Jack said he needed to do some work in his greenhouse. I was sore but didn't want to be alone and offered to help. He seemed genuinely excited and set me up at the table he had made for me. Above the glass roof, the rich blue. The few rags of cloud in the sky had begun to pick up the pinks of a sunset. The greenhouse air was warm and full of earthy smells mixed with the perfumes of flowers.

'This is my special potting-mix recipe for small roots. Some of the babies like that Oncidium there need to keep their toes wet. You'll need this bag of fir bark, some coconut husk and perlite. Two, two, to one ratio.' Mister Shakey slid in and wound himself through Jack's legs as he explained.

He leaned down to give the cat a few scratches on his head. 'This is fine hardwood charcoal. You don't need much. I just salt the mix with it, but it's the secret sauce.' He pulled a pinch of shiny black dirt from a large plastic grocery-store bag. He showed the charcoal to me then Mister Shakey, who gave it a few disinterested sniffs before hopping into my lap and settling down.

We worked quietly beside each other. The cat slept on me, unbothered by the occasional splats of potting mix I spilled on him. The pain was creeping up on me but not enough to end this moment.

'Jack, I want to thank you for helping me out these past months. A lot of what happened is on me. I was a stupid teenage boy ready to burn down everything.'

'Sometimes literally,' he said without looking up from examining a tangle of finger-thick roots below a splay of leaves like green bunny ears. 'But no – I failed you, your mom, us.'

I couldn't have him still holding on to the guilt, shame and doubt teenage me dumped on him.

'Jack, you remember when I said I was going to run off the night before you picked me up. That wasn't true.' As I told him about trying and failing to kill myself, his eyes went wet. Chewing on his bottom lip, he considered the distance beyond the greenhouse to keep himself from crying. I told him about the humiliation of the driver pushing me back into the hospital without acknowledging me. I told him how cruel I felt for calling him earlier that day and having him drive down to Houston to find me dead after not hearing from me for ten years. My need to see him again and say sorry saved my life.

We had stopped working. Jack composed himself before he looked at me. He nodded and said, 'Thank you.'

30

The morning after Jack took me to his AA meeting and I ran away, I was making breakfast for myself. Jack was surprised to see me in the kitchen pouring cereal into a bowl.

'Hey, want to go get donuts with me?'

I raised my bowl and took another mouthful.

'Right. Tell you what. I'll buy you a pack of smokes as well and we won't mention what happened last night.'

I shrugged and put my bowl in the sink.

At the donut shop, a woman was trying to calm her toddler. His butter-yellow knuckles and red fists pulled at his own hair. He choked for breath between cries, pouring snot, spit and tears.

'Hey, kid! Quiet down for a second. You're killing us over here.'

The mother and the child, still hiccupping cries, looked at Jack.

'Cute kid,' Jack said and turned back to me. 'Did I ever tell you about my ditch approach to parenting? I'm going to write a book one of these days. Make my millions. Here's the idea. When you have a kid, you dig a six-foot ditch. Six by six by six feet. You put said kid in the ditch. Give him everything he needs. But he stays in the ditch. About the time the kid is big enough to climb out of the hole, it's about the same time kids are ready to rejoin humanity. It's like prep school for poor people.'

'Your genius is wasted on me.'

'That's the truth.'

We sat, both of us waiting for him to say what he really wanted to say. 'It's too late for rules. You've been running around doing dumb shit, drinking, smoking god knows what. But it's not too late to have a dad.'

I rolled my eyes.

He took a bite of his donut, staring his blank, hard-eyed stare that still gave me pause.

'You're right. Let's cut the crap. This world doesn't give a damn about you.' He paused, letting the weight of his sentence be felt. 'The world will be just fine with one more ignorant pothead who has nothing more to his name than a Waffle House uniform and a bong collection. The good news is you are your mother's son. I want you to have more from life, certainly more than I can give you. I'm serious here, look at me.

'What matters to you? Anything you don't roll your eyes at? You're a teenager for Christ's sake; you should be nothing but passion and hormones. What are you doing that doesn't require police intervention? What would you show Mom if she was here?'

He only invoked Mom's name as a last resort, as if afraid her memory would become a cheat for parental discipline rather than the last bond between us. It was a magic phrase like 'open sesame'. To Jack's credit, he used it rarely.

I shrugged, but the door between us was opening.

'You're already that boring? Sitting around, smoking, talking bullshit is what you should be doing when you're my age—'

'I don't know . . . Art. I like art.'

'Art. I don't know day one about art. Tell me about it.'

I told him. I didn't know anything either, but that never stopped a teenager. I thought I was very clever for liking the Dadaists and the Surrealists like every other arty boy my age. I did have a passion. Although I wouldn't have expressed it that way, I spent whole afternoons hiding in the bathroom stalls at school to pore over stolen coffee-table books, dog-earing pages, scribbling notes, tearing out pictures to give to girls. A few times, I convinced one or another to take the three-hour Greyhound trip to go to the museums in Houston.

He drank his coffee and studied me. 'Would you want to take painting classes?'

'Yeah. That'd be cool.'

'There's a guy from the programme – he used to be famous or something – he was talking about needing an assistant. If you work for him, I bet we can arrange painting lessons or something. He's pretty easy-going. An old hippy. What do you think?'

31

The phone call and the job offer that came while I was in the hospital was a temporary placement doing general office work. The HR woman had put me in an office of cubicles. Someone had printed 'Temp Section' in Comic Sans on a piece of paper. Each morning there was a list of to-dos on my desk. It was monotonous data entry, but I could listen to music while I worked. My desk overlooked an apartment complex. Throughout the day, I liked watching the windows and people going about their days. When I finished my to-do list, I hunched over a book and read or sketched the apartments on pilfered printer paper until five p.m.

An email pinged into my inbox from the front desk receptionist whom I filled in for when she went on her breaks. It was a reminder for a company lunch to celebrate the release of a new product. I wrote a reply.

Dear Mrs. Jones,
I can think of no better way to celebrate this momentous achievement than free sandwiches and soda eaten in the foyer with my esteemed colleagues. I have only been at the company for two weeks, but I am confident

that this new version shall crush all competition in the world of logistics facilitation. Our children's lullabies shall be the lamentations of their women.

Drive safely,

Rev. Jarred McGinnis, Esq.

A response came immediately.

Jarred,

I'm so sorry. I didn't mean to email that to you. I'm afraid the lunch is for employees only. Technically, you are employed by the agency. I'm afraid you can't have any sandwiches. If there are any leftovers, you can have those. ;)

Barb

Stacks of pre-made sandwiches beside bags of potato chips and rows of sodas rested on patterned paper tablecloths. I waved at the receptionist, took a bite of a sandwich, and returned it to the pile.

I popped off the sidewalk and wheeled through the newly planted pansies. A plastic sprinkler crunched angrily under my tyre.

Jack greeted my return home with, 'Something's wrong with your cat. He had a fit. I'm taking him to the vet.'

'Do you want me to go with you?' I asked.

'It's your damn cat.'

'I think I might have gotten fired today.'

'We'll talk about it in the car.'

We were sitting in the vet's office when Jack asked, 'So, what happened with the job?'

I told him.

'Not your finest moment, but you should go in tomorrow anyway.'

'Mister Shakey McGinnis,' the vet called.

The cat was passive as the vet examined him. He held the cat with one hand, petting him with the other. The grey tail swished across the examination table in slow arcs.

'How long have you had him?' he asked.

Jack looked at me.

'Not long,' I said.

'We'll see what comes back with the bloods. The attacks sound infrequent and they're relatively non-severe. At this stage, you just need to keep an eye on him, watch what he eats so we can exclude allergies or accidental poisoning. If the attacks become more frequent or severe, you should bring him back.'

'Thanks, doctor,' Jack said.

'Doctor, could you have a look at Jack? He's been having chest pain but likes to be a hard ass and won't go see a people doctor,' I said.

'All right, all right. Knock it off. Thank you for seeing us on such short notice.'

'No problem, Mr. McGinnis.'

The next day, Jack banged on my bedroom door and told me to go to work. I arrived late, not in a big hurry to be fired and have my wages docked the bite's worth of a tuna sandwich. No one said anything and Barb at the front desk gave me the same perfunctory hello when I arrived. A man from HR arrived at our cubicles and told one of the other temps that Mr. Ghosh wanted to show him something.

As the other temp stood to leave, I whispered, 'Don't you do it, then he'll want to see yours.' The HR man turned to me and said that I had been assigned to Bruce's team and I could find him in the fourth-floor kitchen.

Bruce's middle-aged paunch threatened to burst from his plaid button-down shirt worn dull by years of washing and wear. He sat at the table, drinking coffee from a thermos lid and eating a peanut butter and jelly sandwich. His hands constantly disturbed the red-brown tuft of hair on his head. A smear of peanut butter had given him a cowlick.

I pulled up to the table and watched the television with him. Bruce smelled of soured milk.

'There's a five to ten per cent chance I know that guy on that rope,' he said as he took a bite and nodded at the television showing a commercial for the Army. Heavy metal music followed a serious-faced man climbing down a rope from a helicopter into a frothing sea. The next scenes showed grainy images of armed men yelling and running through muddy puddles.

'Any chance you know those guys too?'

His reply was an unintelligible spray of sandwich. Once he swallowed, I asked about his military service. He proudly talked about developing the meeting-room planning system used in every Army base in the world. I asked Bruce if he was shitting me. Bruce assured me that he was not shitting me.

'Do you know the president? Have you petted his dog?' I asked.

'No, I do not. No, I have not.'

The conversation meandered from topic to topic by segues known only to Bruce. He had a son and a daughter, and he did not like bananas. With Bruce to entertain me, I thought I might be able to behave enough to keep this job.

'Who are you?'

'I'm the temp. HR said I should ask you what you need done.'

'Yes. Yes. I need someone to do web design.' Bruce nodded excitedly then rapidly listed things that needed to be done. Company jargon flew at me in Bruce's clipped sentences.

'Do you know HTML? CSS?'

'No, I do not.'

'You need to learn.'

'Okay.'

'Do you know Photoshop?'

'No, I do not.'

'You don't have any web design experience, do you?'

'Not a dot.'

'You have a lot to learn.'

Bruce's enthusiasm kept me there and nodding patiently, but I was already seeing all the ways I would fail.

'We can do this,' Bruce announced.

I smiled and said, 'When this project is done, they shall sing our praises in the hills for generations to come.'

Bruce walked out. I had already gone too far. I slapped my head just as Bruce popped his head back into the kitchen.

'Let's go,' he said.

'Now?' I followed him to his office. Bruce described software, passwords, access privileges et cetera that I was going to need. Halfway through, Bruce stopped. He ran his hands through his hair. One side of his part said twelve and the other pointed to twenty past.

'Where's your paper and pencil? Aren't you taking notes?' He opened a drawer full of office supplies. Everything inside was perfectly ordered, packed neat and tight. It reminded me of Jack's fastidiousness. He wrenched free a writing pad and tossed me a pencil. Bruce sighed and began again.

'First you have things to learn. I'll give you a day.'

Despite myself, I enjoyed working for Bruce. Each night, Jack and I talked about our work. My days flew past, and I slept the blessed sleep of the exhausted.

When Bruce was happy he did a fist pump and said stuff like 'nailed it,' which made me laugh. If Bruce thought something that I did was terrible, he threw his hands to his head, pulled at his hair, and said, 'Oh man, that's terrible,' with real mourning in his voice. I wanted to do well for him. Only once, in the middle of divvying the day's action points, did he mention my wheelchair, as if only noticing it at that moment.

'Why don't you use an electric one?'

'I don't need to. My arms are fine. Electric wheelchairs are expensive, heavy and, if they break or the battery dies, I'm stuck.'

'Why's that widget so close to the thingie? Move over.'

Some able-bodied people try to pretend the chair doesn't matter. They kneel on their haunches to be at your differently-abled eye level, because they once read wheelchair people like that. For other people you are the embodiment of the stick figure painted on parking spaces and bathroom doors: a curiosity, a subject of gossip or a cypher for disability itself. Finally, there are people like Bruce who, for whatever reason, don't include it as part of their calculation of you.

I pushed back from the computer to let Bruce at his troublesome widget and thingie. He hunched over the keyboard, muttering suggestions as he proceeded to implement them himself by banging at the keyboard and violently jerking the mouse.

I teased him and said, 'I liked the sans serif. It gave a warm feeling to the text. Especially when in bold.'

Bruce turned dramatically, looking behind him. 'What is wrong with you? Warm feeling?' He stood and faced me. I tried not to giggle. His hands ran through his hair creating a different topiary with each pass. We argued. He refused to discuss fonts in nonsense terms like warm and cold. I nodded, conceded his points, and agreed that there was never an appropriate time or place for Helvetica.

'Why do you like this stuff?' I asked.

He tilted his head, furrowing his brow, and gave a quick tug at the tuft of forelock. 'It makes sense to me,' he said.

'But it doesn't really matter. I mean this company doesn't even make stuff. We help people sell stuff that they didn't make either.'

'Doesn't matter? What matters? Listen, you're weird.' He pointed a quick jab of the finger before his hand returned to his head. 'That's okay. You're a good worker. Can you stop talking and do some work?'

'Yes, I can.'

That night Jack brought home Chinese takeout.

'I didn't know what you liked so I kind of got one of everything.'

He unpacked the paper bags until the dinner table was littered with Styrofoam containers full of glistening food, soy and sweet-and-sour sauce packets and fortune cookies.

'How's your Pow Pow Chicken?' Jack couldn't remember what he ordered so he made up the names.

'Delicious.'

'How was work today?' He stabbed a piece of chicken with his fork.

I told him about Bruce and his pronouncement about finding something and making that something matter.

After a bite of his Kung Fu noodles, he said, 'But keep it to yourself, because no one else cares.'

'That sounds about right.'

'Wise and handsome. My blessing, my curse. Now what shall we do to celebrate your first pay cheque?'

'Pay some bills! Pay some bills. Rock 'n' roll. Rock 'n' roll. Rock 'n' roll. Pay some bills,' I sang, banging on the table with a chopstick in each hand.

32

'Where have you been?' Sarah asked. 'I haven't seen you in a while.'

'Up the hill. Working for the man.'

'How's that going?'

'Meh.' I shrugged.

'Amen. How's Incredible Mister Shakey?'

'Furry. We had to take him to the vet but he didn't seem too worried.'

I sat in my usual seat with a view of the counter. Sarah brought me my coffee and sat beside me. She set down a legal pad.

'I've developed a questionnaire for us to fill out. How do you spell your name?'

I spelled it out for her and watched as she wrote my name down at the top of the paper. She had two freckles on her neck where Dracula's bite would be.

'Sarah with an H.' She pointed to herself. 'Give me your personal motto.'

'"We laugh to save ourselves from crying."' I took a sip of coffee, but it was still too hot. I played it off poorly.

'That's a good one. Mine is: "You only get one life so you might as well live it."' She wrote our mottos on her notepad.

'Golden rule? Mine is "Try everything once."'

'"Whatever it is, don't put it up your ass,"' I said.

The tip of her tongue peeked from between her lips as she wrote my answer. She was playing serious and I ate it up. She read the next question, 'Secret pleasure? I was going to write putting things up my ass, but I guess I'll go with "petting alley cats".'

She was flirting. A woman was flirting with me. A beautiful woman named Sarah was flirting with me.

'Something you miss the most?' she asked.

I flinched. I wasn't sure if she was bringing up the wheelchair, but it seemed an innocent question. Still, there were too many real answers to that question.

'I miss the sing-alongs at the men's urinals.' I hid my grin with another sip of coffee.

'What?'

'You know, disabled toilets are off on their own. I miss the fun of men lined up and pissing against the same wall.'

'What are you talking about?'

'Didn't you know men have sing-alongs in the urinals?'

'Shut up.' She smiled. Her left front tooth was a fraction longer than the right.

'I've tried to sing "Officer Krupke" by myself, but it isn't the same.'

'You are a bullshitter. I'm adding that as a footnote. Serious answer.'

'I am serious.'

'I miss just hanging out with people,' Sarah said. 'What happened to showing up at people's doors and hanging out? It seems like now everyone has to make appointments months in advance before they can be social. It's part of the reason I moved back here.'

'Where were you?'

'SF. I was a project manager for a big tech company making database software. This is what you do with a BA in English and forty thousand in student loans. A two-week project management course and I'm playing with spreadsheets and stroking millionaire nerd egos for a living.

'I thought I wanted to be a grown-up when I became a grown-up. But I was wrong. I couldn't take it any more. I was in a meeting and an engineer broke down crying saying he knew we were going to close the group, you know, fire everyone, after we shipped. He said he hadn't seen his kids in a month and we were still going to fire him. I had to say "no, no, no" because we needed him. Meanwhile, on my phone was an email telling me to start closing up the group as soon as we shipped. I knew he was going to go.'

'That's awful.'

'Not being a grown-up sounded like the grown-up thing to do. The sad thing is that I left after we shipped. I still stuck around to make sure that we made our ship date before I took my stand. I hung around the Bay Area, couch-surfing at friends' and pretending to be a bum.'

'I lived there when I was a teenager. Why'd you come back here?'

'My brother is really sick. I came home to help out, but I needed the redo.'

She looked at her notepad. 'We have some more questions. Definition of beauty?'

'I'm sorry to hear about your brother.'

'He's okay now. Everything is okay now, actually.' The smile returned. 'Definition of beauty?'

'The slight curve of the back of a woman's thigh as seen in profile.'

'Creepy. Does that line ever work?'

I flushed with embarrassment. I had no comeback. I wanted to run away.

'Well, Jarred, I think we have all I need here. Back to work.'

She stood and greeted the people waiting at the counter. I had embarrassed myself and left without saying goodbye.

I went back home composing all the other sentences I could have said. Our exchange replayed in my mind until it was full of static and error. My body became an encumbrance. My arms pushed the rim of the wheels, heaving the inert body and useless head. I felt the incline of the road and the struggle against gravity that always wanted to pull me backward. The dog-walker, the mailman, the woman watering her lawn, the child in the back seat of a passing car all had the same expression. Look, he's in a wheelchair. He can't walk. How horrible must his life be? I bet he's bitter and angry and alone. You start out thinking that everyone is sneering at you, then you learn to not care until you finally understand that everyone is so wrapped up in themselves that they don't have time to notice you, never mind patronise you.

When I got home, Jack stepped into my path.

'Hold up. Let's talk. What's wrong? You got a puss on your face.'

'A puss?' I said and turned to wheel around him.

He held the armrest of the wheelchair. 'Hold on a sec. Talk to me.'

I took a deep breath and let go. 'I'm twenty-six. Never going to walk again. I live at home with my dad. I do monkey work for peanuts. In debt up to my paralysed ass. I got you into debt too. I know you've had to borrow money from Patrick and that kills you. God knows what's going on with Melissa's husband and the civil case. On top of all that, I'm telling you my troubles like a lovesick teenager.'

'There are worse things you could be. Elephant inseminator for example.'

I pulled away and headed toward my bedroom. 'Jack, I'm not in the mood.'

'I was watching a nature programme and that was some lady's job in Berlin at a zoo. You could be shoulder-deep in elephant hoo-ha,' he said, following.

'Are those my only options?'

'With your CV, probably. Tell me about this girl.'

We were in front of my bedroom. I turned to face him. I told him.

'The girl at the fancy coffee shop? She seemed like a good one. I'll tell you how you know for sure whether she's interested.'

'Okay, tell me. How?'

'Five bucks.' Jack held out his hand.

'Five bucks? What does that mean?'

'I'm not giving this one away for free.'

'You want me to pay for fatherly advice?'

'Fatherly advice? This is powerful juju I'm peddling. You don't want my help, you cheapskate? Fine with me.'

'All right. I'll bite. Three fifty.'

Jack shook his head. 'This isn't for negotiation.'

I pulled out my wallet and handed Jack the money. He held it up to the light.

'The next time you visit her. Watch her when she first notices you. If she fixes her hair, she's interested. If she doesn't, if she doesn't pause for the minutest moment, she doesn't think of you like that.'

'That was worth two bucks tops.'

'Listen, rubber legs. Women are just as self-conscious and doubtful as you. When she's fixing up her hair, she's thinking of you. More importantly, she's thinking how she looks to you. She wants you to think of her as beautiful. If she doesn't fuss with her hair, you're just a customer. A thing that hands her money and she hands a coffee to. You aren't on her radar. You watch. Try it out.'

'She doesn't care. I'm a guy off the short bus. I said something stupid.'

'You always say something stupid. You worry too much. So what, you look like a giant roller-skate? Women aren't so shallow, not the ones that count. You got my good looks and charm, the ol' one-two combo. Use them. Here. Here's five bucks. The next time you visit her, if she does as I say, take her out somewhere nice. Buy her a coffee.'

I took the money and ignored how pleased Jack was with himself.

'Buy the coffee girl a coffee?'

'You won't have far to go then.'

'Can I ask you something personal?'

'Shoot.'

I hesitated, toeing the edge to test this new ground between us.

'Did you ever date after Mom died?'

'Yeah, of course,' he said.

'But you never wanted to remarry?'

'I meant to. I wasn't against it in theory, but I grew up with your mom. We were high-school sweethearts. I have adored her every day of my life, still do. I became a man with her and raised two kids with her. We took care of each other. After she passed away, I was too busy drinking myself to death. Then I was too busy trying to stay sober. Eventually, a few gals hung around for a year or two, maybe a little more. A lot of them for a lot less. Almost married a lady by the name of Jasmine but she wised up. They all got sick of being second best to a dead woman. I never blamed them for leaving. Your mom ruined me for anyone else. She and I fit perfectly despite everything. Now I'm too old and too used to being on my own.'

Jack's eyes shone. I wanted to put my hand calloused from the wheelchair onto his, but I couldn't command my arm to move.

33

I didn't think anything of it when Jack offered me a ride home after one of his meetings. I went to the diner where he and Thomas sat around playing toss and catch with AA clichés. I still suspected nothing when Thomas excused himself when I arrived. His leaving suited me fine.

'Ta da!' I showed Jack the painting I had been working on with the hippy artist. I was copying an old photograph of Mom taken by him when they were young.

In the photo, she was covering her eyes. Mom always hated her photograph being taken. A curtain of long black hair obscured her face except half of a coy smile. She was in a red western-style shirt, which blended in with the red brick of the fireplace behind her. She was a beautiful woman. Beside her there was a fair-haired man, not Jack, with Seventies helmet hair and wide lapels, holding the infant Patrick. In the painting I had cut them out. It was just Mom.

For the past weeks, Jack and I had been talking about my painting's progress. The first day, he drew out of me how I had stretched and primed the canvas by myself. At first, I was hesitant, unsure of how to be civil. But he persisted, and a father's pride is food for any boy.

Each day, I went to school for a bit to see friends but

usually ran off to the artist's house where I cut frames and mattes for his prints and ran any errand he needed. In exchange, I got some money and some painting lessons. After I got home, I sat on the armrest of Jack's chair. He held the photograph as I pointed out the parts I was working on, explaining how the layers of paint worked together, how to build up blocks of colour to make shapes and even my obsessive musings about the smell of linseed oil. He asked questions I hadn't thought of, which I relayed to the artist and reported the answer back to Jack the next evening.

The painting was almost finished. It was Mom in paint. Her smile was unmistakable.

The waitress stopped at our table to admire the painting. Jack played along, but there was something else on his mind. My feelings were hurt, and I asked him what his problem was.

I didn't know that the high school had contacted him to tell him about my poor attendance, selling cigarettes to freshmen and running a bespoke shoplifting service. I stole whatever anyone wanted and sold it to them half price. My name was coming up too often to be ignored. I had been expelled.

'So what?'

'So what? Finish high school, for god's sake.'

I seethed. I felt betrayed. I decided not to fight back, but to formulate revenge.

Waitresses and diners looked over as he growled and occasionally raised his voice. I held my head repentant. He threatened me with suits of punishment that I trumped. Grounded for a month. No, grounded for the school year. I told outrageous lies. I invoked Mom's name in vain. I did all this so when he ran out of accusations, I could excuse myself to the bathroom without him suspecting anything.

'Shake it more than twice and you're playing with it,' he said.

I took my time. I sat in the stall and stared at the ceiling. I strolled out of the bathroom past Jack's questioning expression toward the exit. I turned, gave my royal wave, quite a signature of mine at this point, and left. I was gone for a couple of months, returned home cuffed and my back pockets stuffed full of promises of court dates, time in juvie and community service.

When the police left, I was expecting a good old-fashioned smack around from his drinking days. Instead, he sent me to my room as if I had drawn on the kitchen wall with my crayons. When I heard Thomas arrive, I went to investigate.

'I said go to your room. You're grounded.'

I laughed. 'I'm just getting something to drink then I'll return to my cell.' That was going to be the end of it. I was going back to my room to finish my book, go to sleep and wake up and disobey him – business as usual – but it was Thomas's eyes that betrayed them.

I went and got my drink then sat on the sofa too close to Thomas, who unconsciously adjusted the distance.

'So, what are you guys up to?' I asked.

'Thomas is helping me do something I need to do.'

'Thomas, that's very kind of you. What are you helping us with? Tax returns?'

He looked at Jack. He looked at me. He pushed up his glasses.

'I'm here to be supportive.'

Jack said, 'I don't know what to do with you any more. You're so angry—'

'I'm not angry. I'm quite content actually. We have a

lovely house with our very own Thomas to curl at our feet on cold winter nights.'

'Jarred, I'd like you to go to your room and wait. I've called the police.' I felt jittering energy race through my body and vibrate in my arms. My thoughts jumbled and pushed each other around my head. Thomas and Jack looked small and far away, as if I was seeing them from the wrong end of a telescope.

'For what? What I have I done?' My voice went shrill and embarrassed me.

'That's not it. It isn't for anything you've done. You need help. I want you to talk to someone.'

'Is this Thomas's idea? It sounds like some pussy talk-about-your-feelings nonsense he'd come up with.'

'No!' The command of his voice had returned. 'Thomas has nothing to do with this. This therapy thing is a whole new world to me, but I think it's right. I don't know what else to do.'

'Fine. You get me to go this time. Are you going to get a cop for every appointment?'

'It's a facility—'

'A nut house?'

I shot out of my seat, but Jack grabbed my shoulders as the police cruiser pulled into the driveway. I used the distraction to go into my room and lock the door. A tentative knock came as I was climbing out of the window.

'One second, please. Just taking my shoelaces out and I'll be ready.'

I went to the front and knocked on the door before running away, across the top of the police cruiser from hood to trunk and down the street.

I don't remember consciously deciding to head in the direction of Patrick's house, but when I emerged from the forest his house was the closest. After walking for several hours, I was drained and numb. Maybe Patrick would let me sleep, maybe give me money for the Greyhound.

I knocked on the door and waited.

My left sock was soaked in blood. Three gashes in my leg had bled a lot but had dried and darkened to a crust rimming my sock. Patrick opened the door while I was still kneeling to examine the cuts.

'Jarred, what are you doing here? What's the matter?'

'I was goofing off in the forest and I fell and did this to myself. Can I come in?'

'Yeah, of course. Where's your shirt?'

I hadn't noticed my shirt was missing.

'The bathroom is just there down the hall. I'll see if we have any antiseptic.'

After I was cleaned up and his wife, Fran, brought me a shirt to wear, we sat on his couch staring at each other like the strangers we were. I became more anxious. Why had I come here? My brother didn't know me. This made my bones tingle with static. I wanted him to not stop talking.

I walked down the hall and investigated the rooms. After a few doors opening and closing, Patrick followed me and asked what I was looking for.

'I forgot how big this place is.'

'It's not that big. The price was right. The seller had to sell. I couldn't pass it up.'

'Holy shit! Is this the kitchen? Is Fran a chef or something?'

'No.' Patrick laughed. 'We really only use the microwave.'

'What a waste!'

Patrick dropped the fake smile he'd been struggling with since I arrived.

I twiddled the knobs on the stove. 'It looks like a

supercomputer. Is that a refrigerator for just wine? You caught Mom and Dad's alcoholism.' I nodded knowingly. 'It's a disease, you know.'

'Jarred, what do you want? Are you looking for money? Or just being annoying?'

'Thank you, Patrick. I knew I could count on family. I need four million in unmarked bills. A dude I met outside a Kwik-E-Mart will sell me a Russian sub. But you can't tell anyone.'

'Why are you here?'

Fran was at the kitchen table. She must have been in her late twenties, but she was dressed and had the hairstyle of a middle-aged woman.

'Fran, whose place is this really? Are you rich?'

'Your brother bought it.'

'So, Patrick is rich. Sweet. Like, how rich? Millionaire rich?

'No, no.' He was smiling, probably thinking, one day, one day. His pride made me want to pull down the unused copper pans hanging above the futuristic space oven or kick the integrated cappuccino machine, ice maker, soda dispenser or whatever it was.

'So Warbucks? When are you going to help Dad out? His house is falling apart since Mom died. He needs a bigger place. Maybe build him a new greenhouse. His old ones keep burning down.'

'You know Dad doesn't ever take help.'

'That's convenient. For you.'

'Are you here to stir shit? Dad's told me about the stuff you're doing.' Patrick raised his voice. Their daughter McKenzie called for Mommy from the back of the house.

'What has Dad said? Did he tell about all the times he used to beat the crap out of me when he was drunk? You missed that, didn't you? You were already out in the world making your piles of money, forcing old women to sell you their mansions. Did you know Mom died?'

Fran looked between us and the hall from which the calls for Mommy came. Her anxiety fed mine.

'Of course,' he hissed.

'That's right. That was the one time you were around. For the funeral. I heard her die. I hear her die all the time. I hear her choking and vomiting as she bled to death in her brain in the living room of that shitty little house Dad lives in.'

'Jarred, you need help. You need to see a psychiatrist.' His face was red with emotion.

'So I've heard.'

McKenzie was in the hallway now, howling, 'Mommy.'

Fran was on the edge of her seat ready to rush to her, but afraid to move.

'McKenzie, little dove, go back to your room. Mommy will be there in just a second,' Patrick called to her, before turning back to me. 'Let me drive you home.'

'I'm staying at a friend's house. Thanks for the lift.'

'No. I think I should take you home to Dad. Fran, can you phone Jack, please?' He kept his eyes on me like I'd do something terrible if given the chance.

34

I borrowed one of Jack's old department-store power suits from the Eighties that was Talking Heads huge on me. I found an old briefcase in the garage into which I put a banana and the neighbour's baby monitor for good luck. I slicked my hair with a side part.

Jack watched, shaking his head and smiling.

'Important business meeting today. Got to look the part. My project is being reviewed. It could mean that head of regional sales position in Topeka I've been gunning for.'

'Are you talking horseshit?'

'Mostly. I did the webpage and graphic design for this new service the company is launching and the project is being reviewed today.'

He looked unsure. His eyes looked around, anywhere but at me.

'Are you still getting pains?' I was worried about Jack and knew he wasn't telling me the whole story.

'Yes, and I'm seeing a doctor next week. That's not it, though. I want to say I'm proud of you.'

My eyes teared up and it was my turn to avoid eye contact.

'Thanks,' I said. 'I'm sure I'll figure out a way to screw it up soon enough.'

'That's my boy,' he joked.

When I arrived at the office, Bruce examined my outfit and hair without comment.

'How'd the review go? Did they like my stuff?' I asked.

Bruce turned around. He looked disappointed.

'What? Did I do something wrong?'

Bruce typed a few sentences in an email and clicked send.

'Bruce. Jesus, don't leave me hanging. What did they say?'

'They were very happy with your work.'

'Great. But what?'

'Let's go for a walk.'

'Are you breaking up with me?'

Bruce marched past. We walked through the parking garage and followed a dirt path on the other side. Bruce turned to see if I was managing but didn't say anything. As we followed the path, Bruce picked up stones and shoved them into his pockets until they were bulging obscenely.

At the path's end, erosion from rain and run-off formed a miniature Grand Canyon. Channels had cut through the layered topsoil making valleys and crooked fingers of ridges and escarpments. A grey tree stump rested ten feet down at the bottom. The centre rings had rotted out.

Bruce emptied a pocket of rocks and handed me one. He threw his rock into the stump's hollowed centre. It clacked against the stones already inside and bounced out.

'That still counts,' he said.

I threw a stone, but it flew wide.

We took turns. When I had hit the mark, we nodded to each other.

'When they built the office, they cut all the trees out,' Bruce said. 'Then this started to happen. The erosion will slowly work its way up that path and they'll have to spend millions making sure the parking garage doesn't drop into the hole like the stump. I told them that would happen.'

'Okay.'

'The project is finished. You're fired. I tried to get them to hire you as permanent, but they said no. They are required to pay a release fee to the agency and they don't want to. I'm sorry. We finished ahead of schedule. You could have had another month of work.'

Bruce thrust out his hand. I shook it.

'You did a good job, but you need a degree. This is how companies think. I'm sorry.'

'Don't be. Erosion shall be my revenge.' I smiled.

Bruce looked out over the yellow scar of dirt.

'Yes. Revenge.'

We shook hands again and I went to the Filling Station coffee shop.

'I've been laid off,' I said to Sarah.

'That sucks,' Sarah said, clearing a table. 'How about a free coffee?' She tucked loose strands of hair behind her ear. Jack was right.

'Do you want to go on a date with a jobless loser?'

'Wouldn't be the first time.'

'Did I mention that I don't have a car and I live at home with my dad?'

'Are you already married with kids? Or gay? Those tend to be the guys I fall for. What time do you want me to pick you up?'

35

At Elysium, a secure psychiatric unit for adolescents, our days began by lining up for a small paper cup. Mine held 600mg of lithium: pink pills with a metallic taste that gave the edges of my thoughts a down-feather softness.

As we waited for the counsellors to give us our prescriptions and check under our tongues, I bitched along with my fellow inpatients. I grumbled and complained, but the truth of it was being an inpatient was the summer camp kids like me never got. I happily did as I was told and played all their therapy games. When the unit was decorated with curses, screams or thrown chairs, my hands would shake with memory, but the bruises were no longer mine. Except once.

Aster was permanently locked in the time-out room and could never be left alone. She wanted to die. The irritant of living inflamed her every cell. Veteran inpatients traded Aster stories like baseball cards and, after I was there for a week, I got my own, a rookie all-star one.

I was padding past the time-out room when its door exploded open. Aster slammed her square body into mine and sent me bouncing off the wall. Counsellor Andy was on the floor. He'd torn her hospital gown trying to stop her and the loaf of her right breast hung out. She wheeled around and stared murder at Counsellor Andy then opened her mouth like a sword swallower and stabbed at the back of her throat with a toothbrush. She stabbed. She stabbed again. A fountain of vomit and blood erupted. Counsellor Andy tackled her and wrestled with her slippery limbs as Aster thumped her fists against his chest and cheek.

I met Fritz later that day, a skeleton with a fading blue Mohawk hanging over one eye. He was sitting cross-legged and whispering at the seam of Aster's door. A 'Caution: Slippery When Wet' sign marked the freshly mopped spot of her suicide attempt.

'Is group now?' he asked.

I nodded, and we walked to the day room, sitting across from each other as everyone took turns doing daily personal inventories: how we felt, what we wanted to accomplish in our therapy sessions and stating a positive word for the day.

My word for the day was 'enthuse'.

While Bulimic Carol spoke, an acid casualty, Redneck Ian, took out his glass eye and stuck it in his mouth. Fritz and I were the only ones to have noticed, and we traded smiles. Ian parted his lips, and the eye moved toward Carol who was reminding herself that she was beautiful, she was a princess. The glass pupil slowly surveyed the rest of the group. I tittered and its gaze snapped to me.

'Shh. Carol is sharing now. You had your turn,' Counsellor Kate admonished.

Fritz giggled, and the eye watched him.

'Oh my god!' Carol screamed.

'Ian!' Counsellor Kate yelled.

The eye spun in its mouth-socket then disappeared. Ian gulped. The mid-schooler named Tracey, who always cried in her AA meetings, squealed.

'Ma'am, I swallowed my eye.'

Counsellor Kate stood up, panicked.

'Just kidding.' He spat it into his hand.

'Ian! You apologise to Carol for this interruption,' Counsellor Kate said.

'Ma'am, I was just giving it a wash. My eye gets right dirty. It's all the porn.'

Everyone in the circle laughed.

Counsellor Kate led Ian away, lecturing him about the sacredness of the group circle.

'I don't think this should interrupt our therapy session, do you?' Fritz said. 'My positive word for today is "Papadopoulos".' He pointed to me – 'Enthuse' then himself – 'Papadopoulos.'

For weeks we were inseparable. Fritz, a couple years older than me, knew about the things I wanted to know: Church of the SubGenius, G.G. Allin and the Murder Junkies, *The Anarchist Cookbook*. Everything important to a fifteen-year-old who longed to be cool rather than strange.

When you are inpatient, it's easy to get to know another person. The doctors and nurses and other inpatients define you. You trade diagnoses with handshakes. Prescription lists are your business cards. The disease they hand you becomes your identity: Bulimic Carol, Alcoholic Tracey, Bipolar Me. Outside the facility, I had never had the comfortable certainty of having all the 'because of's spelled out.

I was inpatient because of self-harming and psychotic episodes, because of the death of my mother and because of the years of physical abuse by my alcoholic father.

Fritz was inpatient because of drugs, because of falling in love with an older man named Jerry, because of his dad molesting him. Fritz didn't believe in 'because of'.

Fritz explained the way we were: 'From the weight of

pain, we singing diamonds are made.' I never asked him what he meant, because I needed it to be true.

I told Fritz everything and told him truly. He wasn't interested in fixing his own life, but he knew what to say to make me want to improve mine. His room was across from mine. Sitting cross-legged in our doorways and chewing his nicotine gum, we talked to each other until lights out.

'What was all that yelling about today? I heard you. Don't take it out on your dad,' he said. Fritz's minty nicotine talks did more for me than the pink pills or Counsellor Andy's nine-to-five concern. It was another month of wait-and-see and I needed it.

'I know,' I said.

'You bottle up everything and pretend like nothing hurts you. You take on all this guilt until you explode. He's trying to help you, your dad. How many times have you been in time-out this week?'

Fritz and I were playing Slap Hand in the hallway. His hands, long and eloquent, rested lightly on top of mine. Counsellor Andy came up to us and seemed pissed off.

'Fritz, Aster is asking for you.'

'Can I go in or do you have to strap her down?'

Counsellor Andy gave him a look like he should know the answer to that and continued down the hall.

Fritz took my hand and led me to Aster's door. We sat cross-legged before it. Fritz leaned close to the seam. 'Aster?'

A moan, achingly slow, an infectious sadness with it, came from under the heavy door. A sniffle. She was crying.

'Aster, you are the gathering of darkness against which they shut their doors and light their fires. But those who dance beneath you naked and unafraid shall see your multitude of stars.'

'Fritz?' Aster's voice asked.

'I'm right here. Go to sleep. I'm watching over you.'

I opened my mouth. Fritz put his finger to his lips. We sat there quietly for a few minutes.

'What happens to her when you leave?' I whispered. Fritz had seven days left. He had been in for the full ninety they gave druggies compared to the thirty days they gave me for being just crazy.

'I don't want to think about that,' he said.

'I'll be out a week after you. We should hang out.'

Aster moaned Fritz's name.

Fritz nodded, but he shushed me again before leaning in to whisper at Aster's door.

A couple days later, we were at the day-room window, waving manically at the pedestrians below and, if they waved back, we licked the window and pretended to masturbate. It didn't take long for Counsellor Kate to stop our game but, instead of calling us both into her office, she told Fritz to follow her. We didn't see each other for the rest of the day and, after dinner, I sat in my doorway waiting until lights out.

I cornered him the next morning. 'I need to talk to you. Meet me in the day room.'

'I'm late for my appointment with Dr. What's-his-face. You should talk to Kate.'

In a world that consisted of locked rooms, two hallways, a nurses' station, a day room and occasionally a yard with a high fence, it was difficult to avoid a person. Fritz managed to avoid me very well until his discharge day. When he tried to say goodbye, I told him to fuck off.

After he left, I moped around for a few days, which earned me an increase in dosage.

'Hey, hey, boy,' Aster's voice called from the time-out room.

Two crescents of eye white appeared in the slit window.

'Hey, hey, boy. Fritz loved you.'

'Aster, please get away from the window,' a voice said from within the room.

The crescents disappeared.

'Fuck you, fuck you, motherfucker,' Aster said.

36

Everything about Sarah's house was a home, a single-storey 1930s Craftsman style, pale green with forest green for trimming. A postcard for this street would have Sarah's house at its centre. Children would be playing baseball watched by a golden retriever and a dad watering his lawn. The card would read 'Wish You Were Here' and mean it. Beneath the eaves, the entire front of the house was a deep porch. A table with chairs was on one side of the door and a swing bench on the other. The broad steps up were lined with clay pots full of blue flowers cowed by the heat. An oak tree, stately and in full leaf, shaded the house. Its shallow roots had cut through the decades-old sidewalk; it reminded me of travelling through Canada as a roadie for a friend's band and stopping to watch a frozen river break up.

As Sarah pulled into the driveway beside the house, I thought about those steps and the inevitable awkwardness of having to be carried up them.

She pulled the emergency brake. I sat embarrassed as she pulled my chair out of the trunk. Clunk. She slotted a wheel into place. Clunk.

She knocked on my window.

'You okay?'

'Yeah, just drifted off.' I locked my wheels, transferred over, adjusted my feet, fixed my pants, and didn't make eye contact.

'We'll go through the back,' she said.

As we passed a window on the side of the house, she rapped the pane. From inside a tinny high-pitched voice howled with unrestrained child's glee. At the back of the house, her mother stood at the top of a long wooden ramp. I was surprised as much as relieved that I wasn't going to be dragged upstairs.

'Hello, Jarred.' Her mom's eyes had the same mischief as Sarah's. Her hair was short with blonde highlights.

'Oooh. That's beautiful.'

'It's Jack the grumpy orchid. Jarred gave it to me,' Sarah said.

'My dad grows them.'

'It's beautiful for a grumpy orchid. Well, Jarred, I hope you're hungry.' Sarah's mom moved her hands and spoke as if she was signing a demagogue's speech and not describing the recipe she found online for potatoes, assuring Sarah it was vegan-friendly. Sarah's dad appeared.

'Hello, Jarred. Welcome to our home.' Her dad spoke like the host of a children's tv show. I bristled, thinking he was being patronising, but it was how he spoke to Sarah and his wife. It was a voice of patience and kindness and seemed ill-fitting on a broad-shouldered man well over six feet. He was bald with a neat copper-flecked white beard.

'I hope you're hungry,' he said.

The house had a hallway for a spine, crammed with photos, paintings and shelves filled with knick-knacks. A handrail ran the length of the hall. The air was filled with the promises of cooking onions, roast chicken and potatoes.

Every room we passed was painted a different colour. I felt at ease in this house amongst this family.

'That's my room,' Sarah said as we passed one with eggplant walls and a messy bed.

'That's my dad's office. He's an architect.' The back wall was all window, the desk and computer sat before the view of a vegetable garden. Shelves of books hid the oyster-shell walls.

'This is my brother Marco's room.' She pointed to the closed door.

She knocked.

'Sarah! Come in!' The voice pronounced the words with a deaf person's imprecision.

We entered a room of sky blue. By the window in a hospital bed an unshaven face lit up on seeing Sarah. The sunken, wet eyes were huge in their sockets. He had the tight skin and lips of an unwrapped mummy. He stretched his arms, opening and closing his hands.

'Sarah,' he squeaked.

'Marky Marco.' She took his hand into hers and kissed his fingers.

'Sarah.'

'This is Jarred,' Sarah said.

Marco held out his hand. I took it and gave it a shake. A tiny tremor of pressure and I understood he wanted to pull me closer. He struggled to lift himself. I hugged the shirtless Marco, felt the thin soft flesh stretched across sharp scapulas, the knotted rope of vertebrae and ribs. The feverous heat. The skull rested heavy on my shoulder. I wanted to weep but I wasn't sure why.

'Nice to meet you, Marco.'

He formed a smile, teeth bared from a flash of pain he didn't name.

Sarah talked to him and he nodded unsteadily, blinking tears, limbs tremoring. I looked about the room: shelves of latex gloves, stacks of diapers, boxes marked sterile and an angry red plastic container stamped 'Biohazard'. A cabinet-sized dialysis machine of tubes and buttons, a 1970s vision of the future, sat beside the bed. An old and battered wheel-chair, not intended for the punishment of the outside world, waited in the corner.

'Bye, Marco. Nice to meet you,' I said.

In the dining room, Sarah's mother and father were setting the table.

'Dinner won't be long now,' her mother said.

A screech came from Marco's room. I looked at Sarah, afraid something was wrong.

'He's singing along to the radio. He's obsessed with R&B. I think that's En Vogue.'

'That's TLC,' her dad said, putting a bottle of wine on the table.

The screech came again.

'See,' her dad said and sang along with the chorus.

Sarah, her dad and mom were all smiling. I didn't know what was wrong with Marco, if he was going to improve or for how much longer he would live. But there in that moment, the entire universe shrank to this family listening to the high-pitched off-key singing of a pop song and despite everything, right there right then nothing was wrong. Nothing was wrong at all.

After the food was delivered to the table, Sarah's mom barely sat down before she popped up for something else. She was either dishing out more food or getting napkins or checking on Marco. Sarah only ate the vegetables. After the meal, we were in the kitchen, wrapping leftovers, washing or drying dishes. Sarah's dad gave pecks on the cheek to Sarah's mom and thanked her for a fantastic meal.

'Let's go for a drive,' Sarah offered.

'Where we going?'

'We're going to feed the Trash Ducks.' She pulled out two empty water bottles from the recycling bin.

We drove along single lane roads beyond used trailer-home dealers and lonely gas stations radiating into the surrounding night their fluorescent-lit promises of junk food and sixty-four ounce soft drinks. The scenery changed from countryside to a mix of empty lots and industrial buildings. Monstrous mud-caked vehicles were scattered about like grazing animals. We turned down a deeply rutted path. Lights and the black lacquer of water glimmered ahead of us. We came to a clearing at the shore of a small lake across from the futuristic cityscape of an oil refinery. Yellow, white, green, blue and red lights outlined rectangles and spires of brushed metal pipes of varying sizes. The billowing steam glowed and a tower belched orange fire that flapped in the wind like a flag.

'It's beautiful. How did you find this place?' I asked as Sarah helped me push across the uneven ground to the water's edge. We stopped at the concrete ledge. She sat and dangled her feet over the edge.

She shook out the last drops of water, screwed the lid back on and tossed one of the bottles into the ill-looking water. It skittered and pirouetted on the water's surface, chased by thin ripples. Its neck stretched forward looking for a mate.

'Trash Ducks,' she said. She tossed the second bottle, and they danced around each other, pushed by the breeze. She rested her elbow on my leg and she showed me how to feed Trash Ducks. We tossed them bottle caps, stones and concrete chips until the wind pushed them further and further.

She rested her head on my lap. I petted her hair. Our closeness was immediate and comfortable. I didn't think to question it. Her presence calmed me, and I thought of nothing but the softness of her cheek as I traced her jaw with my hand.

'Can you see?' She held her hand out, fingers splayed.

'What am I looking for?'

'My fingers.'

A zigzag of white scar ran between her ring and middle finger.

'What happened?'

'I was born with webbed fingers. My mom wanted me to be normal. So, she had them cut apart. Not sure how these ugly scars are more normal, but I still have my webbed toes. If you play your cards right tonight, I'll show you my duck toes. My mom hated me for them. She blamed Dad, refused to breastfeed me until I had the surgery. They had to wait six months until I was old enough to operate on.'

'Wow, Jane seems so chilled out—'

'Jane's our stepmom, but they've been together for so long that she's pretty much *the* mom. The webbing wasn't even that bad; it was completely cosmetic. Sometimes the finger bones can be fused.' She pushed her fingers together. 'Dad begged them to leave my toes alone though. He couldn't stand the idea of them cutting up a baby.'

We watched the refinery and the lake.

'A couple years after me, Marco was born.'

'I thought he was your older brother. I got everybody wrong.'

'No. Dad said when they were explaining all the problems Marco was going to have, they didn't expect him to live to be a teenager. He made a joke to lighten the mood about at least his fingers and toes being fine. He remembers looking at my mom and seeing something in her eyes that told him she was going to run out on us. And she did. She left everything: her clothes, her kids; it was all the same. Disappeared. Dad came home from work, baby Marco screaming and screaming. I don't remember it. I think I was playing in my room. He tried to find out what happened to her. He called all over the place, but no one knew anything. The closest he got was her mother telling him that she said to say sorry and not to call again. When I was ten, he got an annulment letter from California. That's all we ever heard from her.'

'I don't know what to say.'

She looked at me. 'Not sure you're supposed to say anything.'

She put her head back down and I petted her hair. We watched the refinery's reflection sparkle on the water's surface. Sarah said the gas flare looked like a whip-tentacled sea creature floating just below the surface.

'It's watching you,' she said. 'You better be on your best behaviour.'

'Do you want to go see Jack?'

'Yes, please. How're you guys doing?'

I looked at her.

'You said you guys weren't getting along.'

'We're okay right now, I think. Since moving back home, I've realised I'd been blaming Jack for a lot of things that weren't his fault.' I took a deep breath. She watched the small ripples in the water as I brushed a finger along her earlobe. I wanted to tell her about my mom, the lonely teenage years at home with Jack, the lonelier years as a runaway as a way of explaining myself, but I was too afraid of scaring her away.

She looked up and smiled.

'Let's go, kiddo. Let's see Jack,' she said.

We headed back into town. I wasn't sure of the address, but we found the factory surprisingly quickly. We walked the sidewalk that skirted the building. I tried doors as we went. All of them were locked until we reached the loading dock. As soon as I opened the door an orange light spun and an alarm pulsated.

'You have activated the security system. The police are on their way. You have sixty seconds to leave the premises.' Jack's voice came from a call box beside the door.

I mashed the call button. 'It's me.'

'Fifty-nine seconds. Fifty-eight. Fifty-seven.'

'Hello? Can you hear me? It's Jarred. Turn off the alarm.'

'Fifty-six seconds.'

'We should go.' I turned to leave. The alarm shut off.

'I saw you on the cameras. Look up.'

I looked. Sarah waved.

'Is this the girl you've been all gaga for? I remember you from the fancy coffee shop. I'm Jarred's dad, Jack.'

'Hello, Mr. McGinnis.'

We walked through the sugar-scented hallway, passing under banners proclaiming the exciting new flavour ranges of cereals that were knock-offs of well-known brands.

'It smells like childhood Saturday mornings,' Sarah said.

Posters about safety procedures, birthday wishes to Cindee and a softball team sign-up spotted the hall. I wrote my name down for third base. Jack told me to knock it off.

The break room held a few tables and plastic chairs. Along one wall was a sink and refrigerator. A calico of mugs lined the backsplash. Above them, the company's products cluttered the shelves: instant coffee, creamers, teas and powdered drinks.

'If you like your beverages powdered, this is the place to be,' Jack said.

'Nestlé Quik! I haven't had Nestlé Quik since I was a kid,' Sarah said.

'It's fake Quik but knock yourself out. It tastes like sugared brick dust to me. Jarred, what're you having?'

'I'll have chocolate.'

'You guys are guests. Have a seat. What flavour do you want, Sarah?'

'Strawberry.'

Jack pulled down coffee mugs. He scooped the chocolate powder, the strawberry and a scoop of instant coffee for his mug. He took milk from the fridge.

'Is there soy milk?'

'I have no idea—' Jack took out a carton of soy milk. 'What is this stuff? I've never heard of it.' He gave it a sniff before pouring it into her mug. He poured regular milk into his and mine.

'Disgusting. Cold milk and instant coffee?' I said as he brought the mugs to the table.

'Son, let's not pretend. This stuff is horrible.' He took a sip of his cold milk and instant coffee. 'Sarah, I know you work at the fancy coffee shop. But I'm old and that means I don't have to pretend to care any more. You guys want donuts?' Jack stood to grab the box of donuts on the counter.

'I don't think donuts are vegan,' I butted in.

'Vegan donuts? The whole point of donuts is the animal exploitation.'

'That's terrible and makes no sense,' Sarah said.

Jack shrugged and grinned.

'Give her a break, Jack.'

'It's okay,' Sarah said. 'Just because I'm vegan doesn't mean everyone else has to be.'

'That doesn't sound very vegan,' I said. 'Oww! Why doesn't he get punched in the arm?'

Jack laughed.

'Hey, I thought you were supposed to be cutting out the caffeine,' I said to Jack.

'Who's the parent around here?' Jack turned to Sarah. 'You're a pretty woman with a seemingly good head on your shoulders. What makes you want to get mixed up with a goofball like him?'

'I don't know. He has a good sense of humour. He's easy on the eyes.'

'He gets those from me.'

'Plus, have you seen the parking spaces he gets?'

Jack laughed. 'I like this lady.'

We sat at a small round table, sipping at our drinks and talking. Jack told the story of when he found me screaming under the table with a toy soldier's head stuck up my nose. I was hysterical, blood everywhere.

'The kid was smart enough to know the word reconnaissance, but not smart enough to not shove a damn toy up his nose.'

Her laughter filled the room.

'What time do you finish?' I asked.

He checked the wall clock over the door. 'A couple more hours.'

'Do you want us to hang around?'

'God, no. I didn't take this job for the social life. I'll see you at home. Nice to meet you, Sarah.'

'Nice to meet you, Jack.'

★

Sarah dropped me off at Jack's house. The car idling, we sat, staring forward. She filled the silence with a broad smile.

'Do you want to come in?' I asked.

Sarah turned her body to face me. Looking serious, she asked, 'Do you have pyjamas for me?'

'Tops and bottoms?'

'Yes.'

'I think I have something that'll work.'

She was in the bathroom changing into a pair of my boxers and a t-shirt. I got into bed and under the covers. How do I move this half-useless body with any subtlety? She would lie beside me. It had been too long. Even to roll over on my side toward her was going to require an awkward adjustment of my legs, a shift of my hips, a readjustment of my pillows. These are not the movements to seduce.

She closed the door behind her and flashed a shy smile. Even the small shifts of the bed from her climbing under the covers excited me.

'Did you paint that?' She pointed to the painting of my mom.

'When I was a teenager. It's a picture of my mom. She's about our age there.'

'Wow! You were really good. You should paint more. I love how she's covering her eyes, but you can still see her smiling.'

'She was really shy. She hated having her picture taken. I'm glad Jack kept it.'

'Of course he would. It's a painting of his wife by his son.'

She slid her hand under the covers and held my hand.

'You ready?' she asked.

I didn't know what to say. I was an awkward teenage boy again.

'I think you're one of the good ones. You can see my magic duck feet.'

'I don't think we should rush into these things.'

'I know what I'm doing.'

37

The day before my discharge I had a family session with Jack. We sat outside the psychiatrist's office waiting for him to call us in. Jack was already sitting there when I arrived. I sat beside him and we said nothing.

The psychiatrist opened his door. He was stocky and big-nosed. He invited us in with a wave of a meaty hand hanging from his doctor's whites, a thatch of coarse black hair on the back of it. He should have been holding a cleaver, not prescribing antipsychotics.

'Come on in. My name is Dr. McCabe,' he said as he ushered us to our seats. 'Sorry that Dr. Taradash isn't here. He had a family emergency, and I was asked to come in at the last minute. I'm just going through your notes. It looks like this is your last session before we discharge you. I bet you are excited about that, hmm, Jarred?'

'Yes, sir.'

'You'll have to bear with me as each family session is unique to the individual family. I know you have developed the dynamic of these sessions over the course of your therapy and it's not ideal to have that disrupted, especially for the last session. Jarred, can you tell me some of the ground rules you've established here?'

'We try to make our point without blaming the other person and instead frame it in terms of how we feel. Absolutely no yelling, shouting, foul language or fake German accents. Ja?'

The doctor nodded, still looking at the paperwork.

I looked at Jack to see if he noticed the joke, but he was watching the psychiatrist with an empty look. He was a man waiting for his name to be called at the DMV. This was an eye test, a trip to the dentist. Maintenance, but no cure. He was there to sign forms as was expected.

'It says that the breakdown of the family unit was caused by the unexpected death of the mother. Is that right?'

'The mother' as in 'the carburettor'. Something mechanical that failed. To the butcher in the doctor's coat, she was 'the mother'. Fine with me. He didn't have the right to use her name.

After a month of being inpatient I had become adept at using therapy speak and clinical language to slalom between what people wanted to hear without hitting the guilt I felt about Mom's death, the shame of having a drunk for a father, the violence, the directionless anger, the loneliness, the confusion and, most of all, the overwhelming sadness that cored my body. I knew I had to play their game once more, then they would let me out and I would be free to do what I wanted. The psychiatrist seemed pleased with how remarkably receptive I was to all that modern psychiatry had to offer a troubled young man. Jack's name-rank-serial-number responses were the ones that gave him pause. After our session, I smirked when Jack was asked if he had time for a quick private session. I knew from experience that he was going to get a lecture about the importance of engagement in the therapy process.

The next day, Jack signed me out and drove us home.

For weeks, I hid in my room waiting to enrol in an 'alternative high school' where they taught kids about art history, birth control and let them smoke between classes. Then Fritz called.

'What's up?' he asked.

'Nothing,' I snapped, not sure if I was angry or hurt.

'I'm sorry I was such an asshole, but they made it a condition of my discharge that I didn't talk to you. They were worried about "the nature of our relationship".' He said the last part in a mock-clinical tone. 'Do you want to hang out?'

'Don't you live in the boonies somewhere?' I asked.

'No. I'm sharing an apartment with this guy Jerry.'

'Jerry?' In the real world it was easy to forget how we had made knick-knacks of all our problems and secrets. As inpatients, we set them out before us at every group session without thinking about their significance.

'He's okay,' Fritz said.

I rode my bike to the address he gave me. The apartment complex was tangled up in pine trees like a broken kite. Fallen red needles crunched under my tyres and released their waxy scent.

In front of Fritz's apartment, a dusty black kitten complained. I rubbed its head and felt the soft fur and the tiny skull beneath. The cat disappeared inside and a skinny man dressed as an orderly opened the door. His frizzy hair made him look like a redheaded Q-tip wearing glasses.

'Yes?'

'Is Fritz home?'

'In back. Careful, he's on the rag today.'

I stood before the hall and wondered which of the two doors was Fritz's room. The Q-tip stood behind me and held my shoulders. I tensed under his touch and fought the urge to jerk away.

He steered me by the shoulders and said, 'This one. The one on the right's the guest room. Tell him I'm late shift tonight.' The Q-tip patted my back then disappeared.

Fritz opened his door. 'Was that him leaving?'

'Was that Jerry?' I was disappointed by how geeky Jerry was. Fritz was the epitome of cool. Was that nerd really a child molester? Why would Fritz stay here if he was? I was confused and awkwardness settled between us. He gave me a hug. I kissed him. He was warm. I was cold. He smelled of cigarettes.

'Why'd you diss me inside?'

'I told you. They made it a condition of my discharge. I was worried about . . . I didn't . . . I don't know.'

'Forget it. What's that?' I pointed to a bowl of goop that looked like royal blue oatmeal.

'Homemade hair dye. I was just about to do my own. You want to try it? Or I can give you an earring?' Fritz picked up a stud from beside the bowl of hair dye. 'It's a piercing stud. It's supposed to go into a gun, but we can just jab it in.'

We sat next to each other on the couch in the living room, watching cartoons and drinking beer. My ear was hot and I kept touching the earring. We giggled at each other in our shower caps and the blue glop steaming beneath. The kitten hopped into my lap and mewed until I petted it.

'How's your dad doing?' Fritz asked.

'Can I live here?'

'No.'

'Fuck you too.'

'Aster turns eighteen today,' Fritz said.

I raised my beer. 'Happy birthday to Aster.'

'That means they send her to state hospital.'

'I'm sorry.'

We turned toward the sound of the front door unlocking.

'Honey, I'm home,' Jerry sang. He raised a six-pack of beer. 'Hello again,' he said to me. Jerry sat on the floor between the coffee table and us. He cracked a beer and offered one to me. I held up my unfinished bottle to say no thanks. Fritz slammed his and took another. We watched more cartoons and drank more beers. Fritz drank fast and had most of the six-pack. I wasn't sure who he was angry at.

Jerry took out a cigar box from underneath the couch. From it he took rolling papers, weed and a little black rubber ball wrapped in cellophane.

'Jerry, no,' Fritz said.

We smoked, Fritz too, and the world washed through me in calming little waves. I sank deep into the sofa to watch the incomprehensible television. I scared myself thinking how much I preferred feeling like this.

Somehow, I was in Fritz's huge bed. I heard him in the hallway hiss, 'Stay out of our room. Don't you dare touch that kid.' He locked the door and lay down on the floor.

'Goodnight, Fritz,' I mumbled.

In the middle of my dream I heard the door open. I felt warmth on my foot and a tug at my blanket. I woke up but stayed motionless, afraid to open my eyes and see Jerry over me. Something moved along my leg, touched my knee, then my thigh. I held my breath. I felt its weight on the inside of my thighs, pushing them apart. I bolted up and threw the blanket off. The kitten shot into the air, hissing, and fled the room.

'Why's the door open?' Fritz asked angrily.

'I don't know. Cat?'

'You scared the shit out of me.' Fritz shut the door and locked it again. 'Go to sleep.'

38

Afterwards, me on top, tightly embracing, my arms beneath Sarah, I buried small kisses into the flesh of her neck, feeling her warmth against my cheek. I felt her shudder.

When I lifted my head, my cheek was tear-slick. Her eyes were puffy and red.

'I'm sorry,' she choked.

'What'd I do? I'm sorry. What's the matter?'

'Nothing.'

We shifted our bodies so that I was lying beside her. I put my head on her chest and listened to the whisper of breath in and out and the clip-clop of her heart. This heart, like all hearts, could be hurt: heart attacks, blood clots or car accidents late at night after too many drinks. But this heart, I thought, it was going to be me that caused it pain.

An ice-water of panic hit me. I shot up and threw the blanket off my legs.

'What's the matter?' she said.

'Nothing. I need a smoke.'

'Please don't go right now.'

I lay back and she tucked herself against me. My arm and shoulder, her pillow. She fell asleep quickly as I traced her waist and hips with my fingers. Beneath my palm that heart's rhythm. It was not so fragile, but constant. I wanted to be deserving of a person like Sarah. The steady, solid beat calmed me.

'Hey, beautiful. I need to say some things. Maybe I'll be able to say this one day while you're awake but . . .'

Her breathing was quick and shallow as she slept.

'When my mom died, I was there. The same car accident that put me in a wheelchair, Melissa, this girl I knew, died because of me. Now every time I hear brakes squeal or they show a car accident on tv or in a movie I think I'm going to be sick. Melissa dies in front of me just like my mom did when I was a kid, over and over.'

Her lips parted as she exhaled. I traced the outline of her nose with my finger. It was going to be easy to fall in love with her.

'I'm scared that because of me that they'll take Jack's dinky little house from him. The only things I own are bills I can't pay. I'll never walk again and complete strangers treat me like I'm stupid. All that I can deal with, just . . .

'Here's what really scares me. Sarah, I mean, really, really scares me. I'm not sure if I'm ready for things to turn out okay. I'm a coward and I hope you'll forgive me for however I ruin this thing we have going.'

Still she slept. I put my arm around her. The ugliness drained from my thoughts and I fell asleep soon after.

39

Jack was sitting at the table with his coffee and newspaper when I came home the next morning from Fritz's house with blue hair and the earring.

'Help me, my son's a parrot.'

'That's funny. I thought the earring would bother you more.'

'Christ. You got your ear pierced? Unbelievable. Where the hell were you last night?'

'At a friend's.'

'Your friend a pirate? Friends don't put holes in friends' heads.'

A little later, he came to my room.

'You up for a walk?' He handed me two plastic pots filled with scraggles of green. Their small white buds smelled bitter and clean.

We walked to Mom's grave where Jack and I held our truces. We planted the chamomile in front of her headstone.

'Do you remember the times we came out here after she died? We used to sit out here and talk about her.'

'Yeah. Yeah, I do. Sometimes I can't remember Mom before she got sick. I try but I only see her when she was in the coma.'

'You have to picture her doing something. Remember how she had this whole ritual for cleaning the house? She'd put her hair up in a bandana, wear those old overalls she had. She'd sing along to the radio and dance around while she cleaned. Can you see it?'

My eyes closed and I saw Mom sweeping, singing to herself, lost in the happiness of that moment.

'Yeah,' I said and opened my eyes to see Jack grinning.

Jack laughed. 'She'd had those overalls since we were kids. God, that woman couldn't sing. We'd be in the car and I'd have to inch up the volume out of respect for the musicians.'

'She used to laugh at the dumbest jokes.'

'Her family was from the Midwest. They can't help it. There's nothing funny about Iowa.'

'She used to tell me knock-knock jokes.'

'You outgrew them before she did. Do you remember when you were too old to be kissed goodnight?'

'No.'

'She cried and cried: "My baby doesn't need me any more."'

'Really? I don't remember that at all. That makes me feel like shit.'

'You know, it's the same for me. I can't just think of her face. Nothing comes. It kills me. Sometimes, when things are bad, especially between you and me, I talk to her. When I do, I pretend I see her, but it never works. That hurts. I feel like I'm losing her, denying the only thing good in my life.'

I said, 'Even as a kid I knew how much you guys loved each other. I used to get jealous. Sometimes mad.'

'You used to do little shitty things like pour your orange juice in my work boots or write on my paperwork. Supposedly it was normal. I just thought you needed a spanking. She took good care of us. She was worth fighting over.'

Silence and Mom's gravestone stood between us.

'Tell me about this pirate friend of yours.'

'I met him at the hospital.'

'Oh yeah. What's his name?'

'Captain Morgan. I think you guys have met.'

'Jarred.' His voice hardened. 'You can't be doing this. If this is going to work you need to follow the rules. What did we discuss? I thought we were over all the nastiness and lies.'

'I was at a friend's house. I'm still a teenager. That's what teenagers do.'

'Jarred, the hospital told me about your friend. You two have enough of your own troubles without getting them mixed with each other's. Listen, that kid is in recovery.'

'No zealot like the convert.'

He put on his pious face as he pretended the solution to everything was twelve steps away. I preferred the exhausted puffiness of his drinking days. Or the rage he wore when I provoked him. He moved from Fritz's recovery to his own. He talked of amends. He brought up the past where no one was innocent.

I cut him off. 'You don't get to apologise. You fucked up. You live with that. I don't have to forgive you. You burned off years of your life, being a waste. Now because you feel sorry, I'm supposed to give you absolution? Here's the deal. You fucked up. You get to live that fuck-up. That's it. You don't like the deal? Then don't fuck up.'

I started to get that jumbled-thought, light-headed feeling. My vision shifted, the grave stretched impossibly between us and Jack looked far away.

'And guess what? All my fuck-ups. No apologies. Those are mine.'

'All right, all right. Calm down, Jarred. I'm trying to work things out with you. I didn't want a fight.'

He was scared or he was seeing something in me that worried him. Tears were streaming down my face. I fought to put enough breath over my vocal cords to curse him.

'I don't need a dad now. I don't care if you're proud of me or not. I don't need you there to tell me I fucked up. I know I'm fucking up and I don't give a shit.'

'Jarred, you need to calm down. Your lips are turning blue. You need to breathe. Okay, okay. We don't have to talk about this. It's one of the steps of AA to ask forgiveness, except when to do so would injure—'

A kettle whistle screamed in my head.

'Did you bring me here for scene setting? Were you hoping to time it right, so when the sun set over Mom's grave, I'd forgive, and we'd embrace as father and son? Fuck you!'

He became stone, but the old, reliable anger was returning. He was struggling to swallow it down, determined to keep it, digest it, better to fester into an ulcer or cancer, but I wasn't going to let him.

'Look how fucking proud. You love it. Are you apologising or bragging?'

'Jarred, stop. I'm sorry. This was a mistake. Jarred! Stop right now.'

'Nobody wants to relive this shit except you. Go play AA with Thomas. Let him forgive you. Pat your head and lie to you that you were a good husband and father.'

He howled from the bottom of his guts the howl of an animal struck with shot.

'Jarred! Stop blaming everyone else. Be a man for once.'

'Be a man,' I mimicked.

He shoved me and I fell over.

'Jarred. What is going on? What am I supposed to do seeing the scars and cuts on your arms? The weird shit you do. The suicide notes you write. The basketballs, fucking whole basketballs, duct-taped to the ceiling. What does that even mean? The crazy pictures drawn on the wall. What's going on, Jarred? I'm just trying to help.'

'You left me at school. You forgot about me.' I picked myself up and closed in on him.

'My wife was dying!' he yelled and grabbed my collar.

'Go on, hit me! You remember how. Do it. Do it. Fucking hit me. You were good at beating the shit out of me when I was thirteen. Sixteen should still be fun.'

He threw me down and walked off.

40

Sarah suggested we celebrate by pulling down the collection notices. Light barged into my room. We neatly stacked the letters of professionally worded disappointment by colour.

Sitting beside each other on the bed, we were cutting out the thick red-bordered words of FINAL NOTICE, yellow PAST DUE and, our favourite, black and green FRIENDLY REMINDER from collection notices. Her tongue peeked out as she concentrated on her scissors. I reached over and petted her tongue with my finger.

'Hey!' She leaned over and kissed me. 'I don't know I'm doing it.'

She stuck out her tongue again and I kissed it.

'Is that enough for another wall?' Along the ceiling and down the corners of the room legal threats created a coloured border. Plain black and white SETTLEMENT OFFERs and LEGAL ACTIONs covered the wall sockets and switch plate covers.

She stood on a chair and glue-sticked the paper where the wall met the ceiling.

Jack stood at the door, following the border with his eyes. He examined the light switch.

'When are you going back to work?'

'It was her idea.'

'You, little missy, stop encouraging him. What brought this on?'

'The driver of the VW has definitely been charged. He's getting felony DUI. The lawyer said that the husband is done chasing after us. With the driver charged, he's easier to go after and he actually has assets. He suggests we pursue a case as well.'

Jack nodded. 'Some good news for a change.'

'Yep.'

'I brought you some of that stuff you like,' Jack said to Sarah.

'Quasi-Quik. Yum. Thanks.'

'You hungry? We were going to make dinner to celebrate not going to jail or getting sued,' I said.

'Can we have meat tonight? If I see another carrot—'

'Meat is murder, Jack.'

'Duly noted, Sarah, but listen up. I'm a single parent to this fool. I've had to give up drinking, smoking and coffee. On top of that I'm old and I have piles. Now, I ask you this, why shouldn't cows suffer too?'

'Calm down, Grandpa. Jarred'll make you steak,' Sarah said.

'It's not all good news. The moustached marauder is still chasing us for money,' I said.

'What's he said this time?'

'It's just music. Listen.'

'I'll start the potatoes,' Sarah said, stepping off the chair. 'Jack, it's your favourite, oven-baked fries.'

I dialled the messaging service and handed the phone to Jack.

'The first one is Blondie, "One Way Or Another". Then

he phoned back an hour later with "The More You Ignore Me, The Closer I Get" by Morrissey. I don't know the next one.'

'It's Leonard Cohen, but I don't know the song either,' Jack said.

'He's got good taste in music,' Sarah shouted from the kitchen.

'Isn't this harassment? Surely this is illegal,' I said.

'So is not paying your bills,' Jack said.

I went to see if Sarah needed any help. She ran her hand down the back of my head and neck. I rubbed her back. I went to the silverware drawer. Jack was staring. We made eye contact. He nodded and sat to read his paper. I set the table.

'It's nice having a soul like that in the house again. Don't blow this for us.'

I nodded, but I felt the bite of his sentence. A couple of weeks ago, Sarah and I had been at the grocery store. I sat patiently beside her as she examined the labels looking for whatever chemical death she was trying to avoid. I felt a hand on my shoulder. I turned to find a man in an oversized sweater. Everything happens for a reason, he told me. I responded by asking him 'Even this?' and I smacked the macaroni and cheese out of his hand. The blue and yellow box bounced off his face then spun along the floor. He retreated, pathetically holding his cheek. I turned back to see Sarah staring in disbelief. She didn't say anything, but I nodded and went to look for the guy in the sweater to apologise.

Sarah shouted, 'Dinner's ready.'

We sat around the table.

'Dearest one,' I said.

'Yes, love.'

'Give me a break,' Jack teased. He leaned down to drop a chunk of steak for Mister Shakey.

'Is he an indoor cat now?' I asked.

'He's my tv buddy, but he's still your cat. I don't do litter boxes.'

If we weren't at my place hanging out with Jack and Mister Shakey, we were at hers playing cards and having a sing-along with Marco or hanging out with her parents. When she wanted to go out with friends, I stayed home. I saw myself in a bar or a club amongst the whole and healthy, and I felt ill. I imagined drunks tripping over me or laughing at me.

'Oh shit! I forgot to call JJ and tell him I'm not coming out tonight.'

'No, don't do that. I'll come with, if that's okay. We should celebrate.'

'Really?'

'Yeah.'

After dinner with Jack, we went downtown to a bar to meet up with Sarah's friends.

'You know the stories you tell me about your dad and you when you were young? His being a drunk and you two beating each other up. It's hard to see Jack doing that.'

I wasn't really paying attention to her as I played out scenarios of inaccessible toilets and entrances with steps.

'You're grumpy. You're not allowed to be grumpy. JJ and I are friends, that's all. You said it was cool.'

'I'm okay.'

We parked and headed toward the bar. A drunk stumbled toward us talking to himself. A gaggle of college girls curled their lips as they tried to predict his path.

'That's the homeless guy who gave me your cat,' she said. 'Should we see if he's all right?'

'Coffee girl!' the drunk shouted. He tried to focus on me through alcohol blur. His whole body slumped with his sigh. He shook his head. 'No, no, no,' he said. 'It's a good goddamn shame, look at you. Oh god. I'm so sorry you are in a wheelchair.'

A grease-fire flash of rage burst from within me.

'I'm sorry you're a drunk and smell of piss. Let's see who fares better,' I said as I pushed past him.

We navigated through the crowd, Sarah clearing the way with an 'Excuse me' and nodding toward me so the person understood they had to move more than the cursory inch.

Sarah said, 'Jarred, I get it. I'm always one asshole away – telling me I'm prettier when I smile – from feeling awful about myself. I get it; it's not fair.'

We approached a group of people playfully shouting and arguing. 'Excuse me. Excuse me.' We worked our way through, interrupting person after person. As soon as we passed, they went back to cheering and yelling.

'But it's not them you're mad at,' she continued. 'Something inside you believes they're right or that the world believes that they're right, which makes them right. I hate it.'

I nodded, and I was falling in love and admiration.

'You okay?' she asked.

I gave her two thumbs up. 'Can you push? I'm tired.'

She pushed my chair, leaned in and whispered in my ear before kissing it, 'You're not tired. You're lazy.'

Sixth Street was all bars and clubs. The sidewalks thickened with black miniskirts tottering on high heels being chased by popped collars. Sarah weaved us through and I called to go faster. She went faster. We laughed as people jumped out of our way.

I slapped at her hands and shouted, 'Hey, lady, where are you taking me? I don't even know you.'

A man stepped in front of us.

'Help! Help!'

'I'm his girlfriend,' Sarah pleaded. 'Jarred, shut up.'

He gave us a dirty look that made us laugh.

'You're such a dick,' she said.

We arrived at the bar where aluminum poles and a plastic yellow rope penned twenty people with faces blued by cell phone glow. At the head of the line three girls were arguing with the doorman. His eyes streamed tears and, as he told them that they weren't on the list, he wiped his eyes as if truly heartbroken about the oversight.

I went up to the bouncer. 'Excuse me, can I use your accessible bathroom?'

'Go ahead. In and to the left.'

'You okay?'

'Allergies,' he said, swiping away the streams of tears with one huge hand.

The bar was a black napkin and goji berry martini affair and crowded with people who reminded me of my brother Patrick. I suggested to Sarah that most people here had at one time described themselves, without irony, as 'Working hard, playing hard'. She replied by singing, 'Middle managers of the world unite and discuss synergies.' We cut our way through the block of business casual by saying 'Excuse me' loudly, touching an arm here and there, and the occasional bump of my wheelchair against the back of a loafer.

'I'm ready to leave, you?'

Ignoring me, she waved to her friends.

They were perched on stools around a tall table. They fit in with the crowd. They looked up in unison from their phones.

Sarah whispered to me, 'No dickheadery. For me.'

They all kissed cheeks with Sarah. The table was tall enough to rest my chin on. Every time I said something, Sarah and her friends looked down at me from their stools as if I was an amusing pet. I fought a welling ugliness deep in my gut. JJ looked from me to the table and seemed to notice my discomfort.

'Do you mind if we find somewhere else?' JJ suggested. 'This place is full of weekend warriors. It used to be a laidback place like the Crown.'

Because of his past with Sarah, I was prepared to hate him, but with that sentence, he seemed an okay guy.

'I used to work at the Crown,' I said.

'Really? I loved that place. There's nothing like that in New York. I should be asking you then. Where's a good place?'

'I haven't been downtown in a long time. There's probably still some old-man bars on Fourth.'

We found a bar away from the main street manned by dedicated hipsters serving a handful of equally dedicated alcoholics surrounded by Goldenrod photocopies advertising local bands and publicity posters from beer distributors showing pneumatic women with hand-drawn Hitler moustaches and blacked-out teeth.

'It'll only be a matter a time before the Sixth Street crowd find this place,' JJ said. 'Creative industry yuppies like me are the first sign that a place is no longer cool.'

'What do you do?'

'I work for a record label.' He put his thumbs up. 'As an account manager.' Thumbs down.

'Does your sister still work at the hippy store? Can she get Jarred a job?' Sarah asked.

He dialled his phone. 'Yo. What are you doing? . . . That sucks. I got a friend here looking for a job. You guys looking for anybody? . . . Cool. Tomorrow? . . . Cool. Bye.'

We had a good night out. Sarah's friends were nice guys.

They all had office jobs: the managers of people, projects and accounts. The pinball of conversation kept rolling back to the sink of office politics, commutes, vacation days not taken. Sarah was right there with them. It was my first glimpse of her previous power-suited past.

'How'd JJ get a job like that?' I said as we headed back to the car.

'What do you mean?'

'Account manager? Pretty dull for a guy who studied music.'

'It's called growing up. Try it some time.'

'What's that mean?'

'Day jobs are supposed to be boring; that's why they're paying you.'

We reached the car. She unlocked my door.

'He's going to get sucked dry by some company who gets him to drink the Kool-Aid and turns him into a company man,' I said. 'He'll work sixty hours a week to get thrown enough money for him to lease a car, buy a house so he's so scared of missing a payment that they'll work him eighty hours. Then when bosses need to protect their bonuses, they'll come downstairs, be awfully sorry and chuck him out. The guys that fire him will own shares in the bank that forecloses on his house and repos his car.'

I transferred to the passenger seat. Sarah put my chair in the trunk and got into the driver's side.

'Or, another possibility just as likely,' Sarah said. 'It turns out fine. You're too old for hipster cooler-than-thou. Why do you care anyway?'

She started the car and pulled out of the parking garage.

'I can see you miss that shit,' I said.

'Don't pick a fight with me. I don't miss anything. Are you talking about Kevin talking about his promotion? What does it matter to you? He was excited. He wanted to brag. Let him brag. Stop being so self-conscious. It makes you pathetic.'

She checked her mirrors and indicated to get on the freeway.

'You made me look pathetic. Wheelchair boy needed his girlfriend to get him a shitty minimum-wage job.'

She growled with frustration. 'You're making me mad. I am not taking care of you. It's a relationship. We help each other. You need a job. I knew JJ's sister works at a place you'd probably like. If you don't chill out, I'm going to punch you.'

'Fine, punch me.'

'Fuck!' She hit the steering wheel.

'Sorry, forget it.'

'No! I didn't put your wheels in the trunk. I leaned them against the pole and forgot to put them in, because I was busy having a stupid argument with you. Fuck.'

Fear seized my guts and my heart pounded in my chest. Sarah called herself names, apologising for being so useless. It took every ounce of self-control to keep the calm in my voice. I didn't want her to feel bad about this.

'It's okay. They'll still be there. No one is going to steal wheelchair wheels.'

People steal wheelchair wheels.

Sarah broke down uncontrollably when we returned to the parking lot and saw the pole with no wheels below it. I thought about the cost of replacing them, easily $500. I doubted Medicare covered theft. How does a paraplegic explain losing his wheels? I rubbed her back and told her it was okay. She screamed, called herself stupid, a fuck-up.

'Stop that. It's a mistake. It's okay. We'll figure something out. Look, there's a fancy hotel across the street. They always have a loaner wheelchair to get old people up to their room. Just ask them, explain the situation. They're not going to say no, we can't help you and your cripple boyfriend.'

They said no to her and her cripple boyfriend.

I laughed. 'Really? They said no. What dicks. Sarah, don't worry. I'm not upset. It's okay. Come here.'

I pulled her into my lap and held her. She wriggled away, all apologies.

'Stop. You are wonderful. It's a mistake. We'll figure something out. I can get new wheels from the mobility shop in the morning. It's okay, really. We're downtown. There's got to be a DoubleTree or something like that around the corner. This time don't ask, just grab the loaner chair like you know what you're doing. We'll return it tomorrow.'

She parked in the street in front of the Four Seasons. I kissed her cheek and told her it was okay. She nodded and kissed me back. Five minutes later, she was back with a wheelchair with the word 'hotel' stencilled on the back.

'Blue? They didn't have a red one?'

She looked at me bewildered and started to cry again. 'I'll go check.'

She started to turn back and I shouted that I was joking. Calling me a jerk, she loaded the chair back into the car.

'You okay?' I asked.

We kissed and she was okay.

41

Our argument beside Mom's grave was the last time I saw Jack for a decade, but I didn't know that at the time. After the fight, I went over to Fritz's and asked if I could crash at his place.

'Fine,' he said.

'Let's take a road trip?'

'Where to?'

'California.'

'Do you have a car? Do you have money?'

'No.'

'Sounds like a pretty crappy road trip so far.'

I advertised Jack's washer and dryer in the classifieds. As soon as the guy handed over the money and drove off with them bungeed into his truck bed, I phoned Fritz and told him we were leaving that day.

I broke into the neighbour's house and took the keys to their saddle-backed Oldsmobile. By then the neighbourhood knew who was to blame when anything was amiss. We were that family.

I pulled up to Fritz's apartment, tooted the horn and we were off. We shot north to take I-40 West, the interstate highway that had replaced Route 66. Fritz used Jerry's credit card until he cancelled it on the second day. We sang along to the radio and ate junk food. My first road trip and it felt like the solution to every problem I ever had. Fritz said it took a country as big, as open, as changeable as America to discover this thousandth plus one path to enlightenment. The highway is the one promise that this country has kept. He was right.

By the time we hit the Texas panhandle, the mood had changed. Maybe it was the landscape. The flat openness, its measly offering of scrub bush and little else felt threatening. The wind slapped at you with a grudgeful persistence. By the time we were in New Mexico, Fritz was shunning me whenever I touched him. We weren't talking at all by the time we got to Santa Fe.

We were somewhere in the Arizona desert and ahead of us was a man dragging a crucifix along the soft shoulder. I pulled to the side of the road behind him. He didn't stop or look back.

'We should do something,' I said. 'He could die out here.'

Fritz sat up and watched the man. 'What, though?'

'Give him a ride?'

Fritz made a face, but agreed.

I got out and jogged up to the man, the desert heat pressing on us. The bottom of his cross had worn to a sharp edge from being dragged.

'Do you need some help?'

He shook his head.

'You sure? It's easily another thirty miles to the next town.' I talked and walked beside him for a little more but the best I could do was convince him to take our water bottles.

'Is he going to be okay?' I asked Fritz as he drove us off.

'Probably not.'

By the time we got to Flagstaff, we were friends again. The road had done its magic and we sneaked into a bar having a karaoke night. It was fun until I got us kicked out for doing the Buffalo Bill dance to 'Goodbye Horses'. The Oldsmobile broke down the next day so we had to hitch-hike to Phoenix. One phone call later and Fritz's mom had wired him cash, and a plane ticket home was waiting for him at the airport.

'Are you ditching me?'

'I can't ask her for two plane tickets. She'd go nuts. Here's some money for a bus.'

I took the money and walked off without saying goodbye. I pulled out the earring he had given me and flicked it away. My ear felt hot.

As I cursed Fritz and felt sorry for myself, I heard a slow, heavy drip. I stopped walking to consider the sound. I thought of faucets, of trickling streams, of melting icicles. From the corner of my eye, there was a candle wax stain on my shoulder. I touched my ear, and my hand came away bloody.

42

Your ribs are broken. It's going to hurt. Ready? One . . . two . . . three.

'Is he still sleeping?' Jack's voice said from the other side of the door.

'No, he's awake. It's one of *those* mornings,' Sarah said.

'I can hear you two!' I shouted toward the door. 'The hippies can do without me for a day.' The grocery store's real name was The Store. It was the kind of place where customers paid extra to scoop their own granola into a paper bag and make their own peanut butter. The notice boards sold moon cups, meditation classes and hydroponic equipment, all of which signed off with 'namaste'. JJ's sister, Peggy, hired me to work the register. She was a small woman with short hair, huge glasses and contagious enthusiasm. She was good about making sure I could get around the store. Whenever she went into the break room, she always moved a chair out of the way without making a song and dance about it. The customers were a mix of hippies, earnest college kids flirting with right-on politics and complicated dietary rules (no meat or egg but honey is okay) and wealthy soccer moms who had figured out it was less hassle to purchase ethical behaviour than practise it. Every two weeks, I handed over the majority of my pay cheque to Jack. He fussed every time, but I left the cash on the table until he took it with a 'thanks'. It was the first time that I was okay or that I understood what okay could be.

By the time I was up and dressed, Jack was gone and Sarah was sitting in his chair watching tv with Mister Shakey curled in her lap. I gave him a few scratches behind the ear. She asked me if I was ready. Yes.

The moustachioed collection agent was in his car a couple of houses down, but his attention was focused on filling out paperwork. I leaned on Sarah's car horn. He jumped and I got a moment's satisfaction of eye contact as we passed him.

'Do you think Jack has been acting funny lately?' Sarah asked.

'By funny, do you mean not giving me hell every two seconds? Funny like that?'

'I don't know. I just get the feeling something is bothering him.'

'You can ask, but he won't tell you. Only mystery and bullshit lie behind the great brows of Jack McGinnis.'

At the hippy store, I wheeled over to Sarah's side of the car and leaned into the window to give her a kiss goodbye.

'Thank you for being unreasonably patient with all my nonsense,' I said.

'I could say the same thing,' she said.

After my shift I took a bus to Sarah's coffee shop to hang out there until she finished. She had a customer so I waved and blew a kiss as I glided over to my corner. The man at the counter was speaking loudly to his cell phone. He was telling someone not to take less than 'eighty k' and repeating 'fuck him'. He looked at the board above Sarah, not acknowledging her.

'Latte with an extra shot.' He pinched the phone between his ear and shoulder and pulled out his wallet.

'Regular or large?' Sarah asked.

Still talking to his phone, he tossed a bill onto the counter then turned his back on her.

'Latte. Extra shot. Large asshole.' Sarah said to her co-worker making the coffees. Sarah took the bill and made his change. He was still talking on the phone, leaning against the counter. She wadded the bills and coins and threw them. They bounced off the man's back.

'Show me some respect!' she shouted.

Her co-worker and the man both watched, stunned, as Sarah ran from the shop. I found her in her car crying. I tapped the window.

'Licence and registration,' I said.

She shook her head.

'Licence and registration.'

She put her window down.

'You okay?'

'I don't know what I'm doing here.'

My selfish heart stumbled with the fear that she would go back to San Francisco, but seeing her upset hurt more.

'What do you mean? Forget that guy,' I said. 'What can I do for you?' I opened her car door and leaned in to hug her.

'Thank you, Jarred. You've been so good for me.'

43

After Fritz abandoned me, I caught a Greyhound, determined to complete my first road trip. The bus went to LA then up the coast. Viewing the jagged end of this young continent and the impossible grey expanse of the Pacific Ocean did feel like the start of a new adventure, but mostly I remember the loneliness aching in my stomach for the two days it took to get to San Francisco.

When I arrived, I spent hours sitting in coffee shops fly-fishing for eye contact, willing anyone to take notice. Fritz had given me a hundred dollars of his mom's money, but I didn't know where I was going to sleep that night or what was going to happen after I woke up.

I sat on the kerb drinking out of a one-litre Coke bottle spiked with Canadian Club. The black half-moon of Bernal Heights hill rose from a sea of sodium-lit streets. A girl sat beside me and handed me a 7-Eleven Slurpee cup. I peered in to see a toad sitting at the bottom untroubled by his confinement.

'Who does this frog look like?' she asked.

'What?' I asked.

'Who does this frog look like?'

'I think it's a toad.'

'You think so, Mr. Science?'

'Jesus, it looks like fat Elvis.'

'Totally. This is so awesome. I'm Karla.'

Her bleached-to-white hair was bobby-pinned like a braided halo. She was tiny with stick-thin legs that dropped from a short pleated skirt. She was smiling to herself, petting a toad with a bump on its head like a Presley hairdo.

'Want some? It's Canadian Club.'

'Drinking's for losers,' she said and took a swig. 'You live around here?'

'Not sure yet.'

'You can crash with us.' She sat beside me on the kerb, and we stared into the cup while the toad sat motionless at the bottom. 'We're going to call you Fat Elvis. Is that okay?'

We talked and shared my drink. I watched her lips on the mouth of the bottle. She passed it back.

I took a drink and pretended I tasted cherry when she surprised me with, 'My stepdad was a little too grabby-grabby and Mom, of course, didn't believe me. It was all too after-school-special pathetic. I knew the guys from talking to them at shows. It was no big thing to move in. That was a week ago. It's nice. I have my own bathroom, more than I had at home, and everyone watches out for each other. I think you'll like it. Why'd you run away?'

'Mom's dead. Dad's a drunk. No one was going to miss me. Why not?'

'Fair enough. You want to see the squat?' she asked.

'Lead on.' I slipped Fat Elvis into my jacket pocket. He felt cold, jelly and bones. The squat was a condemned hospital near an overpass. She squeezed through a hole cut in a chain-link fence and held it open for me. We followed a path that wandered through waist-high weeds. A grind of guitars and amplified shouts grew stronger as we stepped over toppled piles of bricks and tyres filled with muck and mosquito larvae.

'The straight-edgers are having a show tonight,' she explained. We passed door after door covered by plywood until we reached one that wasn't.

'Hold your nose,' she said. We stepped inside and I smelled a barn full of animals, the blood from a butcher's apron and the men's john at a Greyhound station. The stench clawed at me, watering my eyes, getting up my nose, in my mouth, into my clothes. I pulled the collar of my shirt over my face and followed the tangles of graffiti climbing every wall, thick as ivy.

'Don't worry. Our place is nowhere near here,' she said as we crunched empty plastic vials and avoided bloody wads of toilet paper. I followed her along the hallways illuminated by the lights of the overpass.

For months, we hung out every day. I made friends with the squat kids, the young crusties and the old hippies. There were so many kids in the rooms and halls it felt like a college dorm. We dumpster-dived or shoplifted food. We snuck into theatres and shows. We got fucked up. We did nothing. I made this time and place with Karla home. I forgot about Jack.

It took a day to undo it all. We were awoken by what I thought were the cops bringing us their pepper spray and eviction notices. I told Karla to stay there, and I'd check it out. I unlocked our room by taking down the board that barred the door and rolled the concrete bollard out of the way. A few steps from the door a guy known as Crackers lay with his head cocked against the baseboard as if using the wall as a pillow. He had lived at the squat the longest.

He knew what form to send to delay evictions. He knew what to tell the cops, and how to say it to get them off our backs. He had scams for days and was the RA for our dirty hobo dorm.

His leather jacket had the metal tops of disposable lighters clamped along the zipper like two rows of fat metal teeth and was covered in the patches of all my favourite bands. That morning he was a tangle of limbs, a dead spider in a windowsill. The white face, the colourless lips, told me I had seen my first corpse. Someone had already gone through his pockets looking for whatever he had OD'd on.

I went back into the room to tell Karla. She was close to Crackers. Her tiny body shook in my arms. We decided to get drunk in the park where Crackers used to hang out. We left our room. The body was gone. As we left, Karla cussed a group of people clotted in mourning heaps, calling them tourists and fakes.

By the afternoon we had scored some forties and were sitting on Crackers' bench.

'When I was a kid, I heard my Mom die . . . I was on the phone with her and she had a brain aneurysm. I thought I had caused it.'

'Where was your dad?'

'She was the love of his life. He fell apart.'

'Is that why you ran away?'

We continued getting drunk and maudlin until three teenage micro-gangsters came up to us.

'What's up, pussy bitch?' one asked me.

'Listen, our friend just died. Could you—'

When you aren't expecting it, even a weak punch can knock you down. I went over the bench. Before I got my wind back, they were over me, holding onto the bench to drive the kicks home. As soon as I kicked and punched my way up, I was down again. When you fight two people at once it's better to focus on one until he quits. If you get him, the second will have doubts and nine times out of ten you don't have to fight your way through both. But this time I couldn't land anything. I caught a glimpse of the third kid holding Karla down with one foot. He was laughing at her as she struggled to get out from under his Nike. I moved for him, heard her scream my name but didn't see who or what hit me. I came to with her crying over me, her cheek rouged with a smear of my blood.

In the hospital waiting room, the pain throbbed through my entire body. I held my broken jaw as every motion caused bolts of pain. A grandma in curlers looked at me with worry as groans escaped me. She opened a change purse from which she unwrapped a handkerchief to show me a robin's nest of blue Percocet. Karla plucked out two and went to go crush and mix them in a glass of water.

'Thank you, ma'am,' I grunted through my teeth and fought back vomit.

'Sugar, many, many are the afflictions of the righteous.'

I nodded, holding my jaw, pretending I understood.

After four hours I got my x-ray. After four more I had a bed. I lay there trying not to hear the nurse repeatedly asking the drunk and sobbing woman in the next bed if she wanted the rape detection kit.

Karla kept talking about something, anything, to drown out the conversation. She schemed ways about how to get those fuckers back. I listened, still holding my jaw, scribbling short responses on Karla's notepad.

I wrote, *why don't you go home?*

'I don't want to go home. I want to stay here. Then we'll go home together.'

She kept talking, making sure I was okay, looking at me pitifully.

Why was he called Crackers?

'I don't know.'

Stupid name.

'Don't be an asshole.'

He had a real name and a family somewhere.

'Who were assholes, which is why he left,' she said impatiently.

Maybe it was like in the movies. Somewhere in Wisconsin his mother dropped her tea cup, it shattered, and, as she sopped up the liquid with a Green Bay Packers kitchen towel, she knew her son, who was such a lively little boy, always up to no good, who used to love baseball, was dead. He would never phone her again on Christmas like he did a few years back crying apologies.

I thought of Karla pinned like an insect. She was tougher than I would ever be. She had survived a sicko stepdad and a mom happy to look the other way. But this world wasn't done abusing her, and I was never going to be able to protect her.

I'm going home.

'What?'

I'm going back to my dad's house.

'What are you talking about? Because you got your ass kicked? Big deal. Who hasn't got their ass kicked? Don't we matter?'

You can keep Fat Elvis.

She laughed at me. 'Fine. Fuck you,' she said, her eyes wet, and left.

Jack said once that a boy's hands were too callow for a thing as fine as a girl's heart. He was right about a lot of things.

After four weeks in the hospital, two weeks hitchhiking and one Greyhound ticket scam, I was back. On the road, I had survived on McDonald's milkshakes. By the time I was walking up our street to Jack's house, I was sunken eyes, cheekbones and baggy clothes. Smoke had thickened the early morning mist until it clawed around buildings and tore itself apart in the front-yard pecan trees. It smelled of burnt wood and plastic. The house two down from Jack's was an empty nest of charred brick and beams. The best-case scenario was the family was safe and had spent a sleepless night elsewhere, the smoke still in their nose, the ashes ringing the hotel bathtub. All of them thinking, what now?

Our house, as usual, was unlocked. Jack wasn't home though. I wrote a note, 'I'm sorry', and left. I went to Mom's grave and lay beside it. The chamomile Jack and I planted was bursting with new fingers of green. I plucked a blossom and pulled the thin petals one by one. A loneliness so complete gripped me that I wept.

44

Marco struggled for each breath while his left hand languidly scratched at his bare chest. Dotted with a few notes of grackles, a stave of telephone wires cut across the empty sky outside his window.

Sarah pulled up a chair next to Marco's bed. She reached over the railing to hold his hand. The sealed sterile bags containing tubing or shining metal instruments, continence pads stacked like beach towels and red sharps containers that leered above us on shelves no longer worried me. Amongst the medical supplies was a pencil drawing of Marco I had done for his birthday. Their father had framed it and set it on the shelf.

'Is he okay?' I asked.

'Dialysis wears him out. Sometimes worse than others.'

'We'll hang out here tonight. He likes when I draw for him. We'll have a sing-along. We don't have to hang out with The Store people every night.'

Sarah rewarded me with a smile.

Marco's eyes widened as he forced out a sentence. The noise came as a whimper. His brow creased with effort. Anxiety flitted through me, but Sarah watched calmly to divine his meaning. I still was never sure when he was distressed and that bothered me.

'He wants to show you his quarters,' she said and Marco's head wobbled assent. Sarah pulled out a knitted bag from the dresser.

'I made this for him,' she said.

Marco struggled and sat upright. His chitters and squeaks always made me smile. If Marco didn't suffer as he did, so profoundly and so often, would he still have had his easy and contagious joy. Was that the trade life made for him? Should we be jealous of his serenity rather than pitying his disability? Even if we knew for certain that we would be happier, I suspect none of us would make the trade that Marco had no choice to make.

Marco pointed at the Superman logo on the bag where Sarah had replaced the red and yellow S with an M.

'I've had a lot of time on my hands,' she said.

I hefted the bag, half-filled with quarters, and nodded appreciatively.

'Casino!' Marco's high-pitched voice drew out the last 'o'.

'Did he say casino?'

'Ask him,' Sarah said.

'Sorry,' I said and repeated my question to Marco. 'Did you say casino?'

Marco's eyebrows shot upward and he nodded fitfully.

'Take a chance, make it happen.' Marco sang the theme song for a casino whose commercials were always playing on his radio. He waved his arms and kicked his legs. 'Pop a cork, fingers snapping.'

'He's been obsessed. He does chores for Dad around the house. The quarters are his allowance.'

'What chores do you do?'

Marco made a circular motion, still singing.

'Dishes?' I asked.

'He's been doing dusting too and helping Mom with her garden in the backyard.'

'Let's take Marco to the casino,' I said.

'I don't know. It's pretty far away,' Sarah said. Marco waved his hands like a conductor and I sang along with him.

That weekend, I rapped shave-and-a-haircut on the window, and Marco shouted my name in greeting.

Sarah was at the back door.

I held out one of Jack's old suits. 'For the high roller. We can't just go to the casino. We have to look sharp.' I showed off the lining of the suit I was wearing. It was also Jack's.

'That better be a wig.'

'It's a businessman number four, blue-black.' I doffed the wig.

'And the briefcase?'

'It's for Marco. For his winnings,' I said, following her to Marco's room.

'Are you feeling good enough for an adventure?' Sarah asked.

'Casino!'

She said to me, 'I'll get dressed up. Something Gordon Gecko Eighties seems to be the theme. Can you help him?'

Although unsure of how to help Marco, another grown man, get dressed, I agreed.

'Okay, how can I help you?' I asked him.

'This down.' Marco tapped the bed rail. 'Legs.'

I helped him put his legs over the side and felt the balsa-wood bones.

'Look at those gnarly toe nails,' I said as I put on his

socks. 'After you win your first million, we're buying you some clippers.'

Marco giggled and threw off his blanket.

'Woah! Where are your drawers, son?'

Sarah stood at the door in a long cream-coloured dress. Her hair was pinned up to show off two small pearl earrings. Her lips were a shining autumn-leaf red.

'Marco, is Jarred molesting you?'

Marco pointed at me. 'Pervert.'

They both laughed and Marco waggled his penis.

Sarah slid a pair of boxers up to Marco's knees where he could manage them the rest of the way.

'Look how beautiful she is,' I said. 'We're lucky men, Marco.'

Sarah got shy at the compliment. We helped Marco with his pants and shoes. Sarah went off and came back in heels.

'Look at my handsome men.' She wolf-whistled.

Their dad popped his head into the room. 'You guys be careful. Call me when you get there and when you leave. You have his meds? His day packs?'

'You sure you don't want to come?' Sarah offered.

He hesitated before shaking his head. 'Just text me when you leave.'

I-35 was unusually clear of traffic and the sky was Texas-sized. The trunk of Sarah's car held our two wheelchairs. I had gotten over those moments of sitting uselessly in the car while she dismantled and assembled my wheelchair. It was normal, something all girlfriends did. Marco in the back seat behind me was singing softly to himself until the choruses, which he belted out with screeching glee. Sometimes he reached over the seat and patted my shoulder. Other times he put his hand out the open window and laughed as the wind rudely pushed against it.

Sarah watched him in the rear-view with a smile. His chin was raised toward the fresh air and sun coming in over the trees. She smiled easily but especially for Marco.

'I worked at a casino in Nevada for a few months,' I said.

'That doesn't surprise me.' We drove on and the steady rhythm of the car and the tyres on the road was making us all drowsy.

As we hunted for a parking space, Marco, wearing the black-haired wig, bounced in his seat; he hung his head out of the window to scream the casino's jingle at the people shuffling toward the entrance. Sarah half-heartedly tried to calm him down. She patted my knee.

'This was a good idea. Thank you.'

Marco's song fell away as we entered. His eyes darted as he took in the cavernous space of the casino. The rows of machines glowed and flickered their screens for attention. Clang, clatter, ding-ding, the 8-bit music of winnings, beeping and the noise of conversation bounced around the canopy of the ceiling high above, which had a false night sky, including a shimmering LED Milky Way.

Marco raised his hand, and I gave him a high-five. Sarah pushed him toward a row of slots decorated in bucking broncos and cowboys with guns drawn. I followed. A woman watched us with a mouth like a dog's asshole.

'What are you looking at? The buffet's that way,' I snapped as we continued past her.

'Ha! Fatty,' Marco said.

'Marco! Jarred, don't be an ass.'

'She was staring,' I said.

'What are you? Three? Who cares?'

We found the quarter machines near the back. Sarah put in the money while Marco banged away at the buttons. He clapped at the spinning wheels. He clapped when they stopped. He clapped when a payout came up and the quarters banged against the pan. He rubbed his hands through them, cackling. His glee was ours.

'He's getting low already,' she said. I had been waiting for that and drew out two rolls of quarters from one pocket and three from the other. I let Marco have a sip of my beer. Sarah protested but only a little. After a while, she suggested we get lunch at the casino and head back.

'How'd you do, Marco?' she asked.

Marco rattled the quarters in the briefcase in his lap. 'Pretty good.'

'Lunch is on Marco,' I said.

The restaurant overlooked the casino floor. Marco smiled and watched the people thread between the machines. He squealed any time a machine announced a jackpot. I cut Marco's burger into manageable pieces. It made me feel useful, but he didn't eat much. I worried that I had done it wrong. As we waited for a slice of triple chocolate cake to share, Marco was scratching and staring off into space.

We exited through the gift shop, and I shoved a teddy bear with the casino's logo up his shirt. He hunched over holding the bear tightly.

'Marco, what's the matter? Does your stomach hurt?'

He giggled and shook his toothy grin back and forth. 'No!'

'What are you two up to?' Sarah asked me.

I shrugged innocence.

As soon as we were in the car, Marco chucked the teddy bear into the driver's seat, cackling madly, singing the casino song and bouncing in his seat.

'Marco!' Sarah said. 'You stole this! You are in big trouble.'

Marco was asleep before we got out of the parking space. The sudden change scared me.

'Is he going to be okay?' I asked repeatedly.

'I can't help worrying about him. I think I sometimes worry to worry,' she said. 'I kept us out too long.'

'Shh. We had a fun time. Marco loved it.'

'He'll be talking about this for years. Thank you.' Her phone rang. 'Shit! I forgot to call Dad.' She answered her phone, 'Hello . . . Yes . . . Sorry. We're on our way . . . He's fine . . . Yes, we had a good time . . . He's fine . . . No, he's sleeping . . . I know. I'm sorry . . . Love you. See you soon.'

We crested a hill and before us lay a long line of traffic, moving but slowly. She kept craning her neck to check on Marco in her rear-view.

Marco slept through the whole journey. We pulled up to the house. Sarah's dad was on the porch, pretending not to be worried. As soon as he saw our car, he was standing, arranging a smile and waving. I heard a softly crooned 'casino' as he carried Marco into the house.

'Did I say thanks?' Sarah said, delivering my wheelchair to the passenger side.

'Many times.'

'Did you listen?'

'Once or twice. When we were in the car, you said you worried about Marco, because it was easier than worrying about yourself.'

'Yes,' Sarah said.

'Is that me? For you?'

'Maybe. But it's never that simple. We're all a big bundle of fuck-ups and mistakes. So what? Here's an idea: maybe I like you. What are you going to do then?'

45

At the far end of the parking lot of the hippy grocery store was a picnic bench where the employees smoked and gossiped on their breaks. Sarah and I were sitting at the bench drinking takeout coffees and chatting before I started my shift.

'We should get Jack something nice for his birthday,' she said.

'Buy him dirt.'

'You can't get somebody dirt. I'll get him a satellite radio.'

'Okay, don't listen to me. If you get him something expensive, he'll get embarrassed. It'll go in a closet, never used, because "it's too nice". Buy him orchid pots or vermiculite or some such thing, and he'll act like you bought him diamonds.'

Rose, the assistant manager, pulled up in her truck. She was a heavy-set woman with ropes of ash for dreads. She took the coffee I handed her. I always picked up a coffee for Rose. Sarah gave her sugar packets and a stirrer. She sat heavily and ripped open the sugars one by one to dump them in.

'What's up?' I asked.

'Peggy's quit.'

Sarah and I both showed our surprise and disappointment.

Rose went on to say that head office wanted to be more involved with the day-to-day operations. She didn't know anything more. Peggy hadn't said goodbye and the guy from head office started today.

'You ready to go in?' Rose asked.

I nodded. I kissed Sarah goodbye and told her I finished at six today. We went inside and Sarah went to her car.

'Hello, everyone. Dean James. James Dean. But reversed.'

One of the stock guys whispered, 'We got ourselves a real live corporate asshole here.'

Reverse James Dean talked in company-speak and management jargon sweetened with hippy let's-all-be-groovy sentiments. He laid it on thick with the girls.

After the meeting, we gathered in the break room.

'The t-shirt and jeans are just to try and fit in. At night, he draws the curtains, turns off the lights and puts on his old pinstripe suit and silk tie from his MBA days,' I said.

'I bet he starts growing a ponytail,' one of the cashiers said.

A few days later, Reverse James Dean stopped me on the way to the bathroom.

He was looking at my wheelchair when he asked if I needed anything.

'A raise.'

'We're looking into that. I mean for your special abilities?'

'I'm a cripple, not a superhero. No, I'm fine. Thank you.'

'Okay.' He tapped my small front wheel with his foot. 'My door's always open.'

That night we had a birthday dinner for Jack at our place. His cake was a jelly donut with a candle in it. He beamed when Sarah came out of the kitchen singing 'Happy Birthday'. He blew out the candle and cut it into quarters.

'I don't want you two wasting money buying me crap I don't need.'

'Hush, old man. Open your present,' Sarah said.

Jack opened the box. 'Perlite! Vermiculite!'

'I didn't know which one to buy,' she said.

'I need them both. Thank you.'

I managed to avoid Reverse James Dean for about a week until I was told he wanted to see me in his office.

Everyone working the register had a trick where you passed the item across the scanner but made sure it didn't scan. It was something you did for co-workers, an unofficial employee discount. I had scanned-but-didn't a bottle of wine for one of the girls from the deli.

'Company policy says stealing is grounds for immediate dismissal.'

'Stealing?'

'You didn't charge Suzy for a bottle of wine. I hear you're a good member of The Store's team. You need to understand the seriousness of the situation, but I don't want to have to fire you. This is going to be a written warning.'

I finished my shift and took the bus home. Sarah was supposed to pick me up. She called me but I didn't answer. She texted.

```
Where are you?
                          sorry jumped on bus.
                              bad day at work
   everything okay?
                                          yes
   you want me to come over?
                                           no
   you're a jerk.
                                          Yes
```

Jack was in his recliner reading an orchid catalogue when I told him what had happened at the store with Reverse James Dean. He shrugged and said I should have been fired.

'Whose side are you on?'

'You stole. What do you expect?'

'It's not really stealing.'

'It is.'

'What's wrong? You've been acting funny lately.'

'Telling you to stop being stupid isn't being funny. It's boring.'

'Okay. Okay. Seriously, what's wrong? You look like you're in pain.'

'The doctor put me on some new medication. I'm going back tomorrow.'

'What's going on, Jack?'

Jack looked at me with worry. I wasn't hiding my panic well, but I knew I had to if Jack was going to tell me anything.

'Nothing's going on. Just old person stuff. What about getting me an ice tea?'

'This is your bullshit macho real men don't get sick—' I took his glass.

'All right already. It's fine.'

I yelled from the kitchen as I refilled his tea from the fridge. 'You're lying. If you're going to the doctor that means it's serious.' I returned, handing him his tea. 'Have you seen Mister Shakey?'

'After I brushed him this morning, I let him out,' he said, taking a drink and picking his catalogue back up.

'Will you help me look for him?'

'Nope.'

I went outside to look for the cat. I wandered around, calling his name. I was a few houses down when I heard Jack shouting. He was at the side of the house motioning me to come fast.

'Where is he?' I asked as Jack fell behind and helped push my chair through the thick grass.

Mister Shakey was a large, square-headed animal. A dust-grey beast not far removed from his wildcat ancestors, but beneath the rose bush, lying on his side, he was a child's lost plush toy. I pressed myself into the thorns, bending to reach, but only managed to brush my hands across the poor creature's ribs. His eyes were wide, staring forward while he snapped at unseen flies. Pink foam flecked the corner of his mouth. The front paws paddled as if swimming and the back legs stretched out rigid.

I manoeuvred the chair to bend sideways. Jack held a branch of thorns that was digging into my forehead. Beaded red lines of scratches ran up my arms. A thorn jabbed my cheek. I still couldn't reach him.

'Pick him up!' I shouted at Jack.

'Jarred, I don't think that's a good idea. Let the seizure pass first.'

I winced at each wave of seizure that wracked the small furry body. A growl fell from the snapping mouth and twisting head. The front paws stretched forward. He went limp.

'Get him. Get him!'

Jack laid the animal in my lap. The cat lifted his head and settled it against my knee. I rubbed under the jaw and he lifted his muzzle. A weak purr vibrated under my fingers.

'Hold him. I'll push,' Jack said.

Inside the house, Jack phoned the vet to tell them that we were on our way. My fingertips felt the tiny heart thump unevenly. The small lungs pushed out a wheezing breath. The left front paw stretched forward. I held it, rubbing the pads, willing the cat not to have another fit. A paw shot forward again. The milky claws stretched from their sheaths.

He drew a big breath. My cat sighed long and slow. The purr shuddered to a halt.

'Hang up,' I said. 'Hang up the fucking phone! He's dead.'

I didn't stop when Jack called after me. I headed for the forest. There was a time I was more comfortable amongst the trees and night sky than I was in my own home. By the first line of trees the sand was too thick, and the exposed roots were too difficult. With every awkward push, my cat's limp body slid from my lap as if liquid.

I set the body down next to the nearest tree. I scooted onto the ground. With my bare hands and a stick, I dug. My fingernails turned to black crescents. I attacked the hole, chewed at the grit that flew up. I dragged myself around. My heels drew a twin trail behind me until I found another stick and bashed away at the hole with the body of my dead cat nearby. After a foot, the roots had grown too thick and stubborn to rip away. My knuckles were a mush of torn skin stuffed with soil and blood. I was sweating and sore from the effort.

I brushed the dirt off Mister Shakey. I tried to clear a clump from his eye but my dirty fingers made it worse. I held his body to my chest and wept.

I laid him in the hole.

46

I was twenty-five. In less than a year, I would be in a wheelchair and Melissa would be dead. I was living in Chicago. I was drunk, and this woman's teeth were too small. As she continued to yell, they became the bared fangs of a small dog, something yippy with dripping eyes and greasy hair discoloured at the chin. Her mouth had too much gum as well. Pink and obscene.

I smacked the pizza out of her hand for no good reason. It wasn't until it hit the ground that I realised what I had done.

Like everyone else, awed, I followed the graceful spin of the cheese and pepperoni toward the bar's band-sticker insulted ceiling. Its return to earth began a fraction of a moment after leaving a greasy kiss on a glossy show poster, a perfect pizza triangle outline of reddish yellow grease. After which, it sped toward the beer-stinking cement to land with the fleshy slap of a suicide.

'You cocksucker. Why did you do that? Why did you do that?'

'Cocksucker,' her boyfriend repeated and pulled back to deliver a punch.

I kicked the back of his heel and shoved him to join the

fate of her pizza. I waited to see if he'd get up when pain exploded at the back of my head. I turned around and caught another blow in my temple. An instant headache gripped me. Blood slicked down my face, blinding one eye. The pizzaless girl with the tiny doggy teeth had taken off one of her high heels and was trying to pulp my head. I grabbed the shoe from her and backed up, fingering the bloody wound on my scalp. She tried to follow, comically lurching with one bare foot and one high heel. She leaned down, eyes and curses fixed on me, taking off the other shoe and arming herself again.

I handed the shoe to the bouncer on my way out. He looked at my bloodied face then inside the bar.

'Someone's off her meds in there,' I said and left.

I finished the night at a friend's bar and woke up in one of the booths. This could have described any other morning-after in one of the dozen towns I had lived in since I had run away. That morning I was supposed to pick up my ex-girlfriend for an appointment at Planned Parenthood. She was waiting outside her apartment when I pulled up. I got out to open the car door for her. I kissed her cheek. Her smile disappeared. She looked concerned and tentatively touched the bloodied 'D' marking my temple. She pulled at my collar.

'Your blood?'

I nodded.

'Remind me again. How were you the one who broke up with me?'

'I told you that was a mistake.'

'Definitely not.'

'We don't have to do this.'

'You are joking, right?'

'No. We can figure this out. I'll—'

'You need to stop right now. Just drive.' She got into the car and stared forward. She was fighting not to cry and it stabbed at my conscience. 'Jarred, I am so serious right now. It's hard enough. Stop.'

'Okay, okay.'

We drove in silence until I couldn't bear it. I had to figure out a way to explain myself. To tell her I was worth a chance, but I knew she was right and that was worse of all.

'The last time I saw my mom alive I was coming home from school. I was barely eleven. Their bedroom door was ajar. Dad was giving her a bed bath. A bucket of soapy water was on a chair beside them. He would dip a washcloth into the water and wring it and wash her.'

She turned toward me. I saw her confused look smooth away as she listened.

'"Is that warm enough?" he said. I remember that exactly. I can hear it in his voice just now and I haven't talked to him in, shit, eight or nine years. "Is that warm enough?" and he put the washcloth on her cheek. She nodded. He scrubbed her neck and made a show of washing behind her ears.'

I mimicked the motion.

'She lifted her arms like a kid and he washed them, holding her at the wrist. It was such a delicate thing. He would dip the washcloth, wring it out and wash her. Over and over. I watched, completely entranced. They cooed and talked to each other the whole time. I don't remember or couldn't hear what they were saying. Then she rolled over on her side. He adjusted the towel beneath her and washed her back, following her shoulder blades and spine with the washcloth.'

I traced the motions in the air.

'She was watching him over her shoulder, always grinning. She was a beautiful woman, my mom. I remember he said something, she laughed and he patted her butt.'

I tapped the steering wheel.

'He scrubbed her feet last. After he was done. He put the cloth in the bucket and when he asked her "How was that?" she smiled a smile I've never seen anywhere else. That look she gave him was something beyond love. Adoration? I don't know the word. I don't know if there is a word.'

I shook my head.

'When she died, I was kind of left to raise myself. I hated him for falling apart but now I think how could anyone continue once you've been loved like that? Once you've seen someone look at you like she did.'

She was crying now. I knew I should have shut up, but I didn't. I had never told anyone that story.

'My punishment for intruding on that moment is to know that I will never be good enough, for long enough, to deserve another human to smile at me like that.'

I pulled into the Planned Parenthood office past two bored-looking protesters with posters of a gloved hand holding a tiny arm and skull with red and black gore in the background. Choose Life, their posters said.

I didn't get to finish the story. She jumped out of the car and ran into the building. I didn't say the last thing I saw. After Mom smiled that smile, Jack leaned over to put his face against her feet. She wiggled her toes to brush his lips. He kissed the big toe on each foot. I remember that most vividly.

47

After burying Mister Shakey I went back to the house. Jack was bringing a glass of water to a middle-aged man with a moustache. He looked familiar, but I didn't know why.

'Thanks,' the man said. 'I'm sorry for giving you such a hard time. When Pauline got sick, she didn't have insurance. I got so angry at everything.'

'It's all right. You don't have to explain yourself. You had a job to do.'

'Wait a minute.' I knew who he was.

'Jarred,' Jack warned.

'You're the collection agent. You complete asshole.' I turned on Jack. 'The collection agent? What the fuck is he doing in this house? He should be under it.' I smacked the glass of water so it spilled into the man's lap.

'Jarred!'

'Get out of here. Are you really crying? You're a parasite. Get out.'

The man fled, apologising the whole time.

Jack snapped, 'His wife died.'

'You're here to save everyone, aren't you? The one-car garage buddha.'

'Go to your room, you child.'

'Where were you when I needed saving?'

'It's everyone else's fault, isn't it? I'm done with that, Jarred.'

I screamed.

Jack watched me, tears in his eyes, until I exhausted myself.

'Jack, I don't know what to do.'

'Nobody does.' He grabbed hold of me and we hugged.

48

We found each other behind the dumpsters of a propane distribution company and underneath the building's only window, framing the ceiling and the blue-rinse crown of an elderly woman at her desk as she made sure America's propane needs were satisfied. My roommate had dropped me off on the South Side at a nearby crossover and drove off in my car with a toot of the horn. I had traded the car for the rent I still owed him. The truth was I had to leave Chicago.

There were five of us, probably too many. Four crusty girls of varying degrees of mental ill-health and burnout. Thank god none of them had dogs. The matriarch was a diesel-sooted Mrs. Santa Claus in BO-stinking black but rosy-cheeked with blue-eyed kindness. She knew what she was doing, but the others were dangerous with romance and inexperience. They were on their way to Nevada where a friend had a trailer somewhere, they weren't sure, in the emptiness off Highway 80. Their plans were vague and pointless, and although I could still appreciate why that was a good thing, it bored me. I was tired of needles and the need. Tired of the 'dude'- and 'nigger'-inflected pointless chitchat about stupid yuppies, being free, the bulls, the hotshots, cracking squats, scams, scores, fuck America, the cool, the suck, bands and drugs. I wanted the girls to be scared, and the hours waiting, getting eaten alive by fire ants and sadistic horseflies, I made sure were filled with me and Mrs. Claus trading war stories.

I had scars to show, but it was Mrs. Claus who lifted her shirt to reveal the puckered skin of a stab wound on her breast while casually recounting being raped.

A boy of sixteen walked up to us as if we had arranged to meet him. He sat down next to the girl with a blast of black mossy hair and started talking to her. Now we were six and definitely too many. One of these kids would get us busted; that was inevitable.

Dirty Mrs. Claus pointed out our train arriving. The best part began. We ran for it, slinging backpacks, helping each other up, and that perfect moment when your feet leave the ground and you fly. From the first time with Melissa to this last time I caught a train, it was a victory.

We settled in and the humidity inside the boxcar immediately soaked our clothes in sweat. One of the girls poured water onto her head, but Mrs. Claus wisely admonished her to conserve it. The bounce and shake of the car was the worst I had ever felt. Every tooth in my head ached. The wind coming through the open door only stirred the smell of rotten pigeon shit and the stink of us. After a couple of hours, the girl with mossy hair screamed and screamed until Mrs. Claus held her.

I was sitting cross-legged beside the open boxcar door. The boy sat beside me. The train slowed and stopped as if answering our prayers. In the stillness, our bodies continued to rattle.

'I feel sick.' A girl lurched for the open door.

Soon the heat crawled back in and our fickle hobo prayers switched to willing the train to move again. Mrs. Claus talked over a map with her girls and had them mark their water bottles with a pen to ration their supply. The girls were always embracing or touching, even if it was only a hand left casually on another's knee. They were beautiful in their filthy clothes in the dark space of the boxcar.

Out beyond the car was the endless expanse of the Midwest. It had none of the obvious charm of the Rockies but the colours were all there. A sky bigger than God, clear and rich, so demanding of attention you wondered why it took so long for people to have a word for blue. Below it lay the fat brushstrokes of green and yellow and the daubs of lonely buildings to make you wonder about the lives lived beneath the roofs. A landscape that threatened poetry, but I had none to give.

The boy beside me pointed out a town close to the horizon. 'Look at that shit, dude.'

I followed his finger out to a handful of the roofed squares of houses below the benign gaze of a water tower with a smiley face painted on it.

'Fuck that town and everyone in it. Slaves in air-conditioned cages.' He pointed his middle finger.

'That's not where you're from,' I said and took out my cigarettes and lighter.

'No, man. Some other shit-fuck town full of assholes.' He thumbed behind us.

'You run away?' I offered him a smoke. He grabbed one and nodded his thanks. I lit it for him and he exhaled his answer, 'Yeah,' blowing smoke toward the scenery.

'Why?'

'Old man always on my shit. His new wife loves her some Jesus and wants me to love him too.' He raised his hands above his head. 'Hallelujah!'

'And?'

'And she doesn't like me smoking weed.'

'You get busted?'

'Three strikes and out like a mofo.'

'And you ran off?' I was channelling Jack.

'Ran like a mofo.' He pantomimed his arms pumping, his head down, as if running hard. 'If I get caught this time, it's Fed for me.'

I put out the cherry on the ground by writing my first initial with the black soot and put the butt back into the pack to save it for later. The kid watched me. I knew he wasn't going to listen to me, but I said it anyway.

'That was pretty stupid then, huh? You couldn't just be a little smarter about smoking? I mean it wasn't unreasonable for them to ask you not to smoke weed while they pay your bills, give you a place to stay. Sounds like basic courtesy. Or at least, it's reasonable for you not to be stupid enough to get caught.'

After a silence, he asked me why I was here.

'The freedom,' I said sarcastically.

'New places. New people. That's what this is all about.' He pointed to the girls and me and the boxcar roof. 'Free to see the world. I'm sixteen and I got more experiences than those nine-to-five niggas living their rat-race lives for thirty years. I'm free to do what I want.'

I kept my eyes forward. If I looked at him, I would start crying. I was him and he would be me.

'I'll hop a train to anywhere,' he bragged. 'It's all bullshit, dude.' He fidgeted from my lack of response. The train blew its horn and a shudder ran down the cars. The girls squealed and clapped. The boy retreated to their circle and I was alone with my view.

We had several more hours of the rattling pain. Days later, after my first shower, I had a leopard print of bruises.

The sun set with more poetic flourishes. Mrs. Claus

assured us we were close. They were going to aim for a hotshot west. I still wasn't sure where I was going, but I was done with trains.

The boy announced he had to take a fierce shit.

'I got to take a fierce shit.' He dropped his trousers. His ass, glowing white in the expanding gloom of the car, was pointed at me.

He turned and gripped the sides of the door and squatted. He was grinning and joking with the girls.

The boxcar jerked; the doors shifted. He was gone in an instant, quick enough to doubt whether he ever existed at all. The girls screamed and screamed. They stamped and held each other, held on to me. The last hour was black and silent. The exhausted drawn-out slowing to a stop of the train was more horrible than usual. We alighted emptied of anything human, followed a trail through the weeds to the chain-link fence, mechanically dropped our backpacks through the hole, then pulled ourselves through. The girls walked toward the Super Walmart that we had passed a couple miles back. The moss-haired girl talked about calling 911. I went toward the highway to hitchhike into town.

49

I woke up to see Jack's face close to mine. The black eyes shone under the brow as he studied my face.

'Are you naked?' Jack asked.

I nodded, not sure if I was awake. After I buried Mister Shakey, I called into work sick and spent the day hiding in my room. I had heard Jack talking on the phone to Sarah and Patrick. Something was going on. It reminded me of when he got me locked up in the psychiatric hospital. Crawling under the bed probably wasn't going to help my case if that was his plan again.

'What's the attraction of hiding under here?' Jack rapped the underside of my bed. 'You used to do this as a kid. Always hiding away in closets or under beds. Do you remember hiding in the neighbour's garage? It worked out for the best. Cheaper than a babysitter. The wife used to check in on you from time to time and phone me.'

'Really? I always thought I was on my own.'

'Never in your life, kid. Listen here. Forget about the collection agent. He was here to apologise. To both of us. The guy was messed up. He's in more debt than we are. Forget him. I always have time for you.'

'It's not about that.' I banged the back of my head against the underside of the bed a couple of times.

'Can we have this conversation sitting with both of us fully clothed? I don't really want this moment to go in my memoir just as it is now.'

'Fine,' I said.

'Do you need any help?'

'I'll manage.'

He straightened up. His leather shoes were the colour of brick. The years of scuffs and wear polished out. White socks peeked out from between the shoes and his old-man slacks. The bed creaked as he used it for support.

'See you in the living room. Wear something smart-casual.' The shoes moved over to my wheelchair. The wheels and shoes moved closer.

'About here?'

'That's fine,' I said and used the slats under the bed to pull myself out.

Jack closed the door as he left.

When I had dressed, I found him in the kitchen.

He said, 'Your phone's ringing.' He poured himself a glass of water from the tap and finished it in one gulp.

'It's Sarah,' I said.

'You aren't answering it?' He poured himself another glass and went into the living room.

I followed. 'No.'

'That's not very gentleman-like.'

'Probably not.'

'Did you guys have a fight?'

'No.'

'I'm sure you know what you're doing.' He sat down in his chair, kicking out the leg rest. 'I have to be in the hospital for a bunch of tests. They're tuning my ticker, minor surgery. I'll be in there for a week, which I'm not happy about. I was hoping you'd be okay on your own, but it looks like I need to worry about you again. How are you feeling?'

'I killed my cat.'

'Stop. Jesus, change the record,' he said. 'Are you going to call Sarah and apologise for whatever stupid thing you did?'

'Probably not.'

'I tried,' Jack said. 'While I'm away, Patrick will come by a couple times just to check in.'

'I'll be fine.'

'He's coming for my peace of mind, not yours.'

'Fair enough.'

Jack pulled back the leg rest and stood up. 'You know? I think this world needs a good fuck you. Let it know the McGinnis men aren't beaten yet.'

'What? No.'

'C'mon.' He walked to the front door and opened it wide. 'C'mon.'

'It's embarrassing.'

'When did that ever stop you from acting like an idiot? Get out here. You worried about your reputation? Father and son say fuck you to the world. Let's go.'

I followed Jack outside. The neighbourhood was quiet and still. The day was hot but pleasant. Jack's car sat in the driveway.

'Fuck you!' we yelled.

'Do you feel any better?' he asked.

'No.'

'Me neither.'

'Let's see if donuts will help. My treat,' I said.

50

That lonesome boy disappeared from the open boxcar over and over as I walked into what turned out to be Kansas City. Over and over, the screams of the girls roiled and built to a sound no longer human. Even the memory of their keening sent splinters of anxiety through my bones. I argued with myself about what we could have done, but there was nothing. I tried to imagine happy-ending scenarios for the boy splayed out on the grey ballast in the empty hopelessness of a midwestern plain. I lay there with him feeling the broken bones. We eyed the infinity of rail stretching away from us. Maybe the girls' 911 call saved him. It's possible. The best I could come up with was an instant death. A broken neck and done.

I ended up back in Austin again. I tried to convince myself that it was just a coincidence. I thought about visiting Mom's grave, maybe seeing if I could stay with Patrick or Jack for a few days, maybe looking up old friends, Fritz maybe, Melissa. I didn't, though. I found a room to rent and got a job at an Italian restaurant across the street from the apartment. I had compressed my world down to the apartment, the restaurant and a twenty-four-hour grocery store a block away.

Right down to the dust-covered plastic grape bunches on the shelves, no cliché of an Italian restaurant was missed. The tables all had Chianti bottle candle holders, big-bellied shakers of parmesan and dried red pepper flakes on checkered oilcloths. One wall was a trompe l'oeil Tuscan landscape and framed photos of Italian heroes hung on the others. The portrait of John F. Kennedy seemed to be a mistake until the owner explained his theory on the Italian origins of the former president who had, according to him, been adopted into the Kennedy family from their Abruzzian gardener's widow.

The husband and wife owners completed the exaggerated Italian atmosphere with regular arm-flailing, door-slamming arguments flecked with Italian obscenities amongst bewildered diners and cooling plates of linguini. Her favourite complaint was the husband wearing his wedding band on a necklace rather than his finger, the sight of which would pique her to frenzy. Most of the customers were somehow related to the husband and wife and often took sides.

'Quiet down, Sara!'

'Drop it, Stefano!'

Before evening shifts, the wife prepared a huge bowl of pasta and placed it at the centre of the big round table. As soon as she sat, she impatiently told us to 'Eat, eat' and all of us – the waiters, the dishwashers, the cooks, the wife and husband – would eat, eat. One big service-industry family. We talked about work: shitty tips, horrible customers, menus, bookings. We commented on the food with humming mouthfuls and pleasured nods. The husband expounded on his idea that the Italian race invented everything and all notable persons in history were paisans; mentioning that the Chinese invented the noodle caused a sputtering apoplexy. The wife always fretted over me. I was never eating enough. Such a handsome boy, why didn't I find a nice girl. It was mothering and I devoured it.

After my shifts, I hung around and helped the kitchen or the owners and delayed the time I went back to my tiny empty apartment where I inevitably got drunk or high, watched tv and looked up Melissa on the internet. She had become more beautiful. There were photos of her in a bikini smiling before a plate of food, sapphire sky and sea in the background. Photos of her in what looked like a private jet. Cocktail bars full of beautiful faces full of perfect teeth and her in the centre of them. My jealous heart spat epithets of 'spoiled rich girl' but I knew the truth. The money never saved her from anything. She's doing well despite her childhood. She had a married name now, Al-Thani. A heavy-browed, swarthy, handsome man. The beginnings of a paunch in his tailored shirt and ill-judged sideburns were the only critique I managed. In the photos there was a confidence that stung me. I could have clicked 'Follow' beside her name, could have written a breezy hiya message, could have suggested we meet up the next time she was in town. As far as I could tell she was living in San Francisco.

One Saturday at the restaurant, Stefano gave me an envelope of money and told me to give it to the man coming out to balance the ceiling fans. A little later a station wagon pulled up, and I went to help the stooped figure struggling with the ladder, which had caught on the passenger-side headrest. His too-big jeans and shirt made him look like he was shrinking perceptibly before me. His iceberg-blue eyes must have been striking as a young man. Now, set into the tired skin of an old man, rimmed by the inflamed red of his eyelids, they seemed an unfair reminder of a lost vivacity.

He shuffled and wheezed behind me as I brought the ladder in and set it up under one of the fans. I asked if he wanted me to bring in his tools. He said softly, no, thank you.

Each of his steps up the ladder was the moment before I had to phone 911. He didn't need me to get his tools, because he had no tools. Using the top step as a workbench, he set out a roll of tape and a mix of pennies, washers and slugs. He asked where the switch was. I pointed and he began the cautious descent and trek across the room. He flipped the switch. The fans came to life, turning, picking up speed, all wobbling. Back at the ladder, he paused, holding it firmly, and climbed once again. He studied the swaying fan as it rotated. He made his way back down, across the room, flipped the fans off and he went back to the ladder. A penny was selected. A length of tape was cut between his teeth, an operation too precarious to watch. He pushed the blade, watched its progression, and seemed satisfied. Again, down the ladder and across the room to the switch he went. It worked. The blades followed each other clockwise in a smooth orderly motion. He turned them off again and positioned the ladder to balance the second fan. Halfway through the diagnosis of the second fan, the weight attached to the first flew off and pinged off the portrait of Pope John Paul.

He moved the ladder back and retrieved the penny slowly, carefully, with cracking joints and sighs. He started again. This went on and on. As soon as one wobble was fixed, the balancing weight from another was shot across the room. It was getting close to the dinner shift, and only fan number three was interested in holding on to the bit of metal he had taped to it.

Stefano returned. He stared at the old man. 'What's he doing here?'

I told him what had been going on for the last five hours.

'No. No. No.' His voice rose with each 'no'. 'Give me his envelope.'

Stefano snapped the ladder closed and carried it out to the car, complaining about paying him for nothing. The old man submitted meekly to Stefano's tirade. I stepped outside to have a cigarette, wanting to avoid Stefano, who would continue his complaining all night. The old man was expressionless as he inched back out of the parking lot.

I clocked out and walked home. In my head, Jack became that fan balancer. Was he still working when he should have been able to retire and take it easy? Was he as sad and lonely? Was the pride beaten out of him too? I didn't even know if he was still alive.

I ignored the restaurant's phone calls and the knocks at my door when I missed my next shift.

51

'Hey.'

'Hey,' Patrick said.

'How are you?' I asked.

'Good. You?'

'Good.'

'How are you doing home alone?'

'Patrick. I'm not that crazy.'

'Sorry. We never really knew each other, but you're still my brother.' After I didn't respond, Patrick continued: 'Dad seemed to think you don't need to know.'

'Know what?'

'Dad had a valve replaced in his heart. They used cow tissue, which he was strangely excited about.'

I still didn't say anything.

'He thinks he can be back on his feet in a week. Pretend nothing happened. He's not getting old gracefully. He's becoming a pain in the ass, actually.'

'Becoming?'

'He's got some infection, but it's responding to treatment. Hey.'

'Huh?'

'Dad has really loved having you home. He'd never tell

you that, but it's true. He's kind of woken up this last year. He's been just flat for a lot of years.' Patrick moved his hand to cut the air, signalling flat. 'He's been puttering about in his greenhouse and watching tv. We'd bring the kids to see him. He'd play with them for half an hour or so, but he'd just go blank and quiet after a while. He really likes you. I mean, loves you. We've never been close. I've never felt close to him. I love the guy but we never really . . . we don't have much in common. You should go visit him.' He read something in my expression and added, 'Don't worry. He's okay. He's just going to be in for longer than he thought. Do you want me to take you?'

'I'll go a bit later. Thanks. I can take the bus.'

'He's been putting the surgery off. He was worried about you leaving.'

'Patrick. Please, don't. I don't need anything else that's my fault.'

'No, no, no. That's not what I meant. I was just saying. You mean a lot to him. He's always talking about you.'

'Patrick, do you mind if I take a nap? I'm pretty tired.'

'You sure you don't want me to take you?'

'Please.'

'Sorry. I'm sorry.'

52

The Italian restaurant gave up after a couple of missed shifts. I felt sorry for myself at how quickly they gave up and I never picked up my last pay cheque. I sat in the house and thought about Jack, daring myself to dial his number, hear the three rings and that rumbling voice say, 'Hello, Jack McGinnis.' If I had, I wouldn't have been paralysed and Melissa would still have been alive. Instead she had posted some photos and by the look of them she was in town and at a swanky hotel downtown.

I saw her walking along the sidewalk, doe-legged and ignoring every man who tried to catch her flitting sparrow's eyes. I knew that walk, the confidence and those eyes. After a dozen years, her precocious confidence had steeped into every movement. It suited her.

I called out and, when she recognised me, her eyes lit up. We hugged tightly, and the familiarity of her was immediate.

'Do you still live here?' Melissa asked.

'Well, I . . .' I stumbled. 'I moved back recently. You?'

'God, no. I'm here to just . . .' She pulled away and a sad look flitted across her face. The commuters and downtown shoppers flowed around us. 'It looks like I'm here to see old friends.'

I was a boy again and within her power. 'Man, the last time I saw you—'

'The last time you were setting fire to my house.'

'A tree behind your house and it was more a bush than a tree really.' I laughed. 'You look fantastic. Do you want to get a drink? Let's get a drink. I was just heading across the street.'

She hesitated. 'I'm trying to behave these days.'

'Really? You, behave? Let me treat you. I make a mean Shirley Temple.' I pointed at a bar across the street.

'It looks like a dump.'

'The marketing team prefers the term bijou.'

'Is that your bar?' She waved a hand dismissively at the blacked-out window with a Bud Light neon sign.

'Let me show you around.' I gave her a wink. I didn't know why I was lying about owning a bar.

She hesitated.

'Let's get a coffee then,' I offered, pointing to the Starbucks behind us where I had staked out her hotel.

We talked, but mainly about her. There was world-weariness. She had known she was destined for better things, but what she had found or how she found it had disappointed her. I let her believe I was content with my done-nothing life. There was never any pretence that I would do anything. She seemed to envy that. I was free. Bellboys and executives didn't treat me like a piece of ass. My friends weren't shallow and ignorant. I wasn't married to a rich-boy cokehead whom I didn't love. Most of all, I didn't follow in my mother's footsteps.

'He comes from a very traditional family. Traditional and rich. Total fucking playboy though. He lives these two worlds. Wants to be a good little Muslim, but then he met me at a strip club. I wasn't a dancer by the way. He wants kids. I don't want kids.'

'What's your last name?' I asked, making sure the information I knew from my internet snooping and what she had told me herself was the same lest I accidentally reveal that I'd been creeping on her for months.

'Al-Thani.'

'Melissa Anne Al-Thani.' I laughed.

'My god. I forgot you're probably the only person who knows my middle name besides my mother. My friends now would freak out if they knew I had such a hick middle name. I don't even think my husband knows my middle name, but then again, he doesn't care.'

She took a small bunch of hair and put it in her mouth. 'I met a friend of yours,' she said.

'Who?'

'Fritz.'

'No way. How did you meet him?'

'I was organising parties. That's how I met Frank too.'

'Frank?'

'My husband.'

'Frank Al-Thani?'

'That's what Farooq calls himself.'

'Farooq?' I knew his name already. I knew he was in finance and worked with his four brothers in his dad's company. He was often travelling for work and Melissa usually went with him.

'Anyway!' she said, rolling her eyes. 'Fritz was DJing. We became good friends. I had just started dating Frank but had told him to fuck off, because he was having a hard time, you know, not fucking strippers.'

'It's a challenge for some.'

She stacked our empty coffee cups as she talked. She never took notice of the men going past and stealing glances at her.

'He was begging me to come back. I made him fly Fritz and me all over the world for gigs. Eventually I went back to Frank. I stopped hanging out with Fritz shortly after to be a better wife. So pathetic.'

'That's not the Melissa I remember. You didn't take shit from boys.'

'I didn't take shit from boys like you, but your family doesn't have their own jet.'

'You're right. That is pathetic.'

'Touché.' She looked at her phone. 'Speak of the devil.' She straightened up. Her voice switched to a cold, business-like tone, and I realised we had been talking to each other like when we were kids. The way she had moved, how she had touched her hair, her slouch, all came from that past.

'What? I'm at a coffee shop with a girlfriend . . . Tracy. Does it matter? . . . No, I don't want to tonight . . . No . . . I'm not in the mood . . . Frank . . . I'll see you at the hotel later . . . Fine. Bye.'

'Do you have to leave?'

'No.'

'You sure you don't want to go back to the bar? We can hang out in my office.'

The bar was almost empty, and no one noticed us march to the back, which was little more than a storeroom for crates of beer, liquor bottles and kegs. There was a rickety office chair with one wheel gaffer-taped on. An old Mustang hubcap serving as an ashtray rested on top of a small fridge full of beers.

I opened a beer and handed it to Melissa, who hesitated

before taking it, and opened one for myself. On a beer-stained and cigarette-burned couch slumped against a shelf of bottles, I laughed at Melissa's disgust before laying down a bar towel for her to sit on.

'So, wait, how did you figure out you and Fritz knew me?' I asked.

She brought her feet up onto the couch and gave my shoulder a playful shove with the toe of her shoe. I slipped off the heels and put her feet in my lap.

'When we first started hanging out, we were trading stories about ex-boyfriends. I told him about you and all the dumb stuff we did together. Oh my god, we used to shoplift like every day.'

Hearing her reminisce, I couldn't help grinning.

'Fritz said he met a Jarred after his mom put him in rehab the first time. This town is smaller than you think. We put two and two together. We totally freaked out when we figured out it was the same Jarred. Our first love was the same crazy kid Jarred. It was nice. You were a connection we shared.'

'The way I remember it, you dumped me and he abandoned me in Denver.'

'Oh, that feels nice,' she said as I massaged her foot. 'He felt bad about that. He realised how silly he was being with you.'

'What do you mean?'

'You were straight. He wasn't.'

'He was there when I needed him. I'll always appreciate that.'

She looked me in the eyes. 'He told me about your fucked-up dad and how your mom died. I'm sorry.'

I looked away and took a long pull on my beer.

'I never believed your runaway story.'

'Yeah, I wasn't much of a liar.'

'Ha! You were a big liar, just a bad one. Can I have another beer?'

'Of course.' I stretched behind me and pulled out another beer. 'Do you still see Fritz?'

'I can't believe I'm drinking nasty beers in the back of the shitty bar owned by the guy I lost my virginity to.'

'Living the dream.'

'He lives around the corner,' she said.

'Fritz?'

She nodded as she drank.

'Did he tell you how he knew me?'

'Yeah. You met in the loony bin.'

'Yeah.'

'No surprise there. Keep massaging my feet. That feels good.'

'What do you mean?' I put my beer down and picked up her foot from my lap.

'I refer you to the tree arson, because a girl broke up with you,' she said, and I laughed. I raised my bottle and clinked it against hers.

'Largish bush arson. What happened with that?'

'Mom didn't believe me. She said I had been smoking. I must have gotten grounded or something. I don't remember.'

'How is your mom?'

Her smile disappeared. 'The same. She loves Frank. She'd fuck him if he'd let her.'

While we talked, she drained her beers quickly. She wasn't drinking them but needing them. I thought about all the people I knew whom I had seen do the same thing. It lessened her and I liked that it lessened her. Right there, I could have steered us away from the inevitable disaster, but I wanted to drag someone down with me.

'Jarred, your bar is a dump.'

'That's part of the charm. It's kept tidy. I mean sparkly clean. We then have a team come in to give it character. They come and sprinkle imported piss from beer-drinking Bavarian virgins. Once a week, we stain the stools with artisanal tramp juice using a badger-hair brush. That mouse trap there with what looks like a dried sausage? That was hand-crafted.'

'Tramp juice? Let's go somewhere nice. Frank's treat.' She finished her beer and sat in my lap. We were a little drunk. I held her by the waist. The first woman I loved. A girl then, but the muscle memory of her body was there. I think she felt it too.

'Where do you want to go?' I asked.

'There's Numbers.'

'Absolutely not. That club is full of coked-out middle-aged bankers. Let's have some fun. There's a place I know. It's dime beer night. Don't worry, I know the manager. We'll drink for free.' I winked. 'It'll be great. Dime beer night brings everyone out. The music is all over the place. It'll be great.'

She shook her head.

I thought for a moment. 'Let's steal a bottle of Jack Daniel's and visit Fritz.'

'I haven't seen Fritz in forever. We kind of fell out. He was living with us. Frank hated him. Fritz was stealing shit. It got ugly. He disappeared. Last I heard he had ODed in the toilet of a club in Amsterdam and went into rehab. Typical junkie DJ bullshit. Looks like we all turned out pathetic.'

'Not me. Look at my empire. Living large in charge.'

A man opened the back door. Daylight exploded into the room. He took off his sunglasses and looked at us.

'Oh shit,' I said.

'What the fuck're you doing in here?'

'We should go,' I said to Melissa. 'We're waiting for Scotty,' I called to the man. We moved toward the exit.

'Who the fuck is Scotty?'

'The owner.'

'I'm the motherfucking owner, asshole.'

'Sorry, wrong bar.'

We ran for a bit to make sure we weren't followed.

Melissa said, 'You are still the same asshole. You don't own that place.'

'No. Never been there before in my life,' I said. 'C'mon, let's pick up Fritz and go have an adventure. It's been a long time.'

53

After Patrick left, I went and sat in Jack's greenhouse. I misted the roots of the orchids hanging overhead. The droplets tumbled and drifted in the sunlight. The mist felt nice on my face. A Habenaria – I could hear Jack's voice pronouncing the genus – was blooming on the counter. Nearly impossible to grow and Jack had managed to make it flower. I ran my finger along the long thin spun-sugar petals.

A car pulled into the driveway.

I thought Patrick must have had second thoughts about leaving me alone until I heard Sarah calling my name. I opened the door and there was a moment's pause, both of us unsure and awkward. She leaned over and hugged me. She felt wonderful and I needed her so much at that moment.

'Hey, stranger, you don't answer your phone any more?'

'I'm sorry.'

'I talked to Jack the other day. I'm sorry about the Incredible Mister Shakey. I wish you'd talk to me. I miss you.'

'You'd be better off if you didn't.'

'What does that mean?' Her brow tightened. I took her hand and rubbed her knuckles with my thumb. She pulled away to wipe at her eyes.

She walked to her car and got in. I was about to call

out, but she returned carrying a cardboard box. She put it in my lap.

Her voice on the edge of tears, she said, 'I don't know – you probably don't want a cat so soon, but JJ's mom's cat had a litter. She needs a home.'

'JJ?'

'Don't,' she pleaded.

I couldn't meet her eyes. I reached in and rubbed the fluff of striped orange pressed against the corner of the box.

'I'm sorry. I'm doing what I'm supposed to do and shit still happens,' I said.

The kitten yawned and stretched, showing its tiny needles for teeth.

'You do the right thing because it's the right thing.'

'A cat and a lecture. What else is Jack telling you about me?' I hated myself as I said it.

'Jarred. Seriously? You're doing this?' Her voice stiffened. 'Done.'

'I want to be so pissed off at you right now. But I can't. But I'm not going to put up with your bullshit either. You're a child.'

I turned to leave.

'No. Stop right now.'

'I'm sorry,' I said, turning back.

'Stop saying that. You want to know what else Jack told me, because we do talk. Why aren't you and I talking, huh? He told me about your accident. You've convinced yourself that you killed that girl, which you didn't. You've got it in your mind that you don't deserve to be happy and you're doing everything to make sure that's true. I'm scared for you, Jarred. You're lucky. Your mom died.'

My vision exploded with fireworks. I heard the roar of wind building inside my head.

'You said yourself your mom's last months were beautiful. My mom fucking rejected me, rejected me and Marco. I wasn't worth loving. You think you have issues? Ha! When you figure that out, you can call me. I like you, Jarred. You'd be smart not to mess this up.'

'I have to go to work now. I'll call you.'

'No, you won't.'

I handed her back the box. I heard the car pull away. I grabbed a potted African Violet next to Jack's recliner. The red clay pot shattered when it hit the ground, leaving a blast of soil and a tattered plant.

54

I went to work at The Store. I grabbed two beers from the cooler and drank them at my register. Customers either ignored me or smirked as I sipped with one hand and scanned items with the other. I was called into the manager's office.

'You shouldn't be firing me for this.'

'I certainly am firing you for this,' Reverse James Dean said.

'No, I mean I've done much worse. I've emailed the CEO from your account pretending you had gone full Kurtz down here amongst the "tofu fiddlers" as you referred to them in the email.'

'Hacking is a criminal offence.'

'Not so much hacked as that you hadn't logged out of your computer and I just typed the message and hit send. If you're done firing me, I'll let you get back to growing your ponytail and filling in your NORML membership form.'

'Get out of my office!'

'Whoa, Reverse James Dean. Stay cool. I'm leaving.'

I wheeled to the bus stop. The bus to the hospital was the number 7 going south. I got on the number 7 going north. I sat in the wheelchair space and my teeth chattered.

My sweat-damp work shirt was freezing under the blast of the bus's AC. The bus crossed under the overpass and stopped at the Greyhound station. Beyond the bus window, I saw my mom in her coma after the aneurysm. Grinning and already dead, we just didn't know it yet. She was going to tease us with hope for a few more months. I wanted to see the small moments: feeding ducks together in the park, lying across both their laps watching tv, bedtime stories and kisses goodnight. She was forever reduced to that day and her voice on the phone with an aneurysm about to take her away from us. Any other memory took effort, as if I was convincing myself of a lie.

Melissa too. That long-legged mischievous girl was the body with its head not right and a scalp like a wig gone askew. If I went and saw Jack now, he too would become only a dying old man in a hospital. I would have the drunkard and his violence and a dead old man. The memories of this last year wouldn't hold.

Greyhound stations are disturbingly like hospital emergency rooms worn by the abrasion of unlucky people coming and going. The ceilings, a little too low, weigh on the shoulders and make time there a burden. The swathes of blue paint made this station look more clinical than most. A young man with a shaved head fought nods of sleep and carried in his fist the clear plastic bag of a newly released prisoner's belongings. Two obese twenty-something mothers gossiped and absent-mindedly rocked strollers. The children, too old and too large, screamed and thrashed against their restraints. I lined up for the ticket window and ignored the examining stares.

'Real people take the bus; flying is for rich white folk,' someone said behind me.

Only one ticket window was open and the line ran a

gauntlet of wire chairs with thin metal armrests. The people in line carefully stepped over the outstretched legs and barricades of suitcases the size of small fridges. The tang of piss from the bathrooms on the other side of the building occasionally announced itself. People shouted complaints at the woman with sherbet-bright braids manning the ticket window.

'Shit stinks up in here,' a pasty young tough declared.

An argument broke out at the front and a chorus of clicked tongues sounded through the line. The woman in the ticket booth stared coldly at a man dressed for deer hunting as he exhausted himself cursing and demanding that the Dog needed shooting. An elderly woman told the ceiling, 'I'm going to miss my ride.'

Near me an ancient man was talking to a young teenage girl. He held his knees as he spoke to her, lifting them to punctuate his statements with precise, eloquent gestures. He was wearing a light purple linen suit. His aristocratic face, long and angular, and rod-straight posture stood out from all the others slumped and exhausted around him.

The pink dye in the teenager's blonde hair barely tinted the tips. She wore a Ramones t-shirt. She had a hiker's backpack stuffed so tight that it must have been impossible for her to get on and off alone.

'Look, I know you've seen some trouble, young lady. I'm sorry to tell you this, but you ain't ready for the conse-quences of your actions.' He waved his arms as if he conjured the bus idling outside the window and the people stuffing luggage into its belly. 'You think you're going to be able to haul that bag of yours on and off them there buses for three days? That's if it don't get stolen or the bus don't drive off without it. What'd you pack? You got wet wipes? First thing you need is wet wipes, guaranteed. The bus is cheap but it's raggedy. What about food? You're going get real sick of McDonald's and paying too much for what they're selling in the station. You ready for grease breakfast-lunch-dinner? I bet you ain't even got a pillow. I'm not being cruel here. I don't want to tell you your business. But, you need one of them five-dollar neck pillows. You'll see. Best five dollars you'll ever spend.

'What you're running from, I don't want to know. That's your business and yours alone. If anybody asks you, tell 'em to mind theirs. But here and now, you ain't ready for this bus ride. You need to stop and think about it. If it's home that's trouble, you don't have to go back there. You got friends, I know you do. You're too sweet a young lady not to have someone willing to help you out. You got churches you can go to. Ever thought of that? Go there, get your head straight, think about what you're about to do. If you still think you need to go to the other side of the world to solve your problems, then go. But you said yourself you just got up and went. Didn't think it out.'

As the girl listened, she picked at loose threads on her backpack.

'How much you buy your ticket for?' the man asked. 'Sell me your ticket. I'm going to buy it from you. Don't you worry. I'm an old man. I ain't got nothing I need to save for. It's not my money anyway. This here comes from your guardian angel; I'm just the delivery boy.'

I missed the rest of their conversation as the line moved forward and I went to the ticket window.

'Do you still do travel passes?' I asked the lady with the sherbet hair behind the counter.

'Discovery Pass. How many days? Actually, you should book individual journeys because they have to call in the buses with lifts.'

'Okay, where's the next bus go to?'

'The six forty-five? That one doesn't take accessible people.'

'Which one does?'

'You need to book in advance. At least forty-eight hours.'

55

Sarah was sitting on her porch with JJ. Seeing her laughing with the remnants of a six-pack on the table threw all my plans into confusion. When she saw me coming up the driveway she smiled, but it quickly dropped. I wheeled toward the back of the house and tapped Marco's window. Marco squealed my name in response and that made me smile. Sarah was already at the bottom of the ramp when I turned the corner.

'Hi.'

'Hi.'

I knew what I should say. The apologies and explanations were there lined up at the fore of my mind ready to go. I had revised over and over in my head what I was going to say. I was going to tell Sarah everything I knew for sure. She was kind, intelligent, wise, beautiful. She was the best person I knew and it made me want to be a good person. Not just to her, but to Jack, to everybody. Her kindness saved me. I didn't care how ridiculous I sounded. This was what I was prepared to say.

Instead, other words rushed forward. The easy, hateful words, and I saw everything curl and burn before me.

'Having fun? Going to all those little upstairs haunts you missed.'

'Jarred, you pushed me away, remember? I phoned you a million times. I visited you. I took the hint. I'm not a fuck buddy you put on the shelf until you're ready to make up your mind. You're being ugly. JJ is here because I need a friend right now. You think you're the only one who's allowed to be lonely?'

'I just came to tell you Jack is dying.'

She covered her mouth. Tears welled and her face reddened. She ran up the ramp and at the top she turned. 'Fuck you! You say that shit to hurt me. You're losing a pathetic little argument with your girlfriend, and you'd rather hurt me than admit you're wrong. Fuck you!'

I was almost to the street when JJ called out, 'Dude!'

JJ stepped off the porch and approached me.

'What?' Red veiled the world and JJ.

'She loves you. Stop treating her like shit. Or—'

'Or what?'

'I'll kick your ass.' JJ tried to make it sound like he was joking.

I laughed, locked my brakes, and punched JJ in the stomach. When he bent forward, I hit him in the jaw and threw myself out of my chair. Stunned and confused, JJ held me up as I continued punching him without effect. I slid slowly down his body until we both fell. He scrambled to his feet. I was sprawled, awkward and helpless.

Sarah ran outside and pulled JJ into the house.

'Look at yourself,' she screamed over her shoulder at me.

I sat up and spat dirt. I dragged myself along the ground and, after a few graceless attempts, got back into my chair. On the bus ride home, people stared unabashed.

56

We stole a bottle of Jack Daniel's while the car Melissa ordered waited for us outside the liquor store. The driver took us to the address Melissa read from her phone. Fritz's house was bland and nondescript. The carless driveway was covered in generations of oil stains. The small shrubs had long ago been burnt to bare twigs by the sun and neglect.

'Is Fritz still DJing?'

'Honestly, I don't know,' Melissa said.

A small man answered the door.

'Is Fritz home?' Melissa asked.

The man looked us up and down with exaggerated contempt. It made me giggle. He waited a few beats before saying no, then stared at me.

'Do you know where he is?' she asked.

'Work.'

'Where is work?'

'Who are you again?'

'Friends.'

'Sorry. I don't think so.' He shut the door.

'Wow. He was a pissy little man. What now?'

'I'm sure he's at Area.'

'Okay. Let's go there.'

The bar's marquee promised 'Magnolia Thunderpussy Revue'.

'This will be fun,' I said. Melissa brightened. She became girlish when I spotted Fritz at the bar. She ran up and they kissed.

'Look who I found.'

Fritz looked hard; his eyes were having trouble focusing. 'Jarred? Oh my god. My little punk rocker.'

He leapt from his stool and we hugged. We talked and they gossiped. I kept ordering drinks, working my way through the specials board, and putting them on Melissa's tab and Frank's credit card. It was great to see Fritz, but where Melissa suited adulthood, he had skipped ahead to old age. His hair was stringy and thinning. His face had a greasy sheen to it. He kept rubbing his arm with hands that looked arthritic. At one point, Fritz lined up the orange-uniformed, white-capped soldiers of his medicine bottles. He put his chin on the bar and called their names and ranks: Klonopin 4mg in the morning, 2mg afternoon and evening; Zoloft 50mg twice daily; Wellbutrin 150 mg; Vicodin 5mg; Selzentry 150 mg twice daily. I calculated how old he was: barely thirty.

Person after person, even Magnolia herself, stopped by and greeted Fritz. He used the same exaggerated excitement he had used to greet Melissa and me. Everyone looked amazing and it was always so good to see them. When the conversation dried up, he slumped as if exhausted by the effort.

'One minute,' Fritz announced and disappeared into the bar's gloom.

We sat waiting and waiting.

'Let's go,' Melissa said.

'Are you drunk? It was the Buttery Nipples. We should have stopped there,' I said.

Melissa laughed. 'What the hell were you ordering? Nasty.'

'Let's go. Let's go sit by the water.'

'Are we near water?'

At the exit, Fritz was talking to the man in the booth, leaning in close to whisper.

'Are you leaving?' he asked when he saw us.

'We have a plane to catch,' I said.

'Okay. Have fun. You got my number?' he said and turned back to the man in the booth.

I put my hand on his shoulder. He turned back, and we smiled at each other. I touched his cheek, my childhood hero.

'Thanks,' I said. A thank you for all the calming words he spoke to me when we were inpatients, for the love when I needed it most. I gave him all the affection I had for him. I put it all there in that touch and prayed I never saw him again.

He smiled. 'See you.'

The car dropped us off under the bright yellow moons of street lamps that hovered over the marina. The masts nodded, bobbed and their rigging chirped like roosting birds. Calm came to me with each deep breath of the night's air. Melissa said she had learned how to sail last year in Qatar. I had the idea to steal a boat.

'Don't be stupid, I have a friend who has a boat. He won't mind if we use it.' She pointed to a yacht, the largest one by far, with swoops of white paint and a yellow wood deck that glowed against the night. 'I think it's this one.'

'Who has that kind of money? That's insane. It's disgusting, actually.'

'You get used to it very quickly.'

'It's got a hot tub. A hot tub on a boat?' I pushed a button on the enamelled tub. It rumbled to life and frothed the water. 'Shall we?'

She gave a coy smile and nodded.

I started to undress. 'This is your friend's boat?'

'No, not really.'

A light came on in the cabin. She ran off giggling, still stumbling from the drinks, and I followed with my shoes and shirt in my hands.

57

I was sitting in front of the cardiac unit of the hospital smoking a cigarette. An old man sitting beside me was reading a newspaper. He had a face made for the portrait of a civil war veteran: leathered, crosshatched skin stretched over a skull and eyes like smudges. An ancient burn scar interrupted the unkempt grey beard crawling down his neck. He wore a hospital gown. In the crook of his elbow a streak of dried blood sneaked out from the tape and gauze where he had pulled out an IV. The old man looked at me and said, 'Buy the ticket, See the show,' and tugged at his half-ear.

I thought it had been a few days since I punched JJ. I wasn't sure. Patrick had come by in the morning to check on me, but I went out the back door and around the house before he saw me. I needed to talk to Jack. I didn't want him to die. I drew deeply on my cigarette and hoped it gave me courage. People went in and out, ignoring the man arguing with his newspaper and the wheelchair guy beside him.

'Carl don't like this. They're crazy if they think the people will stand for this. Crazy!' He flipped the page violently, put his nose close to the paper and tsked.

Sarah walked along the sidewalk toward me. A blast of wild flowers poked out of her handbag and nodded with her bouncing steps. Her walk had the skip of a little girl in it. It was one more thing that made her perfect.

'Long time no see,' she said.

I tried to take a drag from my cigarette, but the shaking made it hard. I stared at my hand, turning it over and over, sending sea horses of smoke tumbling.

'You don't look good. You okay?' Sarah asked. She held my hand. I raised the other and she took that one too.

'I'm getting asked that a lot these days.'

She let go. I showed her that the shake had stopped. Here was my chance to say what she deserved to hear.

'The Mexicans! Ho! Carl's got more problems than Mexicans. I'll tell you what. I'll tell you. A farmer hires an illegal; the government should take the farm and give it to the illegal. That'll solve the so-called immigration problem. Ho!'

'Friend of yours?'

'More of a mentor, really.'

'I hate hospitals. They have that smell. When I was little, Marco would disappear and return smelling like hospital. I used to hide from him. He hated it. He'd howl and howl, but I couldn't be near him when he had that hospital smell. I hate that I did that. I was a horrible child.'

'You didn't know any better. You want to sit down?'

She started crying. 'No. You're an asshole. I'm visiting Jack, not you.'

'Ho! Liars!' The man stood abruptly, thrust the newspaper into Sarah's hands. 'Quick, take this from me. It's driving Carl crazy!' He stamped off.

Sarah threw the newspaper away and disappeared into the hospital. I fought the urge to follow. Anger rose up my spine, but I finished my cigarette to let her have her time with Jack. Two old ladies, walking side by side with their arms threaded, gave a startled jump when they passed me. I took a deep breath and went inside. I searched for Jack past the staff-administered procedural kindness and their soft words saying no (it's always no), past babies trying to work themselves into a tantrum while their mothers hushed them, past the bloodied and dazed expressions of the waiting room, the repeated tableaux over and over, framed by hospital curtains, of two people – one in bed, one standing at their side, both trying out words that they hoped would suffice or at the least pass the time – and past police, always in twos, walking the halls. Shooting stars danced in the hallways. I heard the ocean. I felt a sea breeze and tasted its salt.

I followed the sterile right angles of the hospital to Jack's room. Sarah's flowers were in a vase on his sink, but she wasn't there. Jack was sleeping. His sheets were thrown off, exposing thin, almost hairless legs, the colour of fish bellies. I adjusted his dressing gown to cover the exposed buttocks and put the blanket back on him. I held this old man's hand. He kicked off the sheets again and rolled over, grumbling in his sleep.

'What now?' I said. 'What now?'

'Jarred?' Patrick stood at the doorway with his wife and children behind him.

'What now?' I pointed at the children. I slapped my face.

Patrick looked at his wife and, without a word, she nodded and disappeared with the children.

'Jarred, what's happened?' Patrick asked.

I grabbed my hair and jerked my head down to my shoulder. I raised my fist, clumps of hair sprouting between my fingers. I opened my hand and watched the strands fall to the ground. I heard the rushing, pounding sound of a train.

'He's dead. You're only ever here when they die.'

'Jarred, stop shouting. He's just sleeping.'

'You had the best of both of them.'

'Jarred!'

'When did you ever – they sent you to college. Bought you a car. They wanted you.' I tasted blood.

'Dad has done everything for you,' Patrick said, surprised by his own anger. It made me laugh. He dodged the thrown vase of flowers and stepped forward to block the exit. He grabbed my wrists.

Nurses and security swarmed into the room. Golden light flooded my vision to burn out Patrick's face, the hands restraining, the coolness of the floor tasting of chemicals, the shouts.

I heard Jack's voice: 'Leave him alone!'

58

When it happens, there is no taking of measurements or calculation of import. This event. The minimal change in velocity when the weight of steel and glass encounter flesh and bone is just another event in a series. This event that destroys everything. An event that cuts your life into two strands, before and after. The mind encounters it with the same mechanical disinterest as all the other events of the evening. It is the instant when the world wheels, the transfer of momentum, the impolite shove of a silver VW Golf. The noise of brakes doesn't register. Only after everything is at rest, a horrible stillness where even the wind holds its breath, does sound return. The first sound heard is the driver's repetition of 'Oh god!' blurring to a stutter as he paces behind the car, occasionally looking up at you and Melissa. His hands holding his head as it shakes violently. After the event, the continuity of time breaks into flashes of scenes and impressions. Melissa's skirt has ridden up and you expect her to adjust it to hide the perfect, tanned thighs you had been stealing glances at all evening. The mind doesn't reflect on the grave significance of Melissa's body or the gore of her face. That all comes later in pounding, bruising, unrelenting waves when you lie in the hospital praying for the next dose of morphine to push it away. You move your mouth, working the jaw, feeling your tongue, and spit blood onto your chin. Your body doesn't move. You can't get up. You lift your head to look down to command your legs, but they ignore you. Your left arm, it's hard to lift. A knife of bone has cut through a surprisingly bloodless pink gash. You put your finger on its tip. Should you push it back in? You turn your head and watch Melissa and beg for movement. Someone come and help us. You know you need help. That she needs help. Someone please help. Why won't that man by the car help? Please help. He's walking away. No, he's flagging an ambulance. Why did they park so far away? Why aren't they helping Melissa? Go help Melissa. Who is screaming? You are screaming. That. What.

59

It's going to hurt. Ready? One . . . two . . . three.

——

A curtain rail framed the ceiling of the hospital room. Jack stood beside my bed.

'Jack? You okay?'

'Me? I'm up and moving around. It feels like they threw in a box of mouse traps before sewing me up.' Jack pulled down his t-shirt to show the central line for intravenous antibiotics attached to his chest. 'Look, I'm a bagpipe.'

'What happened? Did I do something bad?'

Jack gave a tired smile then left the room.

He shepherded in Patrick's twins. Their wide, fearful eyes locked on me.

'See. Uncle Jarred's okay. Look. Say hello, Jarred. Tell them you're okay.'

'I'm okay. I'm sorry if I scared you.'

They both nodded slowly. Their tiny bodies turned toward Jack.

'You don't have to be scared. Huh? Uncle Jarred is okay.'

They hugged his legs. 'Is he still sick?' the little girl asked, watching me.

'No, I think he's better now. You want to go back to Mommy?'

They nodded.

'Okay, tell her I'll be there in a second,' Jack said.

'What did I do?'

'Woke me up is what you did. Ranting and raving like a wackadoo,' He came toward the bed and put his hands on the rail. 'A goddamn battle royal with the nurses and security. You're in the psych ward. One floor above mine. They're recommending some medication. And you got yourself a handful of appointments with a psychiatrist.'

'That's probably a good thing. A fifteen-year-old nut job might have his charms but it's not cute any more. I'm getting too old for this.'

'You and me both, kid.'

I put my hand on his, and we traded smiles.

'I'll take my crazy pills. I'll go to the shrink, but can we make a deal?'

'Here it comes.'

'No, it's not like that. I mean it. I'm done with causing problems, but I need you to not hide things from me.'

Jack's face fell. He patted my hand and stepped over to the window. He fidgeted with the handle, but it was locked. 'That was me being stupid.' He looked at me and said sorry before returning to looking out the window.

'But you're okay?' I asked.

'Yeah, the doctors seem happy. Stuff just starts falling off when you're my age. There's a handful more things I'm not allowed to do or allowed to eat.' Something below pulled Jack's interest. 'Woah, you should see this guy. He's built like a blueberry. I bet he's going to a disabled parking space. Look at that!' Jack tried the window lock again.

'Jack!'

Jack came over to the bed. 'Too much cake is not a disability.'

'Jack, I'm trying to be serious here. Are we going to be okay?'

He took out his wallet and opened it. In the plastic window where people have their driver's licence was the note that I left him when I first came back at sixteen. The paper was worn to tissue. The folds and creases shadowed, but the words 'I'm sorry' were still visible.

'You laminated it? You dork.'

He took it out. I turned it over in my hands.

Jack said, 'That note saved my life. There were so many times I had thought I had let you down. Let your mother down. That little note gave me the sliver of forgiveness I needed to get through the worst days.'

'Jack, I want to apologise to you right now, apologise for everything. This is my last apology. I'm not going to break anything or anyone any more.'

Jack leaned on the bed rail. 'That's not possible. You can't avoid every mistake. The trick is to just avoid the ones you can. That's where you need some help. You make your life harder than it needs to be.

'You're so keen on everything being broken, because you think you deserve all these problems. This world has nothing to do with deserve.'

'What's the worst thing I ever did to you?'

'Jarred, please.'

'Tell me.'

'There is no worst thing.' Jack straightened and walked back to the window. It was a long time before he spoke again.

'Do you remember I used to take you to your mom's grave? We seemed not to fight so much if she was in our thoughts.'

'Yeah,' I said, my eyes reddening.

'Remember the time I tried to give you your mom's favourite necklace.' The words clunked from him heavy and slow. 'I had given it to her for our tenth anniversary. We finally had some money, had just bought the house, and it was a big deal. We felt like grown-ups for the first time. I told all this to you to make you understand its importance. You stood there with that pissed-off look you always had. I held it out to you. You looked at it like it was a turd and said, "Is this a bribe?" I tried to reason, tried to explain, but you walked off. I couldn't even be angry with you. I hated you, wanted nothing more than for you to run away and leave me alone. Then you did and I felt guilty and angry at myself for the next ten years.'

'Dad.' I called him Dad for the first time since I was a child.

'I know it's not that simple,' he said. 'It wasn't just that moment alone and I wasn't always feeling guilty or angry but that stands out as the moment we, me and you, were beyond redemption. You wanted to know. There you go.' He turned around to meet my eyes.

My voice cracked. 'Dad, I didn't mean it like that. Not at all. I felt awful for taking anything of hers, like I wanted her to die so I could inherit her stuff. I hated the idea that my mom was a pile of trinkets. The woman who drew dinosaurs on the napkins in my lunchbox.'

Jack's eyes shone. His mouth opened, but the emotions reddened his face and threatened to burst. He swallowed, breathed out and tried again.

'She feared everything,' Jack said. 'So I stayed with her. I had plans to see the world. Same travelling bug you caught. But I stayed by her side. She drank because she was scared. I drank to be by her side. You know what? She was worth it.

'I worry, though, that if she hadn't died, we wouldn't have been able to keep it together. I like to think that our love would have been strong enough, but I'm glad it was never tested. That's a hard thing to know. That I kept her sick and she kept me sick. That thought kills me like no other. The only thing I have in this world is that I had a love as rare as rare can be, impervious to the elements, including time. That love is safe, because she died. It makes me grateful, but I still wish it had been me, not her. She would have kept it together and saved you from a lot of hurt.'

'You don't know that.'

'I have to,' Jack said.

'You still think about her?'

'Every day. I still talk to her. And I still mourn her. That doesn't go away either. It just becomes less often and less crippling. No pun intended, rubber legs.' Jack winked. 'Sometimes, though, I feel it so much it pins me to the bed, but I get up and pretend it doesn't matter until it passes. You've got a lot to figure out, but' – he tapped my wheelchair – 'the good news is you're my son. Sarah too is an amazing woman. Each day you two don't take each other for granted, you'll have what your mom and me had, probably better. Then just think, and I sincerely pray to God in heaven that it happens, that one day you'll have a kid just as much trouble as you were, and I will laugh and laugh.'

'I don't think so. There is only so much nonsense from me that someone like Sarah will take.'

'Son, I've called you an idiot a lot. That's probably not what a father should be saying. Self-esteem and all that malarkey, but I have never been so sure as I am at this moment that you are a complete damn-blind idiot. I've seen the way she looks at you. And you look at her. It's for real, dummy. This is it. This is your one. You fit each other. She's visited me every day. Without screaming and shouting and having a fit, I should add. Who do you think we talked about? Hmm?'

'Okay, I get it.'

Jack stands and walks toward the door. 'Good. I'm done talking to you. I need coffee.'

Credits

Author	Jarred McGinnis
Agent	Will Francis
Editor	Ellah Wakatama
Managing Editor	Leila Cruickshank
Editorial Assistant	Aa'Ishah Hawton
Proofreader	Alison Rae
Publicity Director	Anna Frame
Campaigns Executive	Jamie Norman
Cover Designer	Valeri Rangelov
Rights & Contracts Director	Jess Neale
Rights Manager	Caroline Clarke
Rights Assistant	Bethany Ferguson
Head of Production	Kate Oliver
Head of UK & Digital Sales	Jo Lord
Audio & Digital Executive	Katalina Watt
Head of International Sales	Steph Scott
Key Accounts Manager	Drew Hunt
Sales Operations Manager	Nadine Luchsinger
Publisher	Jamie Byng
Typesetters	Jacqueline Simpson and Michelle Forsyth

Acknowledgements

First and foremost I am grateful to the family of readers, storytellers and teachers that I come from. They have given me the curiosity and a love of words from which all else followed.

Before this was a book there were many many people who read the stories, gave me thoughtful advice and feedback or just listened as I rambled on. This list is woefully incomplete, but I must thank: Debbie Bogard, Jamie Coleman, Martin Cummins, Sarah Hall, Ruth Harrison, Peter Hobbs, Sam Jordison, Francesca Main, Jane Main, Adam Mars-Jones, Robert McGinnis, Eloise Millar, Anne Mullane, Robin Pavlik, Christina Petrie, Ben Platts-Mills, Quad Writers Group, Andy Sewell, Natalie Smith, Spread the Word, Karla Steffen, Sam Taradash, Barry Walsh, Willesden Green Writers' Group, Evie Wyld.

And, to every single student I have taught, especially the students of First Story, for reminding me my faith in words was never misplaced.